THE
SICILIAN
WIFE

THE
SICILIAN
WIFE

a novel

CATERINA EDWARDS

.II.

Cover design: Debbie Geltner
Author photo: Fred Katz
Book design: WildElement.ca
Printed and bound in Canada by Imprimerie Gauvin.

Library and Archives Canada Cataloguing in Publication

Edwards, Caterina, 1948-, author
The Sicilian wife / Caterina Edwards.

Issued in print and electronic formats.
ISBN 978-1-927535-60-8 (pbk.).—ISBN 978-1-927535-61-5 (epub).—
ISBN 978-1-927535-63-9 (pdf).—ISBN 978-1-927535-62-2 (mobi)

I. Title.

PS8559.D83S53 2015   C813'.54   C2014-906286-9
                                               C2014-906287-7

The publisher gratefully acknowledges the support of the Canada Council
for the Arts.

 Canada Council   Conseil des arts
                     for the Arts   du Canada

Linda Leith Publishing Inc.
P.O. Box 322, Victoria Station, Westmount QC H3Z 2V8 Canada
www.lindaleith.com

In memory of Antonio Cirincione.

And for Marco, always.

It is mainly by blood that we think,
for in blood all the elements are mingled.

—Empedocles

I
Air

Nature that framed us of four elements, warring within our breast for regiment, doth teach us all to have aspiring minds.

—Niccolò Machiavelli

I didn't regret it then, and I don't regret it now (Sorfarina told the prince). And if you want another slap, you'll get one and how!

—"Sorfarina"

1

Sicily

You leave your childhood home; you make a new one. You invent yourself, and, if need be, reinvent. But for most, emigration from the past to the future is not so simple, and for Fulvia Arcuri, the journey would be a perilous one.

The first time Fulvia ran away, she was eight. A stick-thin, scabby-kneed eight. Big almond-shaped eyes, a nimbus of brown curls, and, bracketed by gaps, two new, large front teeth.

She decided early one July morning. She had been awake for hours, lying on her bed, tingling mad. The air stank of smoke, a thick blanket pressing down on her face, into her throat, winding around and around her chest. She couldn't breathe. She had to get out, get away. Down the corridor, down the stairs, through the first door, the second, then the third. Was she strong enough to pull back the bolts? Her arms were as wobbly as overcooked pasta.

Because of Mamma, who had pounded her with a

wooden spoon. Because Mamma and Papà blamed her and her brother for the fire. "*Deficienti*," imbeciles, which wasn't fair. And Davide insisted it was her fault, her idea. "Fulvia wanted flames."

"You're a big fat liar."

Papà told them he hated tattletales and harangued them some more about knowing better and about responsibility. And how everything could have burnt up, everything.

Papà pulled Davide into the next room. Papà used the belt and Mamma the spoon. Fulvia clamped her lips shut and didn't cry. She could hear Davide's yelps through the wall. Mamma pulled her this way and that, hitting whatever she could, arms, chest, and back, until the spoon broke. Mamma stopped. Papà kept on: *thwack*. Davide deserved it, he did, for the fire and all the other times he bothered her, punching, cursing. Once he shut her kitty-cat, Fedele, in a suitcase. What if Fulvia hadn't found her? Monster. Turdface. He needed to be punished. Why were her parents and grandmother always mad at her? *Filthy child*, stop climbing, stop jumping, stop answering back. Sit down, be quiet, don't squirm. Stay still, stay still, stay still. *Uffa!*

Thwack. They let Davide do anything he wanted, practically. *Thwack*. A ragged howl, and all the places Mamma had hit hurt worse. She covered her ears: enough. She felt queasy and her eyelids prickled. "No more," she said to Mamma, who was lounging in her favourite chair and smoking.

"You idiots have to learn."

Finally, the only sound was the murmur of Papà's voice.

3

"I didn't do anything. And Davide didn't mean to. He was showing me a trick."

"You knew you weren't supposed to go into your father's office, ever, let alone take something, and you did."

Davide had dared her. They did it all the time, when they weren't fighting, dared each other. Fulvia had won full marks for running the length of the stone walls in less than five minutes, for stealing a pack of Mamma's cigarettes, and short-sheeting Nonna's bed. To their surprise, Nonna didn't tell or even complain. Davide managed to smoke three cigarettes in a row without throwing up though he did look a bit green. He sat in the dust and let a lizard crawl up his arm without flinching, but he screamed when he jumped off one of the shed roofs into what looked like a loose pile of hay and broke his arm. Last Wednesday, Davide had dared her to eat a live grasshopper, but she couldn't. So he was ahead one.

Yesterday morning, he caught her cross-legged under an oak tree, reading her favourite book of folk tales. "Hey, Beetlebrain, got a new dare for you." He'd come from the orchard, carrying a pear. He took a giant bite and tossed it at her. It bounced off her shoulder, leaving a mark on her dress.

She jumped up. "Creep."

"Papà's magnifying glass. From his desk. Bring it."

"Won't the door be locked?" She liked this challenge. Fulvia had never been in her father's study; Davide had, though not often. That wing of the house was for business, grown-up stuff. Papà's men went in and out. Nonna and

Mamma stayed away. They had enough to do, Nonna said.

"Nah, not usually." Davide's smile was smug. "This one is easy, easy."

"Except I'm not allowed." A quiver of anxiety in her stomach. Forbidden. Still, she stepped out of her sandals and was off, as brave as any heroine in her book. Soferina or Lettucia or Bette would never hesitate, no matter what the quest. Fulvia ran down narrow passageways and through half-empty storerooms, up curving metal stairs, and across an outer office with a long table and many chairs. A pause to catch her breath, a turn of the knob, and she was in. A dim room, the shutters closed, a big wooden desk with nothing on top except a bronze statue of a blindfolded woman holding a scale, a leather-bound book and, yes, the magnifying glass. No one was about. She could have inspected whatever she wanted, but her instinct told her to hurry.

"One for me," Fulvia said. She and Davide were sitting on their heels beside the tall prickly pear. "Watch," he said, pointing at the cracked, pale earth. The sun battered down on her head and neck. "Look." He pointed out a line of black scurrying dots, then held the magnifying glass over the ants. "Bam," he said, and the ray of light sizzled. The moving dot disappeared. "Killer rays," he said, moving on to the next and the next.

"Don't," she said.

Her brother laughed. "You're gonna care about ants now?"

"No." She'd been bitten too often by the red ones. But watching the specks of life vanish left her dizzy. Maybe it was the heat, pummelling her. Fulvia eased herself up. "Big deal."

"I got more." He looked over at the house and barns. Beppe, the odd-job man was carrying an obviously heavy box across the courtyard. "Come," he said, and she followed her brother to the pasture. "It's magic," he said. "Fire out of thin air." He aimed the glass at a patch of long, dried grass. Fulvia didn't see the spark, but the grass darkened, then there was a small tentative flame, and together they cried out and clapped their hands. Did Davide make a move to smother the growing fire? He told their parents he did. She was staring at those flames, sizzling yellow and orange, dividing and multiplying, flaring up and to the side. This was magic; they had conjured up a force, made from the earth and the air, that ate up the earth and the air.

Davide gave her a kick. "Fulvia, move!" She backed away. He kicked dirt and stomped. And stomped. Fulvia's heart was beating so fast. She should, she must help, but the heat. He was falling back, retreating. The fire jumped, sizzled. Fulvia turned and ran toward the house screaming. Beppe came, and Mamma, in her high heels, because she was about to go out. Toni streaked by, running into the pasture. And Nonna arrived in cloth slippers, her grey hair hanging loose.

"Call the fire department," Mamma said.

"Don't be stupid," Nonna said. "Call the Scammac-

6

cas," referring to their closest neighbours. "And Antonio's people." (Papà's brother had even more men than Papà.) Nonna raised her voice. The fire was loud. Crackles, grumbles, and bangs. "Lela, go and call. Beppe, don't stand there—get the hoses."

Toni was leading Sara the goat up the side path. Her eyes were rolling, showing the whites, and Toni was almost dragging Sara along. But what about the other animals? The rabbit hutch over by the fence? From the other side of the main barn, the chickens squawked, the dogs howled. They were not her pets, but she felt a link, a responsibility.

What if the fire kept spreading and spreading? From the pasture to the olive grove, to the garden and back around to the house? Uncontrollable, unstoppable. A hissing giant snake, swallowing everything in its path.

Fulvia felt as if she were freezing and burning at the same time, scared and exhilarated.

A scream, a cascade of screams, far-off, from the other side of the fire. Don't think about it. "Hail Mary, full of grace," Fulvia prayed, as she never had, "Pray for us sinners..." The words radiated from the centre of her brain out to the edge of her fingertips. More water, barrels full, in the back of a truck, and more men, many more, poured in, brandishing hoses and shovels, taking over. And Papà and Zio Antonio were suddenly there. Ordering the women and children away. Shouting. Cut off the air with water and earth. Smother the fire. Until after an hour or two, embers and finally a field of ash.

Fulvia lay in her bed, the smoky air stinging her nose and throat, scorching her lungs. She was sorry, even if it wasn't her fault, sorry for the grass and the animals, especially the five rabbits trapped in the hutch. She hadn't been allowed to see their remains; "You'll be overwrought," Nonna said. But Fulvia could imagine a pyramid of singed fur. And she still heard their far-off death screams.

She remembered staring at the first flames, unable to move. How long had she been spellbound? Too long. Still, they didn't intend to burn down the pasture. Why wouldn't Mamma and Papà believe them? For sure, the beatings weren't the end: they were going to use the fire to boss her around even worse than before. Maybe forbid her from going to school. Another year of lessons with Nonna.

She had to get out, out into the fresh air.

The birds began to sing before dawn. Fulvia put on a comfortable romper and her sturdiest sandals. She squished two 1,000L notes into a pocket. Fedele padded off his sleeping pillow and rubbed up against her legs. She scooped him up for a cuddle and scratch behind his ears. "If I had a leash, Fedele, I'd take you." Together they walked softly, softly down corridors and stairs. She stopped in the kitchen to place a bottle of water and a cellophane-wrapped pack of cookies in a canvas bag. She poured a few inches of milk into a *caffellatte* cup and set it on the floor for Fedele. Nonna was going to yell when she found it: disgusting.

Fulvia's arms proved strong enough to draw back the

double bolts, turn the knobs, and pull open the three heavy doors. She squeezed sideways through the iron bars of the gate and started down the curving driveway. She could turn right at the road and, after the Inzerillos', slip into the woods.

In the deep dark forest, the stories say, a child can always find shelter in the branches of a tree or a peasant's hut. Someone who is not what they seem, a prince in the shape of a frog or a witch in the shape of a beggar, will appear to help or test her, or to eat her up. Fulvia was a big girl, and she knew the stories were about a time long, long ago, not now, and there were no ogres or wolves hiding in the trees. Still, she took the other way, toward town.

Though her legs, like her arms, were bruised and stiff, she walked and walked. The grey light brightened, the sun climbed into the sky, Fulvia was sticky with sweat. And the air continued to stink of smoke. How far did she have to go? To Alcamo Marina, to the sea, that should do it. She would catch one of the buses in the big piazza. Come on, she told herself, Soferina wouldn't give up. When she heard a car coming, she turned away or crouched in the ditch. Some slowed down as they passed, but none stopped. Not until she was almost in Alcamo. She had allowed herself a short rest in the shade of a leafy bush when the Range Rover rolled to a stop.

Her father had found her. "Fulvietta," he said, his eyes two spots of light in his tanned face. Fulvia stumbled as she got up. He steadied her, then swooped her up into a short, fierce hug. She was buoyed by his familiar, reassuring smell, tobacco and bitter orange. Papà carried her to the car, as if she were still little. She was not fooled: she was in big trouble, bigger than yesterday even. He drove as if she weren't there, in the seat beside him.

"I was running away," she said. From the smoke, the burnt pasture, the dead rabbits.

Papà pulled into the driveway of someone else's villa. His face was expressionless, his voice calm and uninflected, but Fulvia could still feel the flame of his anger. "Such a foolish and thoughtless thing to do. Not that you could ever get very far."

"I might have. Could have taken the train or hitchhiked."

"You're talking like a two-year-old. You must promise me. Never again."

She shook her head. She wanted to cry out in protest, to list all her grievances.

"You swear? Say it."

"I promise." Tucked under her thighs, her fingers were crossed.

"I thought you had a head on your shoulders."

Her stomach flipped and flopped. "Papà, you won't, you won't stop me from going to school?"

"I don't go back on my word. But if you continue to act, to think so stupidly? Fulvietta, you must understand the dangers outside the walls of your home." He gestured at the windshield. "Animals, snakes, bad drivers. Hitchhiking, *Dio*! There are bad men, bad people, in the world."

"I know," Fulvia said, although she didn't. "But do

they hurt little girls?"

"Especially little girls."

And Fulvia thought: they eat them up. They chop them into little pieces. "Like the ogres in the woods?" Fulvia was titillated.

"Just like them, metaphorically speaking."

"What?"

"The point is, all little girls need their families to protect them. And you even more so. Unfortunately. You must stay safe, stay where you can be protected."

"Me? More so?" In her mind's eye, she saw a lumpy, green-skinned ogre crouching behind the bush while she ate her cookies. "Why?"

"Because you are my daughter, and I have enemies. That's the way it is."

"Bad men want to hurt me because of you?" Not just ogres behind every bush, but giants behind every tree.

Papà opened his mouth to speak, then closed it. His left shoulder contracted up and forward, and he backed the car onto the road. "Just remember at Bagna Serena, with your family, you are always safe, protected from harm."

Fulvia was confined to her bedroom for a day, and to the house for an entire week. It was horrible being stuck inside in the hot, airless rooms and harder to escape her brother's sneers, taunts, and sneaky pinches. Or to evade Mamma's and Nonna's eyes and reproaches. Fulvia couldn't even hide out in her bedroom. One of them was always walking in without a thought to knocking, fiddling with her things, remaking the bed, reorganizing the drawers: talking, bossing her about.

2   Sicily
FALL 1962

To release her prince from a magic spell, the maiden sits on the terrace for seven years, seven days, seven hours, and seven minutes—way too long in Fulvia's opinion. "You have to learn patience," Nonna said. "And courage."

Fulvia was allowed to go to school during October and half of November. Then Papà went away, and both she and Davide were forced to stay home. No one told them why Papà left or where he went. When Fulvia asked when Papà was coming back, Mamma knuckled her on the side of the head. Mamma was even grouchier than usual since she too was stuck, unable to shop or visit the hairdresser's. Instead, Mamma sat in Papà's chair at the head of the dining room table, the drapes drawn, smoking, and playing cards or reading books with yellow covers. A bang from the kitchen or even a yell from the garden made her jump.

Nonna separated Fulvia and Davide for their lessons to stop their endless scrapping. Nonna also decided Fulvia needed a friend, so Veronica (whose parents both worked for the Arcuri) arrived every afternoon to keep Fulvia company. And, at first, Fulvia was diverted. A year older, Veronica offered to teach Fulvia everything she should know: how to skip double dutch, play Uno, dance the Twist, and the words to *24,000 Baci*. "It is about what men do to women," Veronica whispered into Fulvia's ear. "How they make babies."

After watching Fulvia hide Davide's slingshot, Veronica asked, "Why do you care if he aims at a bird? He's a bad shot."

"I try to keep the animals in the garden safe and Davide in check. And I wait and I watch."

"You've got nothing better to do? Sad."

How much should she say? That she believed one day the blackbird scolding from the olive branch or the lizard disappearing under a rock would stop and stare back at her? The creature would acknowledge the link between them and reward her. Just like in the fairytales. Three wishes or a special gift. A little horse that would carry her up into the sky. A magic salve that would protect her skin like armour. Fulvia wanted to share. She wanted reassurance.

Later, at the kitchen table, over their afternoon snack of chocolate-filled brioches and glasses of Orangina, she said: "Veronica, don't you ever feel this, this presence, on the other side of what we can see?"

"You are a bit loopy."

"When you're out in the garden? Or when you look deep into your cat's eyes and tell him all your problems.

Have you ever felt he might talk back?"

Veronica shook her head. Her long shiny ponytail whooshed from side to side. "Talking animals? What language would they speak? Wait, I know, Sicilian. But your kitty-cat would use proper Italian."

"They wouldn't use words. I'd just understand, mind to mind. You know?"

Veronica pulled a face. "You're the talking donkey."

Fulvia flushed. "I don't really believe it. It's this funny feeling, that's all."

Veronica leaned over and, with her crumpled napkin, wiped a few crumbs off Fulvia's cheeks. "Not so loud. Your grandmother will hear." Nonna was wiping down the marble counter at the opposite end of the cavernous kitchen. The familiar stink of bleach drifted across the terracotta tiles and circled over their heads.

"So?" Fulvia said. "Nonna talks more to the animals around here than she does to the people."

"But does she expect them to answer?"

Nonna was muttering: the floor needed to be re-washed. "Nonna's deaf, anyway."

"Everyone will think you're touched in the head," Veronica said. "So keep your mouth shut. I'm telling you for your own good."

Keep your mouth shut. Just what Fulvia needed— someone else to boss her around.

Another week, Fulvia was sitting alone, writing out a list of the invaders of Sicily, three thousand years of them, from the Siculi to the Italians. "Ten times and no stopping until you're done," Nonna had ordered. "To help you memorize." To bore her, to cramp her fingers. Fulvia threw the scribbler on the floor.

She opened and shut the kitchen cupboards. She counted the glass jars of home-canned tomatoes: only twelve left. She inspected the door at the end of the pantry, one door of many doors she and Davide had been told not to touch, not to open. "Not for children," Nonna said. "You'll break something," Mamma said.

Curious, Fulvia turned the knob. Break what? She expected a closet, more shelves; instead, she faced a narrow, low-ceilinged corridor. A stone-clad tunnel, Fulvia imagined, projecting herself into another tale.

She was Ninetta, the youngest and the most beautiful of a merchant's three daughters. The father had walled them up in their house to protect them while he was away. But when Brave Ninetta was lowered by bucket into the courtyard well to recover a thimble, she discovered a tunnel that allowed her to escape to a luxuriant palace garden, where she filled her skirt with cherries and jasmine to take back to her sisters. The best fruits and the best flowers were there for her, and each day the Prince watched her forays. The Prince found the girl as beautiful as a fairy princess.

Fulvia stood at the foot of a spiral staircase. As she ascended, the sensation that she was being watched and admired faded. She remembered she had seen these metal steps before, a long time ago. Nonna had been slowly descending, carrying a tray with a food-smeared plate, an empty glass, and a half-full carafe of wine. "What's up there?"

"Nothing," Nonna said. "A storage room of old things"

A thick wooden door, an outside door, to what? A lush garden? No, that was silly. A treasure vault? Fulvia turned the old, rattling knob. An escape hatch? The room was what Nonna had said it was: luggage, a travel trunk, cast-off furniture, dust. A disappointment. A small high window with half-closed blinds let in a grey light. A narrow bed with no sheets, an iron headboard, and a straw mattress. She was suddenly sure that Papà had slept here. Fulvia climbed on and curled up, her back against the whitewashed wall, legs under her. The light, the silence, soothed her. No one knew where she was. She was safe in her very own hideout. She half hummed, half sang a song she had heard on the TV and at the beach. She forced her voice down, guttural. *Stay away from me.* She mimicked the pop star, sneering. *Stay away.*

From then on, she brought Fedele with her. She waited until the kitchen was empty, then scoop, zip, she was through the first door, up the stairs, through the second. She held Fedele tight; if he squirmed hard he could get free and she would have to chase him. "Come, come, come, kitty," she called. "Into the tower." For he liked their secret place. She kept a plush mouse there for him to play with, and a small bag of kitty treats. Fedele explored the corners of the room, then leapt onto the bed beside her. She stroked his back and fluffy tummy; Fedele purred as she told him her versions of the tales of the latest TV show. Gradually, Fulvia sank into the greyness of the room. She wasn't quite asleep, more suspended, eyes open, mind empty. Beauty behind the brambles.

3

Sicily

Two tired men in a small white Innocenti on a secondary road in the northwest corner of Sicily. A black Mercedes followed, not discreetly. Uneasy, the driver of the first car pulled over to the right. When the Mercedes did not pass, he tried to slow down, to stop. He pumped the brake pedal. Nothing. Panicked, he pressed down with his full strength. The Innocenti sped up, began to career around the sharp curves. The Mercedes closed in. A bang, the screech of metal on metal, and the Innocenti catapulted into the air, arching over the mountainside, flipping end over end over end.

The two from the Mercedes stood on the side of the road, peering down the steep hill through the grey light of dawn.

"Down you go," the older man said. He handed his colleague a litre container of gasoline. "We have to be sure."

The younger man slid and fell down the hillside. He cursed the mountain, the mud, the trees, and the two dead men in rhythmic rotation. The curses were his work song. He checked both bodies, picking the pockets of the one thrown against the tree. The other was crushed inside the flattened and smouldering hulk. There was no way he could get at him to remove any identification. The fire should take care of it. He walked back to the heap by the tree and unscrewed the top to the bottle.

"An Innocenti. Two deceased. Could be male or female."

Marisa De Luca, the chief of the Alcamo police station, was at her desk when the words floated over the top of the glass partition that separated her office from the rest of the station house. The squad room was unusually quiet, the clatter of mechanical typewriters still. "Grilled, roasted, deep fried. All identification gone." Marisa recognized *Capitano* Brusca's high-pitched voice. "The blaze could have taken out half the mountain." The man provoked her, even with a partition between them.

She had been making her way through a pile of reports, but now, her concentration broken, she pulled a newspaper out of her briefcase and scanned the front page. The articles on the latest political rows were as dull as the police reports. On the bottom of page two, a headline caught her eye: TERRORIST BOSS FOUND DEAD. Even before she read the details, Marisa's heart began to race.

Yesterday, a guard at the Regina Coeli prison of Rome

had found the leader of the Sempre Guerra movement, Roberto Valente, hanging in his cell. Her Valente. The reputed architect of the Aldo Moro kidnapping and other acts of terror was serving a ten-year sentence for subversion and conspiracy to murder.

Her Valente, caught by her, convicted by her. *The warden pronounced the death a clear case of suicide.* "I don't believe it," Marisa said aloud.

She tried to imagine Valente, always arrogant and sure, overwhelmed with despair. Had the years of imprisonment and the defeat of his ideology destroyed him? She paced in her small office, stopped, and pressed her forehead against the wall. It wasn't her fault. She had done what she had to do as an officer of the law.

She had received a special citation from the Minister of Justice for her *exceptional and heroic work*, which was only right. Her work undercover had helped convict thirty-one members of the paramilitary group. Her boss and mentor, Giorgio Lanza, insisted she was on the threshold of a brilliant career; he would make sure of it. So why the hell was she here in this cramped station house that stank of damp, crumbling stone instead of the headquarters of the *Squadra Antimafia* in Rome or Palermo? Removed from action, stuck in the sticks, and confined to bureaucratic minutiae. Most frustrating, she'd been ordered not to initiate or lead any investigations. The lower ranks would look after minor crimes, and the major ones were to be referred to Palermo. Her job was to supervise, to catch and correct errors. "Too many prosecutions are derailed because of our carelessness," Lanza said. "The Mafia lawyers play every angle."

The need was obvious: on the page before her was yet another interrogation recorded in Sicilian rather than Italian. Still, this position was a waste of her time and her skills. Marisa picked up the report, as well as five other examples of sloppy paperwork, and headed to the squad room, where several officers were on the phone, two others sat and joked, and one typed out a crime report using only his index finger. There was a sharp smell of old sweat and damp wool. Marisa hovered until personal calls were cut short and typewriters began to clack. Then, she passed two of the files to a constable. "Retype, please. I've marked the grammatical and spelling errors." Marisa dropped three files at the next cubicle. "Breaking and entering is a contravention of no. 2926 subsection 5, not 2986, subsection 8. Look it up, each time."

In the tiny foyer, nine civilians stood waiting patiently. An elderly woman perched on a rickety chair. "You have to wait," Grazia, the receptionist, told a red-faced man. "Better come back after lunch."

Back at the door of Brusca's office, Marisa smoothed the hem of her jacket. She took a deep breath and stepped in. Brusca was sitting on his desk, retelling the story of the car crash to Lo Verde and Arcangelo. "It took two fire trucks from here, one from Castellamare, another from Partinico. And the poor souls? Nothing but a few bones and bits of charred flesh."

Despite herself, Marisa shivered.

Brusca bared his teeth in a fake smile. "Do excuse me, *Commissaria*. I continue to forget we now have a sensitive female in the station house."

"Don't be ridiculous. I am a policewoman." She had to stop reacting to his petty provocations. "But remember, I'm not the only woman working here." Two steps and she thrust the file at him. "*Capitano*, this interrogation is in Sicilian."

Brusca's eyes were a clouded and insolent blue. "*Commissaria*, what can I tell you? This is Sicily."

"Look at this: *abbuccarici 'u brodu*. What on earth does that mean?"

"It means he threw broth on him."

"Not literally, Brusca. I can figure that out myself. Do a proper translation. If anyone in Rome looks at this, he'll be totally lost."

"Ah, in Rome." Brusca raised his bulky shoulders and rolled his eyes.

"Again, each report must be accurate and in Italian. And any charges must be classified with the proper designation and number of the law violated. Why is it so hard for you down here to get the simplest thing right?" Marisa regretted the last sentence as soon as she said it. "Ah yes, down here, below the palm tree line," Brusca said. He was projecting, no doubt, to the squad room and the foyer. "Down here, we need to be guided and corrected by all of you from up there."

"Calm down, Brusca."

"Throwing broth means to kill in Mafia talk. They

have dozens of ways of saying this." Brusca slid off his desk so they stood eye to eye.

Marisa took a step backward. "What's this about a car crash with two unidentified victims?"

"An accident on the mountain, rather flamboyant. But nothing important enough for you to be involved." His teeth flashed below his moustache: an appeasing smile.

"No witnesses? No identification? A single car accident on an empty road."

"I visited the site. Too much speed, a nasty curve, the car left the road, down the hill, and then the usual blaze. All obvious and clear."

"And the car registration number? Have you checked that out?"

"The car was in pieces, the licence plate partly melted." Brusca gestured at Roselli a few feet away in the squad room, talking on the phone.

Roselli put his hand over the receiver. "No numbers yet, but the letters are PA, from Palermo." Unlike Brusca, Roselli both respected his chief and was proud of being a policeman. He was in his early twenties, a Calabrese from near Cosenza. *Bimbo*, Brusca sometimes called him. Or *Fesso*: that was another, less deserved pet name, for Roselli was not a blockhead, only refreshingly lacking in self-consciousness. He was unaware of his handsome looks: his long lashes, full mouth, and ears that stuck slightly out.

"Brusca, you take over the phone for Roselli."

"But that isn't—. I don't." Brusca seemed too surprised to rally.

The crash site was twenty kilometres west of Alcamo. Once out of the city, Roselli drove the police car as if it were a Ferrari, whipping around curves, speeding and abruptly slowing, darting around the few cars and one truck they encountered. Five minutes on, Marisa agreed to flashing lights, the public should be warned, but no siren.

Beyond the window, the rolling countryside was spring green. As the car climbed, switchback after switchback, Marisa could see farther and farther to the blue streak of the sea, to the length of the long valley, wooded hills, tidy cultivated fields, the grey snake of the freeway, and the cement outcrop that was Alcamo. Until the scene grew hazy and the smell of smoke intensified.

Another tight corner and they were there. Uniformed policemen, several firemen, their fire truck, and other vehicles punctuated the asphalt. Roselli pulled up behind an ambulance. Two men in white overalls were loading a body bag into the open back. "Stop," Marisa said as she jumped out of the car. "Wait."

"You want to see the remains?" The man looked incredulous.

"I should."

The attendants exchanged a glance. "It's bad," one said.

It wasn't absolutely necessary, Marisa told herself. She could rely on description. "All right," she said. "Not now."

They continued slotting the bag into place beside the other. "Too much for a lady," said the taller one. Marisa bit her tongue.

"The odd thing is the one found in the car was less burnt than the one thrown out," said his stocky colleague.

"How far away was the ejected body?"

"About five metres."

"Where are you planning on taking them?"

"The morgue in Alcamo."

"Take them to the one in Trapani."

"That's two hours, three if the traffic's bad."

"So get going." She turned. "Roselli, phone Doctor Paci and warn him what's coming. And call forensics in Palermo."

Marisa strode the few metres up the road where a uniformed policeman stood motionless, staring down the hill at the crash site. "You, examine the road," she said.

The man had fat lips and a thick, insolent voice. "Done. No tire marks. No brakes applied."

"Traces of another car? Other people?"

"This is a well-travelled road. There are traces of all sorts."

Marisa walked past the last of the scorched tree trunks before she started down the hill. The ground was a stew of ashes, cinders, and wet dirt, and a few metres down she lost her footing. She grabbed a branch of an evergreen bush to stop herself from pitching into a prickly pear. Her feet began to slide in opposite directions. Hoping no one was watching from the road, she hiked up her skirt and managed to right herself. She wasn't going to be able to get closer. Her shoes were heavy with muck and each step was treacherous. She did have a clear view of where the ejected body had landed. The place was properly cordoned off by pegs and yellow tape, as was the vehicle, a heap of black metal crumpled up against a bone-white boulder. A strong acrid smell, like burning hair or smouldering polyester—acrid with an undertone of sweetness.

Her palm was stinging, bleeding, tiny drops pooling in the creases, outlining her love and life lines in red like a garish illustration from a book of divination. "I see much love and strife," a Yugoslav fortune teller had told her once, and Marisa had laughed: "What else is there?" She put her bleeding hand over her mouth and nose to filter the stink. Her tongue flicked up a droplet of blood.

Marisa took the wheel on the drive back. "So Constable," she said, "what do you think?"

"Pardon, *Commissario*?" Roselli's expression showed he wasn't used to being asked his opinion.

"Obviously not an accident. The body outside the car was deliberately set on fire."

"But why do that? Dead is dead," Roselli said.

"To send a message? Though don't the gangs like a big public show, actual blood on the streets?"

"Have you seen the caves in Monte Pellegrino?"

"Years ago, when I was down here visiting a friend. Why? You do mean the ones with the Paleolithic drawings?"

"Those caves, but not the ones the tourists visit."

Those caves. Immediately she remembered a sequence of pictures she had viewed in Rome in preparation for assuming command in Alcamo: limestone caverns, white

25

chambers of horror, white broken by a few black chains, a pair of tongs, a barbecue fork. She remembered a close-up of a clean pyramid of bones, another of a cistern of acid. "The white death, a poetic name for a grisly end."

"The mob isn't subtle," Roselli said. "This crash might be a civilian homicide, a personal vendetta."

By the next morning, several smudged footprints had been found embedded in the mountain mud, two bushes away from the spot where the ejected body had landed. Marisa called the medical examiner. "We need an identification. No fingerprints, I suppose?"

"You're kidding," Doctor Paci said. "Poor bastards."

"Both male?"

"Based on their size. Otherwise, they were burnt, blackened, melted. Deceased A, less so, about thirty percent of his body, but including his hands. Deceased B, third degree burns over eighty percent. You should come to Trapani, see for yourself."

"If only I could fit it in," Marisa said.

"I'm a bit of a gourmand, my dear *Commissario*. I could take you to this out-of-the-way *trattoria* that serves the most exquisite fish couscous."

What an unappetizing line: let me introduce you to the mysteries of pathology and Sicilian cuisine. He was married. She had noticed the ring the first time they'd met, after he had autopsied a young woman who had been strangled by her brother. Did the doctor think she wouldn't care? That his clean profile and practiced smile would convince her?

It took three days for the driver of the Innocenti, Deceased A, to be identified. Forensics extracted the car registration number, and the fire hadn't obliterated his face.
Silvio Inzerillo was twenty-nine years old and unmar-
ried. His father was a plastic surgeon, his mother a former
nurse, and no one in the family had any connection to the
Mafia. They had filed a missing person report after Silvio didn't return the Innocenti, which he had borrowed
from his younger sister. Silvio himself owned a Maserati,
which was at the mechanic's. He did not work; he'd never
held a job. Silvio had told his sister he was driving out
to their aunt's beach cottage on Capo San Vito to spend
some time alone, contemplating his future. So none of
the family had any idea who the other victim could be.
All of the friends they knew were accounted for.

Deceased B was going to be tougher to identify. Marisa
sent Inspector Brusca into the city to excavate the details
of Inzerillo's life: reputation, associates, finances. To find
what he was up to in San Vito, besides contemplation.
And why was Deceased B in that car? Along for the ride?
The questions multiplied. Were both men targets? Or did
one bring death down on the other?

On her walk home that evening, Marisa picked up a small
carton of milk at the *latteria*, and three oranges and a banana at the *fruttivendolo*. She was hesitating between the
rosticceria and the butcher shop—was she up to frying the
meat and then washing the damn pan?—when she noticed a man crossing the pavement before her.

For a moment, a long moment, Marisa saw Roberto Valente, walking in his usual uniform, blue jeans, windbreaker, and exercise shoes, which showed off his youthful, slim, and loose-limbed body and clashed with his grave, mature face. Even as she quickened her step and followed the man into a bakery, she registered that he was not Valente, who was much taller, who had blue eyes, not brown, and a square chin, not a long one. What was wrong with her? Roberto was dead, and this man was alive and talking to her. "Hello, Marisa. This is serendipitous."

He had to remind her he was Alex Zacco, whom she'd met last month at a dinner party in Palermo. The hostess, Ivana, was an old friend from university days. "You have to meet some people, the right people, or you'll never survive," Ivana had said the first time Marisa called. And, still hopeful that there was a way to make this posting more comfortable, that a haven of friendship was close by, Marisa agreed to attend Ivana's dinner.

The right people included a red-haired and freckled architect, a geology professor, a woman who looked like a model and worked for the local RAI TRE station, a correspondent for the national communist paper *l'Unitá*, and Alex, who was introduced as Ivana's cousin. And they were the right people insofar as they were familiar; the rhythm of their conversation made her feel, if not at home, at least at ease. The party could have been anywhere in Italy; it gave off not a whiff of Sicily. All of them seemed to spend their lives in motion: the TV woman had just completed a film on the Haida in Canada;

the reporter and the professor argued over the best restaurant in Berlin; even Ivana and Dario talked about their Christmas holiday in the Maldives. Palermo was just another stop on the itinerary.

For all of them, except Alex. He sounded Sicilian, with his elongated vowels, subtle drawl, and almost formal turns of expression. "Do *you* travel much?" Marisa asked him.

Alex looked at her, as if to ask why she wanted to know. "I visited India, lived in England and Bologna," he said, using the *passato remoto*, the historical past.

"I went to university in Bologna," Marisa said.

Alex didn't seem interested until Ivana, while dispensing advice on the TV woman's sore back, mentioned that Marisa practised yoga. "I'm also an aficionado," Alex said. "I studied at the Iyengar Institute in Poona. A lifetime ago."

"What a coincidence," Marisa said. "That's my style too."

"Have you tried Pilates?" the TV woman asked. "I got bored with yoga." She prattled on, but Alex and Marisa talked around her, as if they were the only two at the table.

And now here he was in Alcamo, standing beside her. "I am visiting our maid," Alex said. "She retired here." One of the shopgirls handed Alex a ribbon-tied package of pastries; the other passed a paper bag with two buns to Marisa.

"You are a good guy."

"She raised me. It is the least I can do." They were

29

standing on the sidewalk outside the bakery. Alex made a motion with his head toward a nearby café. "Could I offer you a coffee? Concetta isn't expecting me at any particular time. We could talk a little."

Marisa was torn. "Not here. Everyone watches." Alex lifted an eyebrow. "Small town, they gossip. I'm from outside, a policewoman. Look, I'll probably be in Palermo early next week. If you give me your number."

Alone in her apartment, over an after-dinner cup of camomile tea, Marisa questioned herself. The report of Valente's suicide had been a shock. She hadn't thought of him in a long time, and to come across it like that with no warning. Someone, Lanza, should have called her. No wonder she thought she saw him. Odd that it was actually Alex. The men did share that way of dressing, that youthfulness. Alex was a different type, she hoped, a better man.

Her thoughts shifted to a more pressing unknown, the unidentified man lying in the morgue. Somewhere there must be someone who had noticed that he was gone, someone who cared. Someone who knew who he had been before he was stripped of wallet, clothes, skin, self.

The man had died in her territory. He was owed justice, though who knew if she could deliver. Marisa could make sure, at least, that he was named and claimed.

4 Sicily/Rome

NOVEMBER 1967 –
MARCH 1968

The second time Fulvia ran away, she was fourteen, gangly. Two thick braids, startling hazel eyes, budding breasts, and a hint of rounded hips. The second time, she was less impulsive; she planned her escape with care. Still, her anger burned hotter—after all, she was fourteen.

In between her first attempt and her second, she had been happy enough, distracted by school and friends, a month at the beach each summer, a week in Rome each fall. Distracted by the endless family gatherings, from baptisms to funerals.

Until one crisp, sunny All Souls' Day. Early that morning, Fulvia dashed back and forth, calling Fedele, searching the garden, the orchard and field, under bushes, behind the pots in the courtyard. When Fulvia came across the other three cats, the outside cats, in the stable, she cried out in frustration. Fedele, Fedele. The skin on her arms and legs prickled into goosebumps. Her knees shook. Where could he be?

The harvest was in, grapes crushed, olives both pressed and pickled. Tomatoes sundried, then soaked in oil or simmered in cauldrons over bonfires, concentrated into sauce. Two weeks ago the courtyard had teemed with workers. Today, it was empty. Who could help her? Toni was leaning against the garage, but he shrugged, mumbled. "The little lady knows I'm blind."

Back inside, Fulvia searched the family rooms again. Fedele could be ill or injured. Or, if someone teased him, angry. She knocked on Davide's door. "I know you," she said accusing him.

"Cut it out," Davide said. "I'm not a boy anymore." Indeed, he had a rifle instead of a slingshot, and went hunting with Zio Antonio instead of stalking the little beasties on the estate. He remained indifferent to Fulvia's panic. "Scram."

She found Nonna in the kitchen, packing up their contribution to the picnic for the annual All Souls' Day outing to the cemetery. "We are leaving in twenty minutes," Nonna said. "Go and change."

"I can't. Nonna, please, I have to find Fedele. "

"The cat will turn up."

"I've looked and looked." Before Fulvia's eyes, black spots multiplied. She fainted. When she came to, she was lying on the tiled floor, the stink of bleach burning her nostrils. The room shifted back and forth.

Nonna bent over, grasped Fulvia by the armpits and

hauled her up. Fulvia clutched the counter. The room was still shifting. "I'm sick. I have to stay home."

"Nonsense," Nonna said. "One day for our dear departed."

"I went yesterday." For the first time, Fulvia had joined the other Arcuri women in sweeping up dirt and dead leaves, washing the stone with detergent, bleach, and water, and polishing the granite. When she returned to Bagna Serena in the evening, she couldn't find Fedele, but didn't worry. Fedele was an independent cat, just as she was an independent girl. But this morning, when he didn't turn up for his main meal, she knew something was wrong. "I'm going to throw up."

Nonna picked a pink apple from a tray of marzipan fruit. "Eat."

Fulvia resisted the impulse to toss the confection and then herself onto the floor.

"You are no longer a child," Nonna said.

Two months earlier, Fulvia had had her first period. Her mother broadcast the news to all the female relatives, as well as to her uncle and father. Zia Miranda and Zio Antonio brought her a present: a gold bracelet. And Mamma presented her with thick hoop earrings, even though Fulvia's ears weren't pierced. "You've become a woman," everyone said, particularly Nonna, and that meant her life was more circumscribed, more regimented than ever.

At the Arcuri mausoleum, a swarm of relatives encircled her with their intrusive hugs and kisses, their inane greetings. No one seemed to notice that she did not speak or smile. She was a hollow angel, like the ceramic statue on a neighbouring grave. Her spirit was in her secret room with Fedele.

She perceived the ceremony in flashes: the sharp spicy smell and fire-bright petals of the chrysanthemums, at least a hundred stems, maybe more, and Zio Antonio intoning the names of the family dead. The rumble of the chorus of voices praying.

In Your mercy, remember Fedele, please.

Mamma, in a new black coat with fur cuffs and collar, held out an oversized loaf of bread, urging everyone to take a piece. Two aunts passed red plastic plates of prosciutto and salami. A gang of children gathered by a cypress tree. In past years, Fulvia had belonged with them, playing hide and seek, the cemetery their miniature town of houses and piazzas. Today she had no desire to run and laugh, but the cacophony of grown-ups was unbearable.

She slipped down the three stairs and through the half-open door of the mausoleum. Mamma had preceded her. She was arranging chrysanthemums in a vase on the small altar. She handed Fulvia a flower and gestured with a small nod to the tomb of Nonno Arcuri. Fulvia had to go up on her tiptoes and stretch to place the flower in the right vase. With a ripple of nausea, she imagined she could see through the granite to the dead, dried to copper brown and black, eyeballs lolling, like the corpses in the Palermo catacombs. "Ma, please, Fedele must be hurt. I feel it. Promise you'll help me look for him."

"As if I had nothing better to do," Mamma said.

"You have to. Promise now."

Her mother brushed a couple of stray leaves off the altar. "*Santa Madonna*, you're annoying. I promise."

Papà would have helped. At least, he would have ordered everyone else to help. Her father was too strict, worse than her mother about rules, but she was his *Beddeletta*, his pretty one, his vagabond, his special girl. "If you were as smart as your sister," he told Davide, when her brother flunked Italian and history in his matriculation exams. "If you had half of your sister's guts," Papà said during another extended reprimand. If her father were home, he would have listened to her.

But he was far away, in a prison at the other end of the country, up near the Austrian border. When Papà had told her he was charged with importing and selling untaxed cigarettes, he laughed. "Ridiculous," he said. "I won't be convicted." Everyone in the family insisted there was nothing to worry about. And for nearly a year, the problem was barely mentioned. Until the trial, until he was found guilty and sentenced. Until he was gone, like when she was a little girl, though this time she theoretically knew where he was.

The conviction changed Fulvia. She began to listen at doors, to note certain facial gestures and grimaces, and to ponder whispers and half-heard phrases. Repeatedly, she asked her family for an explanation. Each of them answered in the same way: your father was betrayed.

By whom?

The Judases. By the police and the court.

Why?

It is their nature. These so-called representatives of the state.

But—

They hate our family. So they trapped your father.

But why?

The *sbirri* are untrustworthy and corrupt. Take this as your lesson.

All of them?

Filth.

One hot afternoon, Mamma answered by cuffing Fulvia hard on the back of the head. "Enough with the questions. You're a broken record."

I'm confused. I don't understand.

"I don't have time for this."

Since Papà had gone to jail, Mamma no longer sat around smoking. She was out all day and some nights, looking after things, she said, and she had a new self-important expression on her face and a clipped tone in her voice. She also visited her husband every three weeks or so. Sometimes she flew, changing planes in Rome, renting a car in Udine. Other times, she drove up in the Mercedes, despite the distance. "It might as well be Germany," Mamma said, "the food, the people, their cursed dialect." To comfort Don Fulvio, she brought him a taste of home. On the plane, she carried two wrapped and beribboned trays of pastries. In the car, she transported cases of fruit: medlars, prickly pears, figs, and, now that it was

November, the first of the blood oranges. She needed at least three cases, what with the guards and Don Fulvio's allies among the prisoners.

After the cemetery, Fulvia made another desperate tour of the grounds, calling. If Fedele could walk, he would show himself. She found her mother in the parental bedroom, packing for her next trip. "Ma." Fulvia had to pause and take a breath.

Her mother held up a pale blue sweater. "Look what I got your father. Loro Piana cashmere."

"Mamma, you promised to help me look. He may be shut in somewhere."

"God knows he needs them up there in that cold, dark north. I decided to buy his coat up there, more choice of winter goods."

"You have all the keys."

"Though if things go as we expect, the appeal will work. He should be home in the spring."

Two days later, Nonna was checking the olives soaking in brine under the side portico. When they were ready, they would be transferred to jars and marinated in olive oil, rosemary, and garlic. As she stirred with a long-handled spoon, a yellow clump floated up to the surface.

When Beppe tipped out the barrel, he and Nonna found a cat's remains: a number of tufts of yellow and black fur and a hairless pickled carcass.

They said it was one of the barn cats, not Fedele. But then Fulvia saw his now-loose leather collar with the star pendant hanging around the shrivelled brown flesh of his neck.

An accident, they told Fulvia, in their kindest voices. No one's fault. The cover of the barrel flipped and rotated on the central metal rod. Fedele must have landed on the wrong spot. Half of the lid dropped and the cat with it.

Davide laughed when he told his friend about the rigid cat. "Marinated," he says. "Tasty. They eat cats in Vicenza, don't they?"

Nonna clucked and gave Fulvia a long hug. "Don't cry," she said to her granddaughter, and "What a waste of good olives," to everyone else. On the phone from the Friulan hinterlands, Mamma's voice was exasperated. She didn't even pretend she was sorry. "Fulvia, I'm sick of this story. It was just a cat. Not your brother or father."

Just a cat? The words were gasoline on the coals of Fulvia's anger.

Just a cat?

Fulvia planned carefully, checking timetables, filling her wallet with money—several years of savings—and buying and borrowing a sort of disguise. In the first-class lounge of the Palermo train station, Fulvia changed herself into an approximation of a city girl, the type she had seen and admired in magazines and on variety shows, Sylvie Vartan or Jane Birkin, sassy, engaging, and unfettered. These young women were elementally different from the ladies of small-town Alcamo, created from air, rather than earth.

Fulvia tossed her school clothes, the past-the-knees skirt and prissy blouse, into the garbage. She pulled on fishnet tights and a Pucci-print mini-dress, both borrowed from her new, slightly older friend Maria Cristina, who thought Fulvia was going to a classmate's party. "My Nonna has banned short skirts," Fulvia pleaded. Though her mother loved to shop, even defined herself through her shopping, it was Nonna who dictated Fulvia's dress-up clothes, who ordered the best dressmaker in Palermo to sew four dresses a year for Fulvia, the winter ones in wool or velvet, the summer in cotton or silk, and all of them still little-girl dresses with Peter Pan collars and smocking across the chest. Her peacoat and knee-high leather boots were passably cool. And the tops and two pairs of pants stuffed into a large bag, with toiletries, underwear, and flannel pyjamas, were less babyish. Nonna didn't care about her at-home clothes. The burgundy leather bag was technically stolen: Fulvia had taken it from her mother's closet, but Mamma hadn't used it in ages. Besides, she had twenty more. Fulvia had bought her first makeup yesterday. Today, she drew black lines around her eyes and piled on the near-white lipstick. She unwound her braids, and her hair sprang out into a mass of curls. She looked a bit older, but not properly mod like the vedettes on TV. Her features were too big, the nose and eyes belonged on a cartoon character. Sighing, Fulvia pulled her hair back with a scarf. It would have to do.

And it did. No one questioned her; no one stopped her. The ticket agent found her the last non-reserved sleeper: pricey, but it brought her privacy and legitimacy. She would save money later, in Rome, once she had joined the students occupying the university, or better still, a radical group,

of shouting, arm-pumping students, astonishing Fulvia by taking the side of the hated *sbirri*. "What's the world coming to?" they repeated throughout the news: not just to the reports of demonstrations, but to any political scandal, to the Vietnam War, and to certain murders—husbands killing wives, mothers killing children. What's the world coming to? Fulvia was sick of hearing that, though some part of her also wondered, what was her world coming to?

Nothing much. Years of sitting on the sofa between her grandmother and mother, watching a flickering screen.

No, Fulvia wanted to be the master of her fate, battling for justice and truth, like the journalist who interviewed Robbie. Oriana Fallaci reported from the global hot spots, from a bunker in North Vietnam, for example, her beautiful face sombre, her light hair caught in two pigtails. And she interviewed the mighty—President Johnson, Pope John, Ho Chi Minh—never toadying to any of them. *La Fallaci* had begun writing for the newspapers at fifteen. Fulvia knew it might not be so easy for her; RAI TV probably did not hire fourteen-year-olds, but she would prepare herself. Fulvia would find Robbie and join the melee.

The shock of losing Fedele had fuelled her getaway. On the night train, in her tiny compartment, she conjured Fedele curled on her front, his head on her clavicle. She could feel the weight of him. The sensory memory floated on a black, cold wave of sadness. She flipped on her side, hugged her middle. She had named Fedele well: he was most faithful, and even now that he was gone, he guided her to freedom.

She slept five minutes at a time, then a curve, a stop,

or the whoosh of a south-bound train would waken her. Alone: the walls of the compartment loomed; the berth was as narrow as a mausoleum slot. Had she really expected to get this far? Breathe, Fulvia told herself, to force down her panic. Breathe. She heard her father's gentle voice, *coraggio*, buck up. Fedele's silky fur beneath her fingers. She was back in her grey room, comforting herself, bracing herself, with the familiar tale of Brave Ninetta.

Once upon a time, whenever a certain merchant had to travel, he would confine his daughters to the house, barring all the windows and walling in the doors. But one day when the most beautiful and brave of the girls, Ninetta, descended into the well to retrieve a thimble, she discovered a tunnel that led to the luxuriant garden of a neighbouring palace. Day after day, she escaped to walk beneath the trees and the flowers. And day after day the Prince watched the beautiful girl from afar. For she stayed only a short time. Too soon she had to enter the tunnel and crawl back to her house.

Fulvia would have to be even braver and more steadfast than Ninetta. She couldn't wait for a prince to rescue her.

The cab driver was incredulous. "You want to go where?" Triple bags hung from his weary eyes.

"I'll pay double."

"Not the place for a respectable young lady like you. It's unsafe. They're insane. Both the police and the students."

"I'll find another cab."

"The roads around that faculty are blocked off."

Fulvia opened the back door and slid in. She repeated: "As close as you can get to the Faculty of Architecture. Valle Giulia." The epicentre of student revolt. The cab driver gave her a long look over his shoulder. Fulvia glowered back: "If you get me to the British School, Via Belle Arti, I can manage myself."

Fulvia's eyes burned, her back ached, and she wished the cabbie would stop yammering. He played the self-appointed guide to the wonders of Rome, the chaos of ancient and modern, Catholic and pagan, church and state, and traffic, traffic, traffic. The cab stopped and started, angling her one way, then another. She grabbed a side strap to help keep herself upright. "Shocking, no? The capital after a small town?"

"I've seen worse." After all, she knew Palermo; she was used to a frantic mix. The cabbie snuck in other leading questions. Was she meeting someone? Eyeing her in the rearview mirror. Instead of answering, Fulvia stared out the window. On a hill, a cluster of ruins. "The Foro Romano," he said.

"Where are you taking me? The long way round?" She had studied the map of Rome until she had memorized the pattern of streets around her destination.

"Where are you staying? Not at the school of architecture, I bet."

"With an uncle." You impertinent fool. She closed her eyes and saw herself in the front line of marching comrades. Almost there.

Or was she? Deposited by the cabbie, for a long moment, she was disoriented, lost. She had not expected the street to be so empty and wide, or the buildings so large and imposing. A flight of stone steps to each colonnaded front. The map hadn't shown the hills, and her luggage suddenly felt heavy. Tinctures of smoke and pepper hovered in the cold air. The climb was steep; her throat began to burn, her eyes to tear. From above, snatches of chants, roars, whistles, and shrieks. Halfway up, her eyes were streaming. She gasped for breath.

For the next two hours, she tried different routes with no success. As the cabbie warned, the so-called forces of order had encircled the area. One approach, she was blocked by a line of helmeted police, on another, a mesh fence. She caught glimpses of a garbage-strewn piazza, of burned or flipped cars. In her only sighting of her imagined liberators, she was so far away they were a seething, multi-coloured blur.

Cold, exhausted, Fulvia retired to a bench in the nearby Borghese Gardens to recharge and rethink her plan. She drank from a bottle of water she bought from a nearby street vendor. She was hungry. She had long digested the cappuccino and *cornetto* from the train station bar.

Under the pale, watery sunlight, she nodded off only to be startled awake by a heavy hand clamping down on her shoulder.

Caught.

Twenty-five years later, she would tell her husband, Sam: "I never belonged in that family. Inside, I always resisted them." In her northern city on the other side of the world from Alcamo, Fulvia hung on to the image of her child self, sitting alone in the silence and the grey light of her secret room. The adult Fulvia rarely talked about her childhood. She did not want to be an object of curiosity, denigrated, or even celebrated, because of her family. She wanted to be judged for the woman she was.

"Don't look back," she said to Sam when he began to wallow in nostalgia. "You'll turn into a pillar of salt."

"Those who don't own their past are condemned to repeat it."

"You're the repetitive one."

"You hate to admit you were a spoiled little princess."

"I was not. You're always so polemical."

"You can't deny the class difference. I was raised in three small rooms. And there were five of us. Just imagine. While you lived on an estate. My mother was a servant, and you had servants."

"You argue for the sake of arguing," Fulvia said.

Sam frequently trotted out anecdotes of his youth for their daughters, Anna and Barbara, who didn't complain, even when they had heard the stories so often that they knew them by heart: The Fall into the Lagoon, Fishing with My Father, Defeating the Class Bully. "Papi, tell us when," they said.

They didn't ask their mother. They were used to her saying she had forgotten. They knew she preferred to read them the old tales. But as Anna turned nine, then ten, and Barbara six, then seven, Fulvia found herself starting to talk about the old life, based on rituals and rhythms of the seasons. How for Saint Joseph's Day, for example, she used to help her grandmother decorate the altar with candles, cakes, and flowers; and then, with her mother, she placed coins and bills in envelopes to be distributed to the needy. How she and Davide had gotten more presents for All Souls' Day than Christmas, which was a lesser holiday. "We didn't have Santa Claus or the Three Kings or even La Befana, the old witch your father told you about. The Dead brought our gifts."

"Weird," said Anna.

"Like ghosts?" said Barbara. "Were you scared?"

Fulvia conjured up Fedele, his china-blue eyes, ivory fur, black paws and face, his sensitivity to her moods. "Fedele was supposed to be Mamma's pet, but he chose me," she told them the night before a visit to the SPCA to choose a pet kitten. "Even when he was tiny, he would follow me around. I made a bed of blankets for him, right beside mine. I had to sneak him in, because he wasn't allowed in my room." Fulvia smiled remembering. "I told him all my troubles. When I was angry or upset, I'd cuddle him and cry into his fur."

"Didn't you have friends to talk to?" Anna asked.

Barbara nodded and clutched her Cabbage Patch doll. "Why would you cry?"

Fulvia had to reassure them. She had had many friends; she had hardly ever cried.

5   Sicily

APRIL 1989

The day after Chief Marisa De Luca saw Valente's ghost, she phoned the office of *Dottore* Giorgio Lanza. He was in a meeting and unavailable. The next time she tried, she was told he was in Rome. She did not want to turn to Lanza for reassurance, but who else knew the complete history of her and Valente's connection? Who else could say with authority *you aren't to blame*?

By the following week, when Lanza finally phoned back, Marisa had pushed aside her vague sense of guilt on her own; she was back to her initial reaction to the report of Valente's suicide: "I don't believe it."

Valente had pulsed with vitality. *Only action*. He spoke fast. *Attack from the front*. He moved, gestured, thought, and planned fast. *Without hesitation. No surrender*. Only his smile was slow, practised, a touch rueful. And his love-making... He had noteworthy stamina. He went through all the *compagne*, the female comrades, taking up with one then another, all the while insisting that the personal was political, which for him also meant that the personal was unimportant and subordinate to the political. But when Valente discovered that Marisa was a policewoman and that his group, *Sempre Guerra*, was finished, he took it personally. She had betrayed him, not just the movement. At the joint trial, the other comrades had hissed and whistled at her when she passed their cage on her way to and from the witness box. Only Valente used words. Marisa could still hear his roar: "*Porca troia*," pig of a whore.

As the mastermind of the group, he had received one of the longest sentences. Still, with time off for good behaviour plus the usual early parole, prisoners rarely served more than one-third of their sentence. Valente must have had only another year left, or less.

"It just doesn't make sense," she told Lanza.

"What are you saying?"

"He wasn't the type."

"Who's to say? A period of despair. You told me yourself he was subject to black moods."

"Can you find out when he was scheduled to be released? The warden of the prison could clarify things."

"My dear Marisa, why do you care? This is why I didn't mention his death to you. He isn't worth a moment's thought."

"I don't speak from concern."

"Be grateful Valente is gone and not out. Not a threat to you." A low blow.

Lanza was asking how things were going: was she

whipping those lazy lumps into shape?

"It's not easy out here in the country."

"Marisa, use what comes naturally. It's worked before."

"Pardon?"

"Your female charm. A little honey."

Marisa stifled the words on the tip of her tongue. *Vaffan culo.* Fuck you. The men would judge any trace of softness, let alone sweetness, as weakness, vulnerability. Still, she decided, a shift in style might help.

Although Lanza had avoided what Marisa wanted most, a rational discussion, and although he had arranged her transfer to Alcamo, she couldn't help counting on his support and guidance. He had mentored her for nine long years, since she had caught his attention at his week-long seminar on terrorism. She had just completed her law degree and begun her police training, and she felt lucky to be taken on by such an important man. "Follow my directions and you'll have a brilliant career," he said.

These were *gl'anni di piombo*, the years of lead: both the years of the bullet and the leaden years. Kidnappings, kneecappings, bombings, and assassinations: terrorism of the left and the right, executed efficiently in this inefficient land. When Marisa graduated with honours from the police academy, Lanza had a job ready for her; she was to go undercover in an offshoot of the Red Brigades. Marisa was reluctant; she had never envisioned herself in such a role. "I'm not an actress. Or a good liar."

A few months later, Lanza convinced her. He appealed to her sense of justice and her love of country; he evoked the Aldo Moro case. The former Prime Minister's kidnapping and murder had come to represent all of the politically motivated kidnappings and murders of the last few years. Moro was martyred, his five police bodyguards slaughtered, and no one had paid. "His executioners and those behind his execution walk free, enabling and committing further acts of terror," Lanza said. "They highlight the state's weakness and incompetence."

It was Marisa's duty to combat this evil by infiltrating an extremist cell, led by a certain Roberto Valente. She was to discover Valente's connection to the Moro case. "He planned the operation, supported it, I'm sure," said Lanza. And though she was never able to find proof of such a link, she did decipher the cell's structure and gathered information on its strategy and planned targets, which led to the thirty-one convictions.

Lanza had arranged for a special commendation as well as further plum assignments. Marisa was more than capable, but she knew the politics of the justice bureaucracy were such that, without Lanza's protection, she might still have been a constable. When she heard that he had been made head of the anti-Mafia squad in Sicily, she felt confident he would appoint her to the team. He had said as much last September when he summoned her to his office. That afternoon, he reminded her of the relatively recent laws against organized crime and the progress of the maxi-trial in Palermo. "We are going to be on the frontlines, Marisa, facing an enemy even more deadly than the radicals." He strolled back and forth before her, gesturing as if he were lecturing a class. On every fourth turn, he would pause and cast a glance at the Roman bust on the tall credenza, which drew attention to his handsome and eerily similar profile.

"De La Torre, Della Chiesa, prosecutors, judges, trade unionists, politicians, shot or blown up. Journalists, a forensic scientist, six *carabinieri* in one shootout. Anyone who stood up, who spoke out against the *Cosa Nostra*, so aptly named, our thing indeed." Lanza said.

He went on, repeating statistics and slogans. Marisa knew all of it by heart, but she kept an interested expression on her face. She sat on a flimsy antique chair and nodded at least once a minute. "Just like the last time, we will defeat them; we will be victorious," he said, his face glowing with certainty. Marisa grew buoyant with excitement. They were going back to the battlefield, and this time she would not be working alone, but as part of a team, with brothers and sisters in arms. Her spirit expanded, floated up and up to the eighteenth-century frescoed ceiling, perching on a country hillock beside a cluster of bare-bottomed cherubs.

Months passed, and the promised call to join Lanza in Palermo did not come. Marisa still had faith. There must be a reason for the delay, she believed, until the official letter arrived: she was ordered to Alcamo. Was she being punished? But for what? Had she simply lost Lanza's favour? She might be stuck for years. Perhaps this new job was a test. She had to prove herself worthy—again.

What if she couldn't do it this time?

What if it couldn't be done? By anyone? Or, at least, by any woman? She wouldn't be the first female to command the main police station in a small city, but she was the first in Alcamo and in western Sicily.

Perhaps it was Lanza who had lost favour, lost power. The latest change in government had brought a new deputy minister of the interior, who might well be replacing the old guard with his friends and allies. That was the way things went. One day you were in, the next day out.

Marisa rejected this scenario the next time she laid eyes on Lanza. He had lost nothing. She could tell even before she sat down opposite him; his face telegraphed preoccupation and self-satisfaction. They were meeting for lunch in an upscale *trattoria* near her office. Marisa intended to ask why she was being denied a place in the anti-Mafia squad, but once she was with him, she couldn't get the words out.

Without asking, Lanza ordered for both of them: pasta with mushrooms and rabbit, a side of garlic spinach, and a bottle of Barolo. Lanza's manner was more formal and distant; she wasn't projecting. Marisa took a big gulp of wine. She was not going to show her dismay. "It will be good experience," Lanza said.

"Good?"

"Useful, first-hand. You'll get a sense of the culture, the roots of the phenomena." Was he offering an excuse? Or trying to reassure her that the posting was not a dead end, but an unavoidable detour? "*Dottoressa* De Luca—

Marisa—you aren't eating."

"I am." She brought a forkful to her mouth. Chewing and swallowing took determination. Her tongue felt as if it were coated in fat. "If I needed to be out in the field, I could have been sent to Corleone, the heart of the heart of the beast." As she spoke, Marisa's cheeks burned and her heart pounded, as if she were a truant child before a school principal.

"Too dangerous. Unthinkable." This from the man who had placed her in a nest of assassins. He was eating slowly, elegantly, pausing to wipe his mouth with the white linen square of a napkin, so in control of the pasta strands not one drop of sauce went astray. She took another gulp of the palate-pricking wine. She had been an idiot to feel secure and appreciated. To presume.

"You will seize this opportunity?" he said. "Give the job your best."

"I always do."

Two weeks after the car crash on the mountain, the second body remained unidentified at the morgue in Trapani. Marisa convened Brusca, Roselli, and another young constable, Arcangelo, around the table in the small meeting space next to her office. A beast, a beauty, and a birdman with long, angular limbs and dark-ringed eyes. And her role? The reluctant cynic, *Dottoressa Diogenes*, in search of an honest cop.

She delivered her prepared talk on team effort and collective responsibility. "We have two men murdered in our jurisdiction. We have to get busy."

"That's a supposition," Brusca said, lighting a cigarette with a showy silver lighter. "No hard evidence."

"I didn't invent the arson, Inspector. Even more telling, there was no trace of a wallet or ID holder, Dr. Paci says, burnt or melted, on Deceased B. I suspect someone took his wallet before the kerosene was poured." Black marker pen in hand, Marisa turned to the flip chart and squeezed in between the chairs and the wall. She wrote and spoke: "Dr. Paci says that the unknown man was between forty and fifty, so probably a few years older than the other victim, Silvio Inzerillo. He also thinks either *Signore* B. was a foreigner or he lived away for many years."

"How can he tell?" Roselli said.

"Pointy head," Brusca joked. "He was an alien."

Marisa ignored him. "He had a dental bridge made from materials not commonly used in Italy or even Europe. Doctor Paci has requested a forensic artist be sent from Palermo, so a likeness can be sketched from the characteristics of the skull. Meanwhile, Arcangelo, you should continue to check the national missing persons list for a possible match."

Arcangelo let out a long, sad sigh. "You said he was a foreigner."

"Yes, but he knew Inzerillo, so he wasn't simply a tourist."

Arcangelo nodded: "Could be an *oriundo*, originally from here."

"Inspector Brusca, what about your interviews with

Inzerillo's family?"

"His mother and sister repeated what they had said to the Palermo constable. They had no idea who the other guy could be. Their dear Silvio had many, many friends. He was such a good son, loving brother, blah, blah. Everybody loved him, blah, blah. *Un ragazzo d'oro.*"

"Well, at thirty-four, his golden shine must have been wearing off," Marisa said. "I also told you to contact his known friends, more distant relatives."

"I'll get to it when I can, *Commissaria.*"

"My title is *Commissario*, Brusca. Or *Dottoressa.*" How many times did she have to tell him?

"It's not going to be worth it. I already spoke to a cousin and two ex-girlfriends, and I uncovered a few things about Silvio, *i beddu.*" Brusca smiled at Marisa as if to say he couldn't help it, only a Sicilian word would do. "He had expensive tastes and limited finances. Of course, so does half of Palermo. He went to university for years but never got his degree. He worked in his parents' clothing store when he felt like it. About a year ago, Silvio took up with a group of high-living aristocrats. Sardinia, Venice, Paris; when he was here, nights of poker with princesses in ruined palaces."

"Good," Marisa said, "progress." She wrote the words loan shark and *cosca*, clan, in big letters on the flipchart. "He owed money to the wrong people."

"Must have." Brusca paused to light another cigarette with the silver lighter. "But that doesn't get us very far. You'd better learn; you won't be able to prove anything."

"Why? You think we can't find out the source of the loan? Obviously we're talking Mafia."

"What Mafia?" Brusca said.

"Are you suggesting that a Mafioso can never be caught and convicted? That we shouldn't even try?"

"First of all, you have the typical northern fixed-idea about Sicily. You see the Mafia everywhere. We have criminals, gangs, like everywhere else."

"Bullshit. Besides, you are contradicting yourself. A criminal, a gang, can be stopped. A conspiracy is more difficult. I was going to ask the three of you to deliver an analysis of the local clan hierarchy and its position in the wider organization, but obviously I can't rely on you, Inspector." She nodded at Arcangelo and Roselli. "A report next Monday. Inspector Lo Verde will help you."

She turned to leave. "Must be that time of the month," someone mumbled behind her. Who had said it? The men were filing out. Which one? Brusca, of course. But how could she prove it had been him? And what good would it do? How could she prove anything?

Patience, Marisa told herself each morning on her way to the station house. Patience, control, patience, control—her mantra as she speed-walked down claustrophobic lanes and broad avenues, through car-choked piazzas, past hives of young and old, past cafés, shops, and baroque churches, under laundry lines and towering palms and a celestial blue sky. Give it time. Nothing was foreordained. She was going to make the best of this posting, this place.

But all day she had battled inertia, and ignored the odd half-hidden obscene gesture or mumbled suggestive phrase from Brusca and his gang. By seven or eight in the evening, on the walk back to her lodgings, Marisa's pace had slowed. Her jaw ached and her back was tight. In the morning she scarcely registered the Norman Castle as she zipped by, but in the evening's darkening light, the ancient structure, with its four towers and massive crenellated walls, loomed large and sinister. Often Marisa stopped in a bar nearby to reinforce herself with a glass of freshly squeezed orange juice or a glass of the local wine, Alcamo White. She had a favourite spot at a small table by the window where she could sip and stare at both the passers-by and the castle. Seven hundred years old, but it looked ageless, unweathered, impenetrable, both empty and throbbing with presence, dominating the centre of town.

Ivana invited Marisa to another dinner party, a small, casual one this time. "Alex has asked about you, twice," Ivana said. "He never does that."

"He doesn't have a girlfriend, then?"

"Not for a long time. As far as we know."

"I liked him," Marisa said. "He seemed genuine."

She decided to make an effort, play up her feminine side: a black cashmere sweater, and a black and white floral skirt. Pearls, red lipstick, and two sprays of perfume. All probably too much for Alex, who arrived in jeans and a white dress shirt and didn't say much for most of the dinner. Marisa talked too much and drank too much.

She and Ivana and Dario grew tipsy as they knocked back Campari cocktails, then Alcamo White and Alcamo Red, with the octopus salad, asparagus, and grilled veal chop. Good thing Ivana had invited her to spend the night in the guest room.

Alex stuck to water. He had the face of an ascetic and his deep, dark eyes reminded Marisa of a Byzantine mosaic. Marisa felt his gaze, his attention. She was suddenly conscious of the sweeping generalizations and pretentious phrases dropping from her mouth. "Sorry. Don't listen to me." She let out a giggle. "It's the isolation. I'm losing it. And I guess I don't get this place."

"Not another tiresome conversation about the Sicilian soul," Dario said, making a face. "We're not so very different from the rest of you on the continent."

"We are so. We're less frivolous, tougher." Ivana put a platter of cheeses down on the table. "Tuma, smoked provolone, and cacciocavallo."

"I don't ever want to hear the words sexism, fatalism, and historical determinism again," Dario said. He offered a cigarette to Alex, and they both lit up.

Ivana returned with two packages of pastries. Alex had brought one and Marisa the other. "We have the horn of plenty here," Ivana said, unwrapping the silvered paper.

"Every damn visitor has their theory."

"Dario, stop it." Ivana lifted up a *cornetto di crema* and touched the edge to Dario's closed lips, leaving a white streak. "Show your sweet side."

"Ignore him," she said to Marisa. And then to Alex,

"What are you doing smoking? With your asthma?"

Alex took a deep drag. Under the table, his free hand brushed Marisa's leg. "Who have you been reading?" His tone was gentle, even intimate. "Lampedusa?"

"Of course."

"If we want things to stay as they are, things will have to change," Ivana recited.

"Fascistic bullshit," Dario said, using a piece of cheese as emphasis. "Human nature is not fixed or unchangeable."

"And Verga," Marisa said.

"The earth trembles with despair," Ivana said. "Even I find that too much."

"Things can improve," Dario said.

"Pirandello," Marisa said.

"Who am I? Who are you? One, no one, and a hundred selves," said Alex. He laughed. He was stroking Marisa's knee. "Try Sciascia. He is up-to-date. And he writes about the Mafia and Sicily with a lot of insight."

"Sciascia broadcasts the same fatalistic message as the other writers," Dario said. Sicily and Sicilians will not, cannot, change."

"I read his article attacking the anti-Mafia," Marisa said.

"You know, then," Dario said.

"He is warning us the anti-Mafia, politicians, judges, and, *salve* Marisa, police, can be both instruments of and aspirants to power," Alex said. "Don't be misled into thinking the legal side is without flaw or represents the good."

We do represent the good, Marisa thought, but didn't say. She didn't want to start an argument. But she felt sure, at least, of that.

Marisa first heard about the Arcuri in the report she had ordered on the local *cosca*. Arcangelo, Lo Verde, and Roselli produced a broad sketch; Marisa turned to a magistrate in Trapani and a captain of the *carabinieri* in Corleone to fill in a few details. The Arcuri clan was old-fashioned, specializing in cigarette smuggling, protection, loans, government contracts, but not drugs. It used to be one of the most powerful families on the island represented in the Cupola, the governing body of the Cosa Nostra. Then, in the late seventies, in the war of the Corleonesi versus the Palermitani, they sided with the latter, the less ruthless, more traditional side. The losing side. The victors gained control of the Cupola and the island's *malavita* by blood and slaughter, not only of their enemies, but any of their own soldiers who hesitated or expressed scruples.

The Arcuri were not wiped out unlike many of the Palermo gangs. Still, six years earlier, Fulvio Arcuri had been machine-gunned to death in his bulletproof Mercedes. In the following months, another Arcuri, a cousin, was found dead in the trunk of an abandoned car an ocean away in Montreal, and Fulvio Arcuri's driver and favourite, Enzo Impastato, disappeared and was presumed murdered. In each case, no one was charged, but everyone in Alcamo from the station house to the hardware store could have told you who was responsible.

Conversely, in the next two years, the local police were able to arrest an unusually high number of the clan's *picciotti*. These foot soldiers were charged, tried, and sent to prison for the usual crimes: robbery, arson, assault, smuggling, and extortion. The surviving top men fled or chose to lay low until the wheel of fortune turned, as it always does. A few of the Palermo survivors, seeking revenge, became *pentiti*, breaking *omertà*, collaborating with law enforcement. Now, at least a few of the Corleonesi were being prosecuted in the maxi-trial. As a result, Antonio Arcuri, Fulvio's brother, returned from Venezuela, and Davide Arcuri, Fulvio's son, from Canada. The clan was resurgent, back on the Cosa Nostra's provincial ruling commission though not yet on the Cupola. "And don't believe that canard about no drugs," said the magistrate in Trapani. "The Arcuri are changing with the times. The new boss, Don Antonio, likes to say he's *a bit of a philosopher*. Well, he's a wily bastard, all right. Knows how to seize opportunities, including global ones." The report gave Marisa a focus, an impetus. Now the enemy in her jurisdiction was less amorphous, though still an abstraction.

Almost a month after the crash on the mountain, an inspector with the Venice police called Alcamo about the unidentified man. A Venetian woman, a certain *Signora* Mazzolin, had gone into the central station and declared her son missing. He had flown down to Sicily in late March, and though he hadn't given an exact day for his return, he was overdue. At first, the inspector hadn't

II
Earth

All at once she threw off the gray cat's fur and appeared as she really was, young and beautiful in her glistening dress.

—"Betta Pilusa"

6   Alberta, Canada

APRIL, 1989

Instead of opening the screen door, the woman stood staring at John through the glass. What's with her? he was obviously not selling or canvassing, he was in his uniform, holding up his badge. "Fulvia Mazzolin?" he said.

A slight nod. Her right hand clutched her bathrobe closer to her throat. Her dark hair looked hacked off, with short bits sticking out at odd angles.

"I'm Sergeant John Buonaiuto of the Edmonton Police Force." She didn't move. "Can I come in, Mrs. Mazzolin?" She was a tall, slim woman, dignified despite the hair and the bathrobe. "It's important."

"The girls." She unlocked the door. "Has something happened at school?"

John stepped in. "Nothing to do with your daughters."

"Well then?" Instead of answering, he bent over, loosened his shoelaces and slipped off his shoes. It was a sign of respect—if he had come to interrogate, he would have kept them on—but it also signalled that he did not expect to be kept at the door. His stocking feet were cold on the tiles in the hall. She led him into a room that could have been in a magazine: modern, sharp-edged furniture, no trinkets or framed photographs, only a beaten-silver bowl, practically big enough to bathe in, and two large landscape paintings, one a yellow canola field under a bright blue sky, and the other a stark, almost menacing mountain scene. She motioned for him to sit on one of the two pale-grey leather sofas. "I'll get dressed before we talk."

He let himself sink back into the sofa. The desire for a cigarette was sharp in his mouth. He had quit six months earlier when his wife had left him, tackling two addictions at once. He had done well, almost no backsliding. Still, intermittently, the urges returned, as insistent as ever. Especially when he was uneasy, when he was the bearer of bad news. It didn't matter how often he did this.

Before John made detective, he had been assigned to North Edmonton, which included both the original Little Italy with cafés, stores, church, and park, and the more up-scale, low-crime suburb to which many of the Italian immigrants had moved. He soon became the go-to guy for notifications of death to Italian families. John had protested he was second generation, he didn't speak Italian, but the head of the communications decided John knew how to handle any excessive expressions of grief. "You guys tend to get emotional, the way I hear it."

John was tired of the *you guys*, of the jokes. Hey John,

"But you aren't certain it's him?"

"It is a tentative identification, which is why we need his dental records. He had a bridge, North-American made."

"He did." For a long moment, Fulvia Mazzolin did not say a word, but stared at the painting behind John's head. "I told him not to go." Her voice remained steady. "I told him."

John put all thought of Samuele Mazzolin aside. He had played his part, notifying the widow.

But a week later, a telephone call brought the man back.

"Sergeant. Buonaiuto?"

The voice was female and foreign. He thought he knew it.

"Fulvia Mazzolin?"

"Concerning her, yes. This is Marisa De Luca."

"Pardon?" Trying to remember if he'd heard the name before.

"I'm the *Commissario*, the chief of the Alcamo district police."

A female chief in Sicily. "Did you receive the dental records? Has the identity been confirmed?"

"Yes, it was Mazzolin. There is much investigation to be done there, in your city."

"Investigation?"

"Someone deliberately set this man on fire," she said, "after he was dead."

"You think there was foul play?" John could taste the surge of adrenaline.

"Play? Sergeant Buonaiuto, you don't speak Italian?"

"Call me John. No, I don't."

"Can you understand? Sometimes, a person cannot speak, but."

"Afraid not. Well, not enough anyway. But you speak good English." He could now distinguish her voice from that of the widow. The policewoman pronounced the words more precisely, with a British intonation. Her voice was husky, melodic. What kind of face went with the voice?

"It was a deliberate act, as if to obliterate his very presence." He pulled his attention back to the *Commissario's* words. "And we found footprints on the hill that must belong to whoever set the fire. I think the brakes of the car were sabotaged. We can't prove that; the car is in a pitiful state. We did find traces of silver paint on the section of the bumper that wasn't burnt. They were forced over the edge. And then whoever was in that second car climbed down the hill and finished the job."

"Who was the other victim? And what were they doing driving on that road?"

"Yes, exactly. The other man, Silvio Inzerillo, was from Palermo. His family claimed he must have been driving home after a few days of relaxation at their summer house. Alone, as far as they knew. The place is isolated, by a national park, handy for smuggling. Drugs, of course."

"But there's no evidence?"

"Not yet. But we think these guys were amateurs. Inzerillo had no previous history. He was seriously in debt. We need to know about Mazzolin. About his history. Why would he be involved? Was he also in debt? And then there's his wife's family, his in-laws. What is their role in all this?"

"The wife I met?"

"Of course. She's an Arcuri. Her father used to be the local boss of bosses. Now her uncle's in charge."

"I never would have guessed."

"Was Mazzolin working for them or against them?"

Toward the end of the call, Chief De Luca announced she was flying to Venice the next day to attend Samuele Mazzolin's funeral and interview his family. She asked that John look into the man's life in Edmonton: "Jobs, friends, finances, everything you can find." She also wanted him to go over the Mazzolin phone records, noting any calls to and from Italy in the last five months.

"I'll need an official request with a rationale," John said. He was going to have to file an affidavit, an Information to Obtain, and go before a judge to be granted a warrant.

"What a hassle. And it's going to take time," John told Lloyd as they pulled up in front of the Mazzolin house. "I explained we aren't allowed to go on a fishing expedition. She seemed a tad surprised."

"They must have a sizable budget there for phone calls," Lloyd commented. "Sounds like the lady went on

69

long enough."

"She's used to giving orders, that's for sure." John turned off the car engine and looked over at the house. It bore none of the usual signs that the home belonged to Italian immigrants: no wrought iron ornamental fence, no brick arches, and no stone lions. It differed from the homes on either side only in the trapezoidal rock garden in the front yard and the curving red stone path to the door. "So I'll be jumping through hoops. And for what? Who knows if she's on the right track. Were they importing drugs? Were these Arcuri were involved? Hard to judge over long distance."

Lloyd said. "You don't know how good her instincts are."

"Are we supposed to be suspicious of Mrs. M. just because she's related to a nasty bunch?"

Lloyd flashed his familiar I-have-a-lot-more-experience-than-you smile. "Seems wrong. Still, the fruit doesn't fall far from the tree." Lloyd rang the doorbell and almost immediately the inside door was opened by a little girl of about eight, wearing an oversized Mickey Mouse T-shirt and shorts. She gazed at them solemnly, opening the outer door only after the two officers introduced themselves. When they stepped in, she ran off to call her mother.

Mrs. Mazzolin appeared in a black robe. "Was it a mistake? Was it someone else?" Her hair no longer looked as if it had been chopped off with gardening shears. It was even shorter but followed the shape of her head.

Instead of answering, John introduced Lloyd. Only after she led them to the living room did he say: "I'm sorry to say a match was made. Your husband was in that car crash."

She did not react.

"I have some questions for you."

"Questions? Why?"

"The crash was not an accident."

That startled her. "Not? What do you mean?"

"The car was deliberately forced off the road. Your husband was tossed out. Someone poured gasoline all over him." She didn't flinch. "Murder," John said.

"No, this is too much."

"There is solid evidence. But nothing we can talk about yet," Lloyd said, masking how little they knew.

"Nothing indeed. Fantasies of the Sicilian police," the woman said.

"With a shock like this, it doesn't seem real at first. It's normal to feel numb," Lloyd said.

"Lieutenant, I don't need to be told what's normal."

"Do you need some time? We can come back," John said.

"I don't need *time*." Her mouth twisted.

John opened his notebook and began his questions. She answered mechanically until he asked, "When did you last see your husband?"

"He left this house on January 20."

"And when did you last hear from him?"

"January 20."

71

"You were estranged? Separated, Mrs. Mazzolin?"

"Not legally, but that was why I didn't know he was missing." Her mouth turned down in a tiny grimace at the end of each of her statements, placing visual quotation marks around her words.

"Did you know he was in Italy? And that he went to visit your mother?"

"I did. Sam went to pay his respects to my family."

"Why would he do that?" John could not imagine himself visiting his in-laws at the moment of his and Janet's separation.

"Maybe he wanted their relationship to remain cordial. Maybe he wanted to convince them I was in the wrong. To see if they could influence me." She smiled wanly, as if at the ridiculousness of the thought. And then, again, the fleeting grimace.

"Did he succeed?" Lloyd asked.

"At winning over my mother? I don't know."

"Surely they wouldn't take his side?" said John.

"My husband wanted all of us to return to Italy. My mother did too."

"And you?"

"Holidays, business, fine. But to live? We tried going back four years ago. Now I have a business here, a clothing store in LeMarchand Mansion."

John looked up from his notebook. "Any reason why your husband decided to go when he did?"

"A sudden flood of nostalgia. His excuse was a job someone scared up for him in Venice." Her voice was weary.

Another girl, this one about eleven, stood in the doorway, cradling a grey cat. "Anna, please, stay with your sister. We're almost done."

"Why should I?" The cat's legs were flailing. "I get to know why the police are back," the girl said. "He's my Dad." Anna must have relaxed her grip. The cat streaked to the mother's feet.

Mrs. Mazzolin bent and smoothed its fluffed up fur. Her voice had turned gentle. "Anna, a few more minutes, and we'll talk." The girl lifted a hand to her mouth. She bit down on the tip of her index finger, then turned, and with a last glance at John and Lloyd, was gone.

Lloyd leaned forward. "We still have some questions, Ma'am."

"Another day." She paused, her face telegraphing a real exhaustion.

"We know it's tough," Lloyd said, playing his most sympathetic side. "If it wasn't most important." As he often told John, "Push them when they're tired."

"Tomorrow, in the afternoon."

"Aren't you going to go to Italy?" John showed his surprise.

"I couldn't even if I wanted to, which I don't. I asked him not to go, and he didn't listen. It wouldn't have happened, if he had listened. I had had my operation. I'm having treatments. He insisted I could join him later, when I was stronger, knowing, knowing—"

The doorbell, three long notes, interrupted her. Mrs. Mazzolin's entire body twitched. The older girl loped through the living room and down the hall. The bell rang again. "We can come back," John said. "But today we need the names of his last employer, of a good friend, of anyone you think might be useful."

Mrs. Mazzolin did not answer. Her attention was on the approaching voice, loud, gritty, and unintelligible. The source, a stereotype of a Mediterranean crone, barged in, bustled over to Mrs. Mazzolin and plopped down beside her. The newcomer acknowledged Lloyd and John's presence with a glower. She was short, thickset, and wrinkled. Her salt and pepper hair was pulled tight in a bun. She spat out some words at Mrs. Mazzolin.

Mrs. Mazzolin answered her with an introduction. "Sergeant Buonaiuto and Lieutenant. Dudley, my aunt, Mrs. Dolores Grignoli. They are here to ask questions about Samuele."

Mrs. Grignoli's voice was just as harsh when she spoke English. "Questions. *Dio*, can't you see the state she's in?"

"*Zia*, they think the car crash was not an accident."

A couple of tongue-twisting words, insults no doubt, and then the aunt turned to the policemen. "Lies. Stop this harassment; she's sad and she's sick. She told you she had a tumour in her breast?"

"*Zia*, please."

"And reacted against the radiation?"

"There's no need."

"Show them the chest." The woman pulled aside the lapel of her niece's robe, exposing a trail of red, weeping sores.

Mrs. Mazzolin jerked the robe back into place.

"Enough," she said. "Sergeant Buonaiuto, if you pass me that pen and a piece of paper, I'll give you what you need." She wrote quickly. The aunt kept up a low grumble. "Last employer and two friends. I don't know the addresses off the top of my head. I'm sure you can find them."

In the car, the two men were silent almost until the station house. At the last intersection, where the red light seemed to go on forever, Lloyd said, "That's one angry woman."

"You mean Mrs. M.?" John said. "I get it. Years of marriage, two kids, and he walks out just when she needs him most." Lloyd had been married to the same woman for twenty-five years and didn't understand what it was like to be abandoned. "And then the son-of-a-bitch goes and gets himself killed."

Lloyd didn't reply until they were inside the station and had filled their mugs. "He was up to something. I can see why the lady chief is thinking drugs."

John took a sip of coffee and made a face. "This stuff is worse every day. Look, what if he wasn't planning to abandon his family? He had this opportunity and was trying to force her to join him. A power move. You know how stubborn some women can be."

"I recognized the aunt, old Dolores Grim-and-mouldy at once."

"I've heard the name before."

"She and her son Joe are heavy into slum housing. broken plumbing, broken windows, bad wiring, no heat, no insulation, overcrowding. Not all their rental properties, but too many. They rent to desperate cases, people on welfare, drunks, anyone who has trouble finding a place. To hear the son explain it, they're serving the public. And everything is the fault of the renters. But letting the houses fall apart is part of the plan. Downgrade a street, buy up some more houses cheap, and then bulldoze them all and put up new ones. They made a mint until the real estate market crashed."

"Wasn't the son charged with something?"

"Arson. One of their walk-ups in Strathcona. Maybe five years ago. The charges didn't stick. We thought Joe hired someone to do the deed but couldn't prove it. The insurance refused to pay up."

"It didn't deter them?"

"No more fires. I met the old lady when I arrested her for assault."

"What? At her age? That's impressive."

Lloyd leaned back in his chair and put one foot up on the edge of his desk. "Tough old buzzard. She knew me right away too. That's probably why she acted all protective of her niece. They own fewer places now, but they still bully the renters. I arrested her after she whacked a poor old man with a two-by-four. He was standing up for his rights, wanted a wall fixed. She brought a piece of plywood, told him to do it himself. They had words; bang, he fell down some stairs. Wasn't the first, but he came to us."

"Fine and probation?"

"One hundred and fifty hours of community service."

"The usual slap on the wrist." John hesitated. "I figured the family connection in Sicily didn't mean anything. She'd left and didn't want to go back. But then the aunt came in. So the family here's not entirely on the up-and-up either."

"You have to look at family, friends," Lloyd said. "It isn't everything, just another piece of the puzzle. I watched Mrs. M.'s face when her aunt walked in, and she was upset."

"She probably thought their association would reflect badly on her. She'd know we'd figure out who her aunt was," John said.

"I guess. But the look in her eyes: it was disgust, pure and simple."

7

Sicily
1 9 6 8 - 1 9 6 9

Who had turned her in? Must have been the cab driver, bag-eyed bastard. Fulvia kicked the metal legs of a chair, and pain flared through her foot, up her leg. Maybe not. She had thought she could blend in, pass for one of the thousands of university students. Wrong.

The cops in this neighbourhood station house had not questioned her or searched her bag, yet they knew who she was and where she was from. They called her "little lady," their voices amused, and "Miss Sicily." They took turns offering food and drink. A panino, a coffee, a lemon soda? One smiling *sbirro* held out a plate of chocolates. "Excuse the long wait."

Fulvia was not fooled. She was a prisoner, caged in a narrow room with plate-glass walls.

Around eight in the evening, a blond woman in civilian clothes entered the room. "Fulvia," she said, "your uncle is coming to fetch you." Zio Antonio—Fulvia's chest tightened. She was in for it now. She waited, swinging her legs, flexing her feet. Half an hour, an eternity, and the woman returned, smiling. "Come on, you tired girl. Your uncle has arrived." She ushered Fulvia into the muddle of desks and people that was the main squad room. Fulvia looked left and right: no uncle. An ugly old man was walking toward her down the central aisle. The smiling woman gave Fulvia a little push. "You see, rescue."

Who was this stranger? He couldn't be here to fetch her. He didn't look like one of Papà's men. He had hunched shoulders, big ears, and magnified by his glasses, protruding eyes. More like a priest, but he wasn't wearing long skirts or a dog collar. And he was escorted by two tall types, guards with thick necks and shaved heads. The trio drew the attention of everyone in the room: typewriters fell silent; chatter faded. The smiling woman had her hands clasped as if she were about to pray. "Honourable Minister," she said. "I am overwhelmed by your presence."

The Frog King ignored her.

He stopped in front of Fulvia and extended his arms as if to clamp her into an embrace. "You have been a naughty girl," he said.

Fulvia stepped back: "You're not my uncle."

"I'm here for the family." Behind the lenses, his eyes were opaque, like the unseeing orbs of a ventriloquist's dummy. "Your poor mother, your Nonna Rosa, frantic with worry."

She was sure he didn't know either her mother or her grandmother. "He's not my uncle," she said louder.

No one heard her. They had all fallen under the Frog King's spell. The smiler was still talking: honourable minister this and honourable minister that. There was an open door at the other end of the room, but even if there weren't twenty people in the way, even if she made it out of the building, where would she go? They would hunt her down. Fulvia had no choice but to give in, to follow. She was a package, tied up, marked for delivery. She was expressed out of the building and into the back seat of a big black car.

The Frog King sat beside her. He smelled as if he had scrubbed himself with a harsh laundry soap. The car sped through the city, its way cleared by police cars, sirens, and blue revolving lights. Once past a wasteland of suburbs, the clamorous escort fell back. Now only the growl of the engine, darkness, then the intermittent flare of an oncoming headlight. The Frog King did not speak to Fulvia or glance in her direction, even when her breath grew raspy, and a half-strangled sob slipped out. At a checkpoint, a booth and a barrier arm, the car stopped; the left front window slid down. A uniformed soldier leaned in, looked straight at her.

Where was she? In the lair of the Frog King. She strained to see one sign, then another, but couldn't make out the words. Through the windshield, she saw a cluster of lights, cars, and people. And off to one side, a small plane. When the car stopped, she managed to whisper "Did Papà—?"

The Frog King's face remained expressionless. His voice was as quiet as hers. "Your father requested that I expedite matters."

For a few seconds, when the plane lifted off the earth and began to climb, a spasm of excitement loosened the black fear that had her by the throat. For a few seconds, she was flying. If only it were day and she could see the land below, the patterns of hills and sea. Instead, darkness and isolated clusters of lights. The plane shuddered and dropped. Her stomach was a bouncing ball of anxiety. Again her throat and lungs tightened. She ached with exhaustion, craving her bed and her room. Despite the soporific drone of the engine, the comfortable leather seat, and the dim lights, her body resisted sleep. She was on guard.

After the plane landed, the Frog King was the first one up. On his way down the aisle, he stopped and turned to Fulvia. Leaning over so his mouth was close to her ear, he said, "Tell your father, tell your uncle that there will be no paper trail. No sign you were in Rome." His breath smelled of sharp mint and wet earth, swamp. "And tell them I am a true friend and happy I could be of service."

They had arrived not at Punta Raisi, but at a deserted airstrip. At the bottom of the exit stairs, one of the bodyguards tugged on her elbow and steered her away from the Frog King and his little crowd of retainers. Her brother was a few metres away, leaning against the Range Rover. "Thank you," Davide said to the guard who handed him Fulvia's bag.

"*Sorelluccia*," Davide said, his eyes amused. But then his face changed; he assumed his role. "*Stupida troia*," he spat, and Fulvia was no longer the cute little sister, but a stupid whore. His forearm smashed into her face, knocking her off her feet onto the muddy ground. A kick, like a sword piercing her side. She jumped up almost as fast as she went down. *I'll scratch his eyes out.* But she could feel, as his fingers dug into her flailing arms, how much bigger and stronger he now was. Her head and side were ablaze with pain. Her face was bleeding. Her stockings were ripped, her coat and Maria Cristina's pretty dress coated in yellow mud.

"Good thing I carry a big towel," Davide said. As if he hadn't just smashed her into the dirt.

They arrived at Bagna Serena with the sunrise. They entered not by the usual way around the side, but through the massive front doors that crowned the double staircase. Each step of Fulvia's return must have been planned, choreographed. Instead of a servant, Mamma, in nightgown and robe, let them in. "Thank God, you're home," she said.

In the following weeks, Mamma harangued her. Selfish, selfish, selfish. I was worried, worried, worried. Nonna added to the chorus. You'll be the death of me.

Fulvia apologized repeatedly. She was embarrassed, for their charges were true: she never considered their feelings. Still, her punishment was excessive. She was confined to the farm for three months, allowed to go to church but not to school. At first, Fulvia didn't mind, not wanting to be seen with her swollen nose and bruised face. Her injured side made it difficult to sit on a hard chair. But once the bruises faded, she grew resentful. She begged, for it was her first year of *liceo classico*, of ancient Greek and Latin. She was going to fall behind and fail. "I can't teach myself Greek," she told her mother.

"You can switch to the *magistrale*," her mother said. "You'd be with Veronica and most of your other friends."

"I want to learn Greek, art history, calculus," Fulvia said.

"You are perverse. Who would *want* to study Greek?"

"Mamma, you know it's compulsory to get into university."

"*Testarda*. You are obstinate." Mamma's hands gestured the rest: dream away.

Maria Cristina brought Fulvia her lessons and took back the completed assignments; she had forgiven Fulvia for the ruined dress, probably because Mamma bought her two replacement dresses, actual Puccis that cost ten times more than the original. Fulvia was grateful and resentful: Mamma never bought her a Pucci, or anything fun. Nonna's rules: "You must look like what you are, a *ragazza per bene*." A girl from a good family.

Not that it mattered on these dreary days. Who was going to see her anyway? The farm hands.

Then Nonna arranged for Dorina, a third cousin with a university degree in archeology and no job, to tutor Fulvia. Years later, Fulvia would still be grateful, for Dorina brought Fulvia not just homework help and language drills but an appreciation of ancient myths and philosophy. Dorina analyzed the stories for every possible feminist nuance from Medusa to Artemis, from Antigone to Medea. Dorina also told Fulvia that Sicily was *Magna Græcia*, that Archimedes ran naked down the streets of *our* Siracusa, and that Icarus and his father were escaping Crete, on their way to Sicily, when Icarus became so intoxicated with the joy of flight that he flew too close to the sun. Persephone was picking flowers on the banks of *our* Lake Pegusa when she was captured by Hades. Demeter was standing on the mountain of *our* Enna, gazing down at the central valley, when she saw her child seized.

"We must go together." Dorina's face shone with earnestness. "To the lake and the mountain."

"Yeah, for sure." As if her parents would let her past the front gate.

"To Agrigento to visit Demeter's temple. It is over a fissure in the ground and unlike those dedicated to the male gods."

"I can't wait," Fulvia said, as if she could wish away her house arrest.

8

Sicily

1 9 6 8 - 1 9 7 2

When Fulvia's father arrived home from detention in mid-September, she told him, "If you'd been here when I lost Fedele, I wouldn't have run away." For Papà commiserated with her about the cat. He hugged her when she cried, remembering her sweet, fluffy Fedele. He offered to get her a new kitten. "No, thank you." Fulvia said. She still felt Fedele's presence, lying at her feet, grooming himself or watching her with his head cocked.

Despite Papà's sympathy, he didn't spare her. She was subjected to another tirade. "You promised me you'd never run away," he concluded. "Promise me again and mean it this time."

"I can't promise. I might have to." Because of boredom if nothing else.

"You'll only get caught again. Humiliating."

He knew her. She still squirmed from the humiliation of her return, the sudden shock of the fist smashing into her face, the shame of lying helpless in the mud. "Did you tell Davide to hurt me?"

She expected a denial; instead Papà a caress to her forehead, under her chin. "You're an Arcuri through and through. *Fulvietta*, listen, understand, I am a man of honour." He said it as if the phrase only signified his distinction and worth. Fulvia knew that not just on the farm but beyond the gate, people deferred to him. *Whatever you wish*. Or they used the old feudal greeting, *I kiss your hand*, to demonstrate their allegiance. A few actually bent over and kissed the back of Papà's extended hand, the way Fulvia had bent and kissed the bishop's ring at her confirmation. But his honour, Papà insisted, depended on the family honour, which was determined by how Mamma, Nonna, and Fulvia acted, by who they were. "Your foolishness weakens me," he said.

Fulvia was aware of the ambiguity of the phrase *man of honour*. She had heard it used to describe a *boss, a latitante*, a fugitive, on the TV news, but that was not her father. He deserved deference. Still at fifteen when she heard the word honour, she felt a buzzing in her brain, a tightening in her throat.

Your foolishness weakens me.

Years later, despite a new life in a new place, the word honour still agitated her. Though Fulvia wanted to be open and honest with Sam, no dirty secrets, she didn't tell him who the Arcuri were, not during their courtship or their engagement and not for the first two years of their marriage. Not until after they began their own family, until she felt the baby quicken inside her. And she began to brood. What was she passing down to this little one? Dark brown hair? Long slim feet? Guilt by association? Original sin?

No, this baby was untainted, free. She had to tell Sam the truth, to warn him, if nothing else. On a wintry Sunday over breakfast, Fulvia forced the words out: "My father is a man of honour."

"What? What do you mean?"

"A boss." Four short weeks later, her father would be dead, but that Sunday morning, she had no inkling. "A power, a force to be reckoned with."

"You're kidding." Sam let out a short bark of a laugh. "No wonder you didn't want to go see the *Godfather*." A beat. "Why didn't you tell me before?"

Her fingers and lips were numb. "I planned to, but—" Her eyes stung. "I guess... I tried to block it, out of my mind." Why was she speaking at half-speed?

"*Ostriga*, Fulvia, you should have let me know who you really were. What family I was marrying into." Sam looked more amused than angry. Yet, her heart thumped. This agitation couldn't be good for the baby.

"It isn't who I am." Fulvia touched Sam's arm. "Please, you didn't marry into anything. I left the Arcuri behind, over there. They have nothing to do with us or our child."

"You said you were estranged. I presumed your parents were a pain in the ass, like mine. My mother is a shrew, my dad a drunk. I never imagined Don Corleone." He flashed his ironic smile and patted her extended hand.

"My little Mafia princess. It explains a lot."

"Damn it." She aimed a piece of croissant at his head. "It does not."

"You're refined. I knew you'd grown up with money, so I imagined you'd been indulged."

"Far from it. Nonna ruled over me. She was a high priestess in the cult of family honour. I told you about my tutor Dorina. She was so enthusiastic about the Vestal Virgins, dedicated to the Goddess Hesta, goddess of the hearth and home. The only priestesses in Rome with any power, she used to say."

Sam got up, went to the stove and poured himself the final bit of espresso. "And the connection between the virgins and your upbringing?"

"The Vestal Virgins kept the sacred fire burning. If they did not tend it night and day, it could go out. If they were not spotless, if they transgressed, it could go out. And then Rome would be destroyed. The Arcuri women had to dedicate themselves to feeding the flame of honour, keep themselves spotless, or the family would be seriously threatened."

Your foolishness weakens me.

"Did you always know? That you were born to it?" At least Sam no longer looked elated.

"I knew I was raised to behave better, to be better, than others."

"So you didn't suspect?"

"That I was being raised by wolves? No, no. But I wanted to get away, even as a teeny girl."

At fourteen, fifteen, and sixteen, Fulvia couldn't stop herself from noticing certain inconsistencies, evasions, silences. But she pushed away her anxiety. She rationalized: so what if Papà claimed he is flying to Berlin while Mamma said Milan? Fulvia didn't know all of Papà's businesses: he must need so many strong young guys. And the handguns? She noticed Enzo first, probably because he was as square-jawed and cute as Gianni Morandi. From her bedroom window, she saw Enzo step out of the business wing of the house, holding a long-nosed revolver. As he crossed the courtyard toward her, he shoved a cartridge into the handle, then slipped the gun into the back of his pants. His movements were quick, practised, but nonchalant. First Enzo, then one day, one of the guards, Totò, adjusted his trouser leg and exposed a holster strapped to his calf. Still, she resisted.

"Fulvietta, safe in her fantasy world," Davide said, apropos of nothing. Since the beating, Davide didn't tease and harass her the way he used to. He was not at Bagna Serena much: he passed the weekdays in Catania—learning, Mamma said, how to run a pizzeria. Or he would be off travelling—Tunis, Philadelphia, and Montreal—for Papà, for business. But when Davide was home, he ordered her about. I'm hungry/thirsty/sleepy/bored. Get me this, make me that. He came into her room, turned off her radio, interrupted her study or drawing or phone calls with Maria Cristina or Veronica. Nonna was getting old. She was spending more time in her suite than in the kitchen. And Davide was telling Fulvia to take up the slack, to submit to her only possible future—tending the home fires.

Fulvia didn't argue or answer back. She avoided speaking to him. She looked past or around him. The times she couldn't block out his physical presence altogether, the fleeting glimpses of his red-spotted chin, newly broad shoulders, or wispy moustache made her queasy.

"Where are you today?" Davide said. "On the other side of the looking glass?" He was at the kitchen table, she at the counter putting together a panino of caciocavallo and Parma ham. Bringing him the plate, she saw it, a grey gun, laid out before him, so she couldn't miss it.

Nonna rarely left Bagna Serena anymore. She had stopped shopping, visiting relatives, and attending Mass. She no longer cooked or sewed. She ordered her food to be prepared separately and *in bianco*, white meat only, light and lean, with no spices. The same bland diet Nonna had imposed on Fulvia and Davide in their childhood. Nonna had always waged war on dirt and bacteria. Bathrooms, kitchens, and all the floors had been cleaned every day and wiped down with bleach or disinfectant once a week. But now she shuffled from room to room, brandishing a rag and a spray bottle of rubbing alcohol, repeatedly swabbing the telephones, the doorknobs, the backs of chairs, anything touched by human hands. She insisted on using only her own dishes and cutlery and, after they were washed, wiped them too with alcohol. "We're going through more rubbing alcohol than olive oil and wine combined," Mamma said.

Nonna decided she should also, with diluted bleach,

rinse the hands of the women who sometimes helped in the kitchen—Pinetta, who had been working for the Arcuri for forty years, and Veronica's mother, who was a distant cousin on Mamma's side. After the first time, when they were taken by surprise, the women rebelled. "Your mother has lost her mind," Mamma told Papà. "She'll poison us all." Mamma had had more than enough, twenty years of servitude. Now she was having her own revolution, overturning the ancient regime or, at least, taking possession of the palace.

Fulvia spent her days studying. The courses of the last two years of *liceo classico* had not changed in forty-two years: Greek, Latin, Italian literature, French, history, art history, philosophy, biology, chemistry, and mathematics. Although Fulvia had her moments of boredom, particularly in chemistry, more often she felt a clean, precise pleasure at learning how to make the connections, to catalogue, classify, recognize, and name. She mastered subject after subject. She asked her parents for extra lessons, private lessons: English, tennis, painting.

Her father approved of her diligence. "You are a serious young woman."

Her mother added, "Among people of our level, it's more than appropriate for a wife to be cultivated."

Wife? Oh no. Fulvia had thought she was safe for a few more years, even though the brides of the different weddings the family had attended in the last few years were all eighteen or nineteen, twenty-one at the most. People called Dorina an old maid, and she had just turned twenty-five.

Wife. How much longer did she have? Did her parents already have someone in mind? An up-and-coming *picciotto* in one of the other Cupola families? A dynastic marriage to seal a détente? Her stomach twisted itself into a knot. They couldn't force her to marry, could they?

Better to focus on her studies, her calculus homework or the declensions of Greek nouns. She had a report due on the life cycle of the *Anguilla vulgaris*, the mysterious freshwater eels that journeyed*I* from the landlocked ponds of Europe to the Mediterranean, the Atlantic, and finally the Sargasso Sea. She worked late into the night. "Before death they spawn a thousand fathoms below the surface," she typed, "in a region of perpetual darkness." What guided them, Fulvia wondered. What instinct compelled them?

Outside, dogs barked, a car pulled up, and Papà was finally home. It was one thirty in the morning; Fulvia heard a creak, and the doorknob turned. Nonna pushed open the door. She was a ghostly vision in a white, high-necked nightie, yet she, rather than Fulvia, shrieked, "Enough."

"What's wrong, Nonna? Are you feeling ill?" Nonna was breathing deeply, almost gasping.

"You're the one ruining your eyes and your health. It is the middle of the night."

"Can't you sleep, Nonna?"

"I sleep less and less. I worry." Nonna tugged on Fulvia's arm until she got up from her desk.

"Papà's home."

"God bless him." Nonna pulled off Fulvia's dressing gown. "None of you have any idea of the dangers out there. Deluding yourselves that there can be peace." Nonna gave her a little shove toward the bed.

"What? Nonna, I haven't finished. The report's due tomorrow."

Nonna lowered herself slowly onto the desk chair. "You can lose your mind. Tancredi, my brother Calogero's youngest, he was like you, studying all the time for his *maturità*, not sleeping, not eating. And it drove him crazy."

"You told me." About a million times.

"He tried to shoot himself. Luckily he was shaking so bad, he only nicked his ear. And anyway his mother heard and stopped him from trying again."

"I know." Fulvia would be back at her desk as soon as Nonna left. "Maybe you need to talk to Papà about the dangers."

"So many of them. If I catch you again, I'll burn your books. I promise you."

Fulvia didn't believe her grandmother. Still, she kept the important textbooks with her at all times, carrying them in a large brown leather satchel. By the time the diploma exams began, she had driven herself to exhaustion and the edge of hysteria. She had to excel: she was earning herself a future. The competition was national and of such importance that the written topics were reported on the evening news. And the written tests were followed by a string of orals, each one conducted by a different group of teachers. Identify the four kinds of force in the atom. Describe how Empedocles accounted for change in his theory of the four elements. Fulvia couldn't feel her body; she was a voice answering other voices. Enumerate the difference in principles behind Renaissance and Baroque architecture. That day she felt an ache behind her eyes, as if her brain were in pain. Explain Rousseau's theory of education in *Emile*. The June heat was punishing. Translate aloud this passage in Latin and identify the source and the subject:

> *At regina gravi iamdudum saucia cura*
> *Vulnus alit venis et caeco carpitur igni.*

The Aeneid, Book IV. Queen Dido ached with longing for Aeneas, Fulvia said.

> *She is eaten by a secret flame.*

Fulvia received the top total mark, not just for her high school or the district, but for the entire island. She won a bunch of awards. Her picture appeared in the Palermo paper, *L'Ora*, breaking the Arcuris' unspoken rule that the family members should never draw attention to themselves. Papà seemed proud; he invited the entire extended family, as well as Enzo and Totò, to a celebratory dinner at the most elegant seaside restaurant on the northwestern coast. "I'm not surprised," he said in prelude to his toast. "Fulvietta has a will of iron." He lifted his glass.

Evviva, Fulvia.

Nonna stayed home, gripped by the flu. "Besides," Nonna said, "I don't understand these seafood extravaganzas, twenty antipasti, five *primi*, wasteful, unseemly, homicidal for the digestion. And for what? To honour your grabbing the spotlight? It can only lead to trouble. Mark my words. *Malocchio*. You will draw the evil eye."

Fulvia made a show of shrugging off Nonna's comments, but inside she was not so sure. Even before she had aced her exams, she heard her schoolmates, her friends, whisper, "Brown-noser, show-off." Veronica called her Princess Dweeb to her face.

When Davide returned from Tunis, he brought Fulvia a gold chain and an amulet in the shape of a hand with an eye carved into the palm. "This is a surprise," Fulvia said, "You marking my achievement."

Davide grimaced. "Nonna's orders."

"Of course." Fulvia fastened the necklace around her neck, settling the amulet under her cotton top. "She says the Eye of Fatima is supposed to protect me from envy, from the dark gaze."

"Why would anyone be jealous of you?"

"Go, get lost, break someone else's balls. I did stupendously well."

"And that will get you what? A husband? I don't think so."

"I don't want a damn husband. I want a life. I want the world. And my marks are my beginning."

Davide laughed. "Wake up. Haven't you heard yet

what people are saying?"

"What do you mean?"

"You didn't earn those marks."

"You think I cheated?"

"Nah, not you. But I don't think you're any brain either."

"So how did I do so well?"

"There's speculation. You can ask Veronica."

"What?"

Davide smiled. "Everyone thinks Papà got you those marks as a graduation present."

"I don't believe you. You just want to annoy me." Fulvia started to get up off the sofa, but her legs wobbled. "I deserved those marks. They were honestly won. Papà had nothing to do with it." She took a deep breath. "Did he?"

"Not as far as I know. But it wouldn't be the first time." He so obviously loved disillusioning her. "Look at Cousin Angelo. Why do you think he has such a modest practice? The family helped him get through medical school, leaned on a few of the professors. It was fine till that kid croaked on the operating table, and the gossip started. It's no wonder when you turned into a *secchiona*, an egghead, people thought it was a big joke."

"You just have to spoil everything," Fulvia said, clenching her teeth, prepared herself to wait.

9

Sicily
APRIL 1989

After the long-delayed, official identification, what had previously been only charred flesh and scorched bones, the remains of Samuele Mazzolin took on a different presence. Mourning could begin; the rites of death had an object. Marisa De Luca had decided to accompany the coffin on its journey to Venice. She had never felt the need to oversee the delivery of a body before, but she trusted the impulse. Since she'd learned his name, she felt more responsible than ever: she owed him justice.

She arranged for a hearse to pick up the coffin at the morgue in Trapani and deliver it to the Punta Raisi airport. Her own trip to the airport would be more circuitous. She was going to stop at police headquarters for a meeting with Lanza and then connect with Alex on the way.

The baby-faced Roselli picked her up before seven. Now that Mazzolin had been identified, Roselli was driving into Palermo to reinterview Inzerillo's relatives and friends. The day before, Brusca had argued he should be the one to go into the city. He had conducted the first round of interviews. And he was the captain; he had the necessary experience.

Marisa countered with the need for different approach and a fresh eye. She wasn't going to let herself be stuck alone in a car with Brusca. She said, "Besides, you'll be busy, organizing and executing a search of the vacation house on San Vito where the two men were staying."

"It has been searched."

"It has been visited and given a surface inspection."

"Waste of time," Brusca said. "What's the logic?"

"I'm thinking drugs."

"Drugs? *Mizzica*. Our *Commissaria* has an imagination," he said.

"It is not far-fetched," Marisa said to Roselli as he drove. "Types like Inzerillo, they dabble in recreational drugs."

Roselli kept his eyes on the road. "Dabbling isn't importing."

"I keep coming back to why Mazzolin was in the car with Inzerillo. His family was modest, and he was middle-aged. Besides, he is not from here, and he and Inzerillo weren't even close friends. So why were they driving down Monte Bonifacio at dawn? And why were they staying at the Inzerillo holiday home in San Vito in early April? What connected them? "

"Those pants I found on the chair in the cottage were soaked in sea salt," Roselli said.

"One of them had been wading in the ocean. In April. Why? Unless he was hauling a boat in."

"Inzerillo's aunt and uncle do own a speedboat. It's anchored at a marina on San Vito."

"You see," Marisa said. "Just right for a quick trip to Africa."

Roselli's handsome face clouded. "Possibly. But would they be that stupid? This is not the place for freelancers."

"At first, I thought that was the answer. They were stupid. But now we know who Mazzolin was, and his relationship to the Arcuri."

"You think he got a blessing from the in-laws?"

"A blessing if they were importing something the Arcuri had no interest in. Otherwise, a franchise."

They made good time: in forty minutes they had reached the outskirts of Palermo. There the crowds, the buses, and trucks, even the mountains of garbage bags surrounding the overflowing bins placed at the centre of many intersections slowed the car to a crawl. At Marisa's prompting, Roselli flipped on the siren. He swerved in and out of traffic lanes and sped through a couple of red lights.

"A friend," she said, thinking of Ivana, "found herself in the middle of a shootout in the Piazza San Domenico. A couple of men burst out of the bank with guns drawn and guards at their heels. She threw herself behind a mound of garbage bags. She said she never thought she'd be grateful for spotty garbage collection.

They zoomed around the corner into Piazza della Vittoria, which with its green space of manicured grass and towering palm trees and after the pandemonium of the main streets, was an oasis of calm. Roselli turned off the siren and drove sedately past the Sicilian legislature to the police headquarters at farthest corner of the square. He deposited Marisa, with her briefcase and carry-on bag, at the entrance to the courtyard of Palazzo Sclafani, which was being guarded by a soldier cradling a machine gun.

In a dingy office, labelled POLIZIA SCIENTIFICA, in the basement of the building, Marisa's supposition about the victims and drugs was partly confirmed. A lab assistant brought her the results of the analysis she had ordered on a small, scorched mass extracted from the trunk of the burnt Innocenti. The bald, thin, morose monk of a man announced: "It's hashish all right, North African, possibly Tunisian. Three hundred and fifty grams, wrapped in several layers of tinfoil, which kept out the oxygen so the drug was baked, further baked that is, into a cinder-like rock."

After the laboratory, Marisa climbed the wide stone stairs up to Lanza's office on the third floor. They had an appointment, but his secretary told her she would have to wait. Down the hall, Marisa found the anti-Mafia squad common room—long, narrow, and windowless, crammed with desks, typewriters, files, and people; ringing phones, raised voices, and the odd laugh punctuating the clatter.

A young woman in a black and white wrap dress broke off from a cluster of men around a book of mug shots and came to meet her. "I'm Sandra Fazio," she said. "And you are?" Marisa gave her name and rank. Sandra showed no sign of recognition. Her thick eyeliner, black bob, and stiletto heels made her look out of place, even exotic. Was she a receptionist? She wasn't dressed for that role either. "Join us," she said. "We're about to order coffee."

Marisa shook her head. "I just had some questions about the importation of soft drugs to the area."

"Suit yourself." Sandra steered Marisa toward an officer at a desk, bald with two days' growth of black beard. "Saviano will help you. Massimo, this is our lady in Alcamo. I leave her in your hands. I have to see Lanza." And off she went.

"I had an appointment with Lanza at nine. I was told to wait." As soon as Marisa heard herself speak, she regretted her words and her wistful inflection.

Saviano gave her a knowing look. "Don't let it bother you. Sandra has privileges none of the rest of us have. She's his new star, lighting up the sky."

Marisa could feel the blood rushing to her cheeks. She made herself smile. "Ah, office politics." So that was it. Marisa's position, that of token woman, had gone to Sandra, who was younger, smarter, sexier. Marisa had never played that card with Lanza. They had remained professional. She should not presume that anything improper was going on between Fazio and Lanza. If there were any hint of impropriety, wouldn't Saviano have made some allusion? In Marisa's experience, in their profession, men tended to ascribe the ascension of any woman not to competence, but to sleeping with the boss.

But still. Sandra was as pretty as a *velina*, a showgirl.

And I have made too many mistakes, Marisa thought. Or, at least, I've been too honest about those mistakes, running to him for advice and comfort, when I should have pretended I was invulnerable. Not this time. Ten minutes later, when Lanza asked her if she were still feeling overwhelmed at the station house, she told him that she was making progress, taking more control.

"*Brava*," he said. With his silver head of hair and grey Zegna suit, Lanza was more than ever the picture of authority. "And you are staying clear of the local families?"

"I haven't questioned a soul."

"But you've turned a car accident into a murder."

"Unavoidable."

"Be careful."

Marisa forced herself to nod and smile.

"I also hear you've found an excuse to visit Venice."

"Lucky me. The family of the Venetian has been kicking up a fuss. Throwing around accusations."

"You couldn't have sent one of your inspectors?"

"Have you met my inspectors? No finesse. Besides, I need to get away."

First Lanza had made her wait, now Alex. Marisa waited at a table by the floor-to-ceiling window of the Bar Alba. lingering over a dish of lemon gelato. Alex didn't have a job to detain him. Perhaps he'd forgotten he'd offered to drive her to the airport. Or been derailed by an unexpected and important phone call. Perhaps a car accident. Perhaps.

Alex was hard to read. He wasn't like the men Marisa

usually found attractive, the Roberto Valentes, arrogant, decisive, and ridiculously charming. Alex was reticent and without bluster, separate and self-sufficient, yet—she saw when she stared into his deep, dark eyes—he took everything in.

Last week, they had met at a pizzeria in the medieval centre of the city. She'd worn high heels—date heels—foolish, not realizing she wouldn't be able to find a parking spot anywhere close, forced to walk back down two dark, empty streets, click, click, past the ruins of the palaces bombed in World War II and never rebuilt, click, click, back to a triangular piazza and the restaurant marked by a string of lights. "You could have parked there," Alex said, pointing with his cigarette at a spot a few metres away.

"You mean under the No Parking at Any Time and Stopping Forbidden signs?"

"You tip that guy," he nodded at a dishevelled man leaning against the wall of the restaurant. "Give him enough, and he'll make sure your car won't be ticketed or vandalized."

"This is a quintessential Sicilian moment," Marisa said. "Ignore the rules. Buy yourself protection."

"Come on. What's the harm?" He smiled.

The restaurant consisted of three connected rooms, each overly bright, noisy, and crowded. She and Alex had to lean toward each other and raise their voices to be heard. Alex signalled their glowering waiter several times before he brought the wine, which proved rough and sour. If Marisa had been alone, she'd have sent it back.

Alex said, "What shit" and immediately downed an entire glass. At least, when the pizzas finally arrived, they were thin-crusted delights, and Marisa and Alex gave themselves over to eating.

She shouldn't have accepted his invitation. What kind of man didn't work for a living? Besides a rich one. Ivana had confirmed that suspicion. "He inherited large amounts of property," Ivana had said.

"What do you *do* all day?" Marisa almost asked Alex, as he walked her back to her car. She hung onto his arm for help navigating the cobblestones. "Damn shoes." She stumbled and fell against him. His lips brushed the edge of her mouth, lingered on her cheek. Then his teeth caught her earlobe. She breathed in his scent, musk and tobacco. And she felt—what? A spark. The possibility of a flame.

It was almost noon. Alex wasn't coming, and she wouldn't be able to get a cab. She was going to miss her flight. Why had he insisted? He'd made a joke about setting his alarm since he would have to get out of bed before his usual time of one in the afternoon. Perhaps he did need an alarm, and it hadn't gone off.

Again, Marisa scanned up, down, and across the street. Her eyes stopped at a woman in tight jeans, boots, and an oversized jacket. Her body was arched; she was making a show of lighting a cigarette. A working girl, odd in this middle-class neighbourhood. The woman flopped down at one of the outside tables. When she turned her head, looked back into the *caffè*, Marisa recognized the black spiky hair and pale pinched face.

. LuLu, she called herself. One of the constables had brought her into the station for questioning a couple of weeks ago. He claimed he'd been tipped off by an anonymous accusation. Marisa was busy with the usual, checking arrest reports, when a confusion of shouts and curses distracted her. Marisa found a screeching LuLu in the largest interrogation room, surrounded by a pack of policemen. "Dickheads, cuckolds." Her words and outfit, white-leather shorts and a white bustier that only covered the bottom of her brown nipples, contrasted with her weary expression.

"What's going on here?" Marisa said.

Brusca gave LuLu a shove; she fell back into a chair. He bent over her so his moustached mouth was inches from hers. "Shut your filthy mouth or I'll gag you with my cock."

"Captain, stop this." Not one of the men turned or acknowledged Marisa's presence. Not even Roselli, squeezed into a corner of the narrow room.

"A cocktail wiener. Two little bites and I swallow."

"I come in king size."

"Stop. Now." Marisa pushed her way into the circle. She grabbed Brusca's arm. "*Capitano.*"

Brusca straightened and turned. His blue eyes and yellowish teeth snapped. "I'm handling this."

Marisa picked up the big ball of white fluff on the table, LuLu's coat, and draped it over the woman's bony shoulders. "You can go."

Five minutes later, Marisa confronted Brusca, Arcangelo, and the overzealous constable in her office. She was her most severe. There was a standard of conduct to be followed. What were they thinking? Besides gratification. As if there weren't enough real crimes to investigate.

Arcangelo and the constable justified themselves. The woman was planning to open a brothel, and even if they'd found no signs and no other imported women, they were protecting the citizens of Alcamo. Still, at least these two looked chastened.

Brusca still looked exhilarated. "We were trying to shake her up a bit, convince her to leave and not come back," he said. "We didn't mean to offend you. We forget you're a woman. That you might have delicate ears."

She dismissed him with her hand. "Get out."

Marisa forced herself to stop staring at LuLu. She picked up her spoon again and scooped up the last dribbles of lemon gelato. On her tongue, the peppery taste of her resentment melted into the icy-sweet tartness. Again, she glanced out of the window, and this time she saw Alex. He was kitty-corner to the bar, a slender figure in a plaid shirt pacing and waiting for a break in the traffic. Thirty minutes late.

She stood up, knocking over the metal dish and just missing the glass of water. She didn't pause; she grabbed the bill and her bags and headed for the cashier. She wasn't going to let Alex find her passively waiting. She pushed through the glass door and stopped. Where was he? Then she saw him with LuLu. Standing beside her, his head inclined, talking.

"Excuse me," said a grouchy voice close to Marisa's ear. She was clogging the entrance. She took several steps in the direction of the couple. Alex spotted her, waved. Now he was coming to her.

"You're late," she said in greeting. "I almost called a cab. We'll have to leave right now, if you're still driving me."

His hand was on her elbow. He was turning her, propelling her back into the bar. "Plenty of time for a quick coffee. Haven't had a chance yet this morning." At the counter, he signalled two espressos to the bar man. "I am sorry I'm late." He began an excuse involving his sister and some papers that suddenly needed signing. Marisa heard very little of it, preoccupied as she was by the idea of him and LuLu.

She would never have pegged Alex as the type of man who visited prostitutes. Maybe he had peculiar tastes or wanted special services. Her hands trembled as she tore open three packets of sugar and poured them into her cup. Alex said something about making sweet the bitter, and she tried to smile. Her mind was busy imagining what his preferences could be, projecting a sequence of lewd slides. She downed her espresso in two swallows.

His car was an old, yellowish-green Fiat 126, not at all what she had expected. He moved a mess of tapes from the passenger seat to the back before he let her in. The right door had no inside handle, and the engine rattled. "Don't worry," Alex said. "I'll get you there on time.

Dorotea, the car, is battered but not beaten."

Marisa focused on the traffic, which was barely moving. "It's easy to see why there are no getaway cars, only getaway scooters here," she said as she watched a scooter zigzag its way down a line of cars.

Detach. Breathe. "You said you did yoga."

"I haven't had a class in a while." She was suppressing the urge to ask him how he knew the whore. "You went to Iyengar Institute in Poona, right?"

They chatted about yoga and his travels around the Indian subcontinent, their words stopping and starting with the traffic. Alex was trying to describe the allure of that country when he said, "I can express it better with paint."

"You paint?" That was a relief. He wasn't idle: he painted.

"Not lately. I smoke too much when I paint, and I'm trying to quit."

"Good for you."

"It triggers my asthma. At least, it has in the last while." He looked over at her. "I'll get back to it, once I'm clean."

"Clean?"

"Once I'm over the craving. Once I've stopped completely." A pause. "What about you? Any secret pursuits?"

"Me?" She laughed. "Nothing artistic."

The car was now out of the giant knot of the city and was speeding along the freeway by the sea. They would be at the airport a little less than an hour before her flight.

Clean, craving, she turned the words over in her mind: rehab language. Of course. Drugs. She should have guessed when she had first seen him talking to LuLu that their link involved artificial rather than natural chemistry. Just like Mazzolin and Inzerillo, their connection had seemed unlikely until the hashish was identified. And she'd been proven right.

Alex and Inzerillo were both from respectable upper-crust Palermo families, and though Alex was a few years older, Marisa bet they knew each other. She could ask him. And smother any possibility between them. Would she learn anything from him she couldn't get from others? Wasn't she just looking for an excuse to cross-examine Alex? Confirm this new hunch. What do you know about drug usage in the circle of wastrels? And, more important to me, what about your own usage?

The man from the mortuary in Trapani was waiting impatiently for Marisa in the freight office. The necessary forms were signed and stamped. The remains of Samuele Mazzolin, enclosed in a body bag, a metal casket, and a shipping container, were already being loaded onto the plane. With ten minutes until her boarding call, Marisa commandeered a phone and a cubicle in the custom offices.

"Marisa! How are you?" As usual, Ivana's tone was urgent, as if she were expecting disaster.

"Fine, busy. I have a question about Alex."

"I thought you'd call last week after your date."

"I can't chat. I'm at the airport, back Friday."

"You've fallen for Alex, haven't you?"

"He is attractive. But…"

"But. Yeah, thinking it over, I shouldn't have set you up with him."

"Why not? What's wrong with him?"

"Nothing. Well, he's had his problems, but he is a good guy. When you get back, we'll talk."

"Is it drugs? Ivana?"

"Are you asking as a woman? Or is this a police investigation?"

"As a woman. But because of my work, I do have to be careful." A matron bedecked in gold necklaces was staring at Marisa through the glass. Marisa lowered her voice and turned to face away.

"He's been to rehab twice," Ivana said. "The last time seemed to take. His brother, who's a psychiatrist, arranged it."

A rumble over the intercom. Was that her flight being announced? "But he still has access to the subculture?"

"Subculture? What do I know? I should tell you my little brother and Alex were both arrested, oh, about ten years ago. Importation of hashish from India. My Uncle Luigi got Giacomo off, and Alex got a reduced sentence. Alex's mother refuses to admit it ever happened, even to her best friend. But everyone knew. It was on the front page of *Il Gazzettino*."

Marisa was the last person to board the second of the shuttle buses to the plane. All the seats, straps, and poles were taken. She had to rely on the others, wedged in all around her, and her own nimbleness to keep upright on the short and bumpy ride. She kept her knees bent, ready to react.

10   Sicily
1972

He didn't know who she was: Fulvia was sure of that. The young Adonis the other side of the crowded room wouldn't be staring at her so intently if he did. In Alcamo, no one would ever dare. Not that she minded. On the streets of Palermo, where she was anonymous, men assaulted her with their eyes. Unless she was escorted by a chauffeur, and sometimes even then, they made obscene gestures and muttered indecencies.

This young man's gaze was different. He looked not at her but into her. He was making his way across the room, pausing to exchange a word with one guest, then another. Was he coming to her? Or to the refreshment table? Fulvia turned and picked up a plate.

Claudia, a senator's daughter and a new friend, was hosting the afternoon soiree, an English tea. On the long table, she had laid out gold-trimmed china, embroidered napkins, two triple-level stands of triangular sandwiches, three platters of cakes, and a silver teapot. "As they say, I'll play mother," Claudia giggled. "Milk? Lemon? It's Earl Grey." She nodded at the dark-eyed man, who had reached the other end of the table and was loading crustless sandwiches onto a small plate. "Alex brought this special tea for me, all the way from London, Fortnum & Mason. He is such a darling." Claudia leaned over and whispered in Fulvia's ear. "He wants me."

Don't count on it, Fulvia thought, suppressing the urge to give Claudia a shove. Claudia had asked everyone to dress British; the girls were in high-necked blouses and tweed or tartan skirts, the boys in tweed or pinstriped suits. Only Alex was up-to-date: bell-bottomed jeans, shiny paisley shirt, and long hair almost to his shoulders.

As she introduced Alex Zacco to Fulvia, Claudia caught his right arm and held on. Alex lifted an eyebrow and smiled at Fulvia. Claudia was burbling on: Alex spent the summer in England studying the language, weekends in Dorset, thatched roofs, narrow country roads, roses. Claudia was making clear how well she knew him. When she paused, Alex said: "It's not the landscape or, dear God, the wretched food. I wanted to stay because of the reasonableness of the people."

"Me too," Claudia said. "They stand in line there, patiently."

"They tolerate eccentrics," Alex said. After Claudia left them to greet new arrivals, he added, "Didn't I see your picture in the paper last spring? The best of the best?"

"Oh, that." Fulvia blushed.

"Yet you didn't go away. You chose our third-rate university."

"I wanted to go to art school in Milan until my father convinced me law here was more practical." Papà hadn't convinced her. He told her she had no choice.

"A contradiction in terms, so to speak, law in Palermo."

"Ouch!" Fulvia smiled despite herself. "I'm taking a side course in art history. For my sanity."

"I'm stuck here myself. Doing philosophy, which is appropriate here in this birthplace of rhetoric, and centre of solipsism. And those eternal Sicilian questions: Who am I? Am I myself? Am I another?"

No one had spoken to her this way before—smart man to smart woman. She managed to say, "Why eternal Sicilian questions? Doesn't everyone face them?"

"Not with the anguish of the Sicilians. Think of Pirandello, Lampedusa. Sciascia."

"Of course," she said, though she wasn't sure what he meant.

A few days after Claudia's tea, Alex walked past Fulvia at the university *mensa*. He was talking to a pony-tailed guy and didn't notice her. She went weak in the knees. *Un colpo di fulmine*; her desire hit her like a lightning strike. A week later, he crossed a stream of students to greet her. Her legs nearly buckled. They continued to run into each other. They began to arrange meetings, lunches in the *mensa* and then nearby cafés. They weren't alone, but they felt as if they were. The lightest, the most casual of touches, his leg brushing against hers, his hand on her shoulder, his lips grazing her cheek, sparked a charge.

A beginning, chapter one of their story: their short chats evolved into a continuing conversation. *Don't you think?* he said. *Don't you love?* she said, this song, that movie, this book. Which life? They agreed—an authentic one. Fulvia found *Steppenwolf* boring, and that was Alex's favourite book. Alex shared her enthusiasm for *Baron in the Trees*, but for the wrong reason: for the allegory, not for the character of Cosimo the wilful boy, who climbed up a tree and never came down. It was easier to agree on music. He introduced her to Dylan and the Doors; she led him to Donovan and Faithfull. He spent hours translating lyrics, partly to convince her that they should get stoned together.

Open the doors of perception. Free mind, free love, free world. Fulvia had long been intrigued by such mottoes. Her high-school tutor Dorina often spouted her favourites: *The Earth is Our Mother. Back to nature. Save the planet.* So the ideas that Alex and his *ragazzi*, his circle of friends, debated were not completely new. But the thorough and endless discussion was. "Should Sicily fight for its independence? Was Italy doomed? How about capitalism? And the earth? Nuclear war or environmental devastation?" On and on, with references to Sartre, Gramsci, Foucault, and more.

Although Claudia must have been disappointed, even hurt, by Alex and Fulvia's sudden relationship, she did not rat Fulvia out. Alex still hadn't heard any innuendos about the Arcuri. Claudia continued to act friendly to

Fulvia: wasn't she coming to study, to the movies, to the disco? Fulvia was not fooled: it was a show. From time to time Claudia gave her true feelings away with a sour facial expression, an ambiguous phrase, or a smirk. The first time they met, Claudia had said, "We're going to be such friends." From then on, she peppered Fulvia with invitations. Too much, too soon.

The Arcuri were expanding into construction, bidding on regional government contracts. Was Senator Lombardo her father's ally? Fulvia asked Papà if he knew the Senator. "Of course," he said. "Good man. Why?"

"I've become friendly with one of his daughters."

Papà nodded; he knew. He must have arranged it.

Too much too soon: that didn't apply to her and Alex. Because he wasn't put up to it, he wasn't acting. He was real, and they were real. *Un colpo di fulmine.*

Alex accepted without question that her parents were old-fashioned and wouldn't allow her to date. Such strictness was common enough in Sicily. "We'll have to fly under the radar," she said. "A secret love," he said, though not a secret to their friends. He was adept at finding dark corners on the campus, concealed spaces in his building and hers. Quick, over here, squeezed between a door and a wall, behind a column; wait, in an empty classroom. His lips, his tongue, his fingers, the swell of him pressing against her abdomen. Delicious, and soon as necessary to her as bread.

Alex bribed a janitor for use of his closet. In the midst

of mops and brooms, her white flower perfume and his patchouli oil commingling with the chemical bite of cleanser fumes, she flicked her tongue under his eyelashes, into his ear. They could hear student voices and laughter from the corridor outside. He unbuttoned her shirt, pulled down her bra. Under the fluorescent light, he gazed at her bared breasts. "My Venus." His caresses were feather light; she was touched to her core.

They both wanted more. Fulvia stepped up her lies, inventing shopping trips with girlfriends, study sessions with fellow students, or compulsory lectures by visiting experts. "I'll be late again tonight." Being able to deceive the family, having the moxie to do so, made Fulvia feel confident, in control. She was not being monitored the way she used to be. Because the family accepted her as an adult? Probably not. Her parents were distracted, her grandmother oblivious.

A year earlier, Zio Vincenzo had died. Their very own *Americano*, who, when Fulvia was little, brought her bubble gum and Barbie dolls and candy cigarettes, and who, when she was bigger, brought her blue jeans and hit records and taught her American slang. Papà said Zio's car was hit by a semi-trailer truck on a freeway in New Jersey and demolished.

Was it true? Fulvia couldn't tell. For sure he was gone, however it happened. For sure the family mourned.

"Bring my boy home," Nonna said. "We'll have a proper burial."

"His ashes, "Papà said. "Antonio and I thought it was

best. The damage." He contracted his left shoulder up and back, a habitual gesture when he was uneasy.

Nonna inched her way out of the room, muttering and striking the stone floor with her cane at each slow step. *Another... one... massacred.* Fulvia heard her grandmother's howl through the closed bedroom door: a howl that morphed into a strange, high-pitched moan that stretched on and on. A moan that made Fulvia's stomach writhe and her brain burn.

Two days later, when Nonna finally emerged from her room to attend the memorial mass, she had hacked off the long grey hair she'd always worn pulled back into a bun. She'd used nail scissors. Mamma let out a loud sigh. "Come on, Rachele, it isn't the eighteenth century."

"Actually, Mamma, the custom of shearing one's hair to signal grief is much older than that. It goes back to classical times," Fulvia said.

Lela threw her a look. "Even worse. Listen, *Signorina Pignola*, make yourself useful. Get one of your grandmother's black hats."

After that loss, Nonna abdicated her role as matriarch of the family. She stopped presiding at the head of the dinner table, then stopped even coming to the table. "*Meglio così,*" better this way, Nonna said, since she ate earlier and differently from the rest of them. Now and then, she wandered into the kitchen and watched Mamma cooking or Pinetta cleaning. Nonna still scolded: too much olive oil, more tomato. "You call that clean? Try some bleach." But she didn't seem to expect instant obedience.

Several times Fulvia caught Nonna having only *caffè e latte* and dry bread for dinner. She began carrying a tray to Nonna's room with boiled veal, a poached egg, or a bowl of vegetable soup. "Come on, a couple of bites for me."

Mamma was happy to be in charge of the household. "About time," she said. When Fulvia was a child, her mother had been restless, fearful, and idle. Now Lela was busy and full of purpose, giving orders at home, as well as driving all over the island, attending meetings and carrying messages.

"The fucking police don't pay attention to women," the ever-irritating Davide explained.

Meanwhile, Papà was transforming himself into a construction tycoon. When he lingered at the table after dinner with Mamma, Davide, or Zio Antonio, he mused about possible developments, a high-end resort for Alcamo Marina or a new suburb for Palermo. Fulvia had no interest in the talk. But one of her chores was clearing the table, so as she collected all the dishes, scraped the tablecloth with the ivory handled crumber, and put out bottles of *amaro* and liqueur on a silver tray, she couldn't help overhearing. "Imagine a bridge," her father said, "over the Strait of Messina, linking the island to the continent."

"So it's even easier for Rome to break our balls?" said Uncle Antonio.

"No, no. So we can win the contract, be in charge. So we can break their balls."

"It's going to be easier and easier to get away," Fulvia told herself. Drive away, sail away, fly away. The times are a changing. And Sicily and the family are changing too.

By February, Fulvia was skipping at least a third of her law classes. Instead, she attended some of Alex's philosophy lectures, content to sit beside him, to cover pages of her notebooks with doodles or write endless notes back and forth, critiques of the professors or the other students. Interpretations of her drawings. Confessions; when I was seven, when I was twelve, at fourteen:

I missed months of school because of my asthma.

I ran away and got as far as Rome.

I nearly died twice. I couldn't breathe.

My brother beat me.

What? Why?

To teach me a lesson. And because he gets off on it—inflicting pain.

Alex borrowed his sister's car. The two of them would drive off to Mondello, which was semi-deserted in the winter. If it was raining, if the windows misted over, when they found any semblance of cover, they fell on each other with joy.

"I'll make a fallen woman of you yet," Alex said in his fondest tone.

"I'm already fallen. I jumped."

They wanted more space and time for the complete act of love. But where and when? They discussed birth control. Condoms, they decided, were easier than the pill. She was both eager and hesitant. Her family, her culture, and her religion had drummed into her that her worth depended on the physical fact of her virginity. She must remain pure, untouched, and impervious to all men outside the family. *L'uomo è cacciatore.* Men were by nature hunters, and if a woman is bagged before marriage she will be *rovinata*, ruined, like spoiled food or a broken appliance, fit only for the scrap heap.

Even before Alex, Fulvia objected, though not out loud, to this claptrap. When she heard the word *rovinata*, her aunts and Nonna gossiping, her schoolmates whispering about some poor girl who'd run off or been sent off, the skin between her shoulder blades prickled Mara, a second cousin on Mamma's side, had her head turned, it was said, by a young man as beautiful as a movie idol, and they were seen together on the mountain, at the beach. Mara was obviously ruined. Worse, he was a *carabiniere*, low grade. It was said they went to Milan, where he deserted her, of course, and what could she do?

Before Alex, at sixteen and seventeen, Fulvia had decided her value would not depend on a flap of skin. She would make the loss of her virginity a careless, insignificant act. Instead of waiting passively for a family-approved Prince Charming, she'd track down a stranger, a cute one, a gentle one, somewhere, somehow, and free herself. With Alex, she changed her mind. Their coming together should be meaningful and liberating. She contemplated sneaking out of Bagna Serena at night, imagined their first time under the stars. Dressed in black, she would slip out through her bedroom window, climb down the olive tree, and avoid the patrolling guard. Best on a Monday or Thursday night, Totò wouldn't stop her. Would he? But if he didn't and her father found out, what would happen to Totò? To her and Totò? Fulvia had never seen her father make a violent gesture, let alone strike someone. Yet.

She dismissed her plan. She needed a hidden door in the stone wall that encircled the estate or, better still, a tunnel that surfaced miles away. Didn't the Boss from Corleone, twenty years on the lam, have one under his Palermo villa, so he could come and go as he pleased? Maybe she should suggest it as a necessary feature. *Papà, you never know when it might come in handy*. Maybe one already existed, like the secret room that was her childhood hideout. The memory of her silver cat surged over her, a wave of longing for Fedele. And in that wave, a dark undertow, a feeling of desolation that encompassed more than the loss of a pet. Even in these last months, underneath the exhilaration, below the fire of love and defiance, a dangerous, gritty pull.

Swim up to the light. Or you will drown.

Alex reminded Fulvia that she suggested they meet one night somewhere magical, by the sea or the temple ruins of Segesta. "I thought about it. I thought and thought, but I can't. There's no way I can sneak out." Fulvia enumerated the levels of security at Bagna Serena.

Alex looked bewildered. "Dogs? A patrolling guard? That's unusual."

"There have been some robberies in Alcamo. A home

invasion. It's recent." Fulvia stopped.

"I heard the town was unusually safe. Because of the ruling *Mafiosi*." He paused and, as the truth sunk in, leaned back. "*Dio mio.*"

She could not continue holding back. "I didn't tell you before, because I thought it would put you off."

"You know me better than that. You aren't your parents. You're you."

"I don't believe my father has done horrible things. Yet I'm ashamed."

"I don't give a shit about the things they care about, status and money. Fulvia, you should have trusted me."

"I trust you. I wanted you to get to know me without the taint, the preconceptions."

For I was born to original sin and need redemption.

They often spoke, dreamed, of travelling together: England, of course, the Scandinavian countries, or Goa, Nepal, and Tibet. They could do it cheaply, hostels and backpacks. "Nothing weighing us down," Alex said.

After her confession, such conversations were more urgent. "I have to get away," she said. "It's the only way for us," he said.

Was he serious? He was.

They were going to have a new life together? They were.

Not just a trip or an interlude, a better life?

How about America? A country as far away as the moon.

Perfect, for the moon was how far she must go.

11   Venice
MAY 1989

When Marisa arrived at the hotel on the Lido di Venezia, she was twitchy and on edge. She had had a long day. She had been disillusioned in the morning, then disappointed at midday, irritated and bored by having to wait for the coffin to be unloaded and the undertaker to arrive, and for all the paperwork to be completed and stamped. She had brought Sam Mazzolin home to his family. Now she needed information. What sort of man had this Sam been? A smuggler? Professional or amateur?

A fool? Obviously.

She had a rationale for wanting to attach an identity and life to the pile of bones that lay for those weeks unnamed and unclaimed in Trapani. How else would she ever discover why he and Silvio had been killed?

Or would this case lead nowhere too?

The Mazzolin's family apartment was close, a few blocks down and one off the main boulevard of the Lido.

The rain that had blotted out the lagoon on Marisa's boat trip in from the airport had stopped. Marisa walked at her usual fast pace, circling some puddles, jumping over others. Last week, when she had gone to Alcamo Marina to investigate a string of burglaries in the vacation homes that lined the sea, people were already on the beach. Here the air was still chill, the bushes only beginning to flower.

Though it was not yet eight o'clock, the grey light was fading to black. The shops were closed or closing, the road traffic spotty. From the canal that bordered the side street, a whiff of stagnant water, a stink redolent of Venetian rot.

On the front steps of the apartment house on the cross street, a figure from carnival: a Pulcinella mask floating above a black cloak. At least until Marisa drew closer and was able to see the presence was an old woman, with a crooked nose and a curved chin, a black coat draped on her shoulders. Marisa understood she was Mazzolin's mother.

Marisa put on her official reassuring face. "*Signora*, I am—"

The crone grabbed her hands and squeezed. "*Commissario*, you brought him home to me. *Mio figliolo.*"

Marisa opened her mouth to respond, but Mrs. Mazzolin continued to talk, to lament her boy, vanished from the face of the earth, a good boy, a good man, the best. She shepherded Marisa through the metal and glass front door, across a lobby, and down some back stairs. Massacred. Burned. Those damned Sicilians. That woman. Through a glass door, down a long, dark hall that stank of fish, and Marisa found herself in a kitchen. Two lamps cast circles of light, but the room was large, and most of it remained in shadow.

How to interrupt the cascade of words? Marisa tapped Mrs. Mazzolin's arm and plunged in. "Did you live here while Samuele was growing up?"

The woman shook her head. "While he was at university. I was hired here as concierge his last year of high school. That made it more possible. Before, five of us in three rooms, misery. My husband was useless. And Samuele so smart, so smart, he was the first in the family to study. A golden boy, but unlucky. The professors were against him because he was no *figlio di papà*, not a spoiled rich boy like the others. And he didn't have a godfather, a connection, to help him along. So he went, he emigrated, he left us. What an ugly destiny."

She uttered these phrases not once but several times in varied order. Marisa had the sense that she would go on repeating them for months, maybe years, to whomever she met.

Still, she managed to sit Marisa down at the table, to put on a fresh pot of coffee, and to pick up a few scattered dishes. What had her son majored in at university, Marisa asked Mrs. Mazzolin?

The old woman's voice lost its screeching tone. "We hoped for engineering. But he wanted architecture. Well, he was an artist, brilliant, doing well, but then the strikes started and the politics. He got into trouble, but it wasn't his fault."

Of course, Marisa thought, in your eyes he was always right. "What sort of trouble?"

"Nothing, they used any excuse." Mrs. Mazzolin poured the coffee and offered a plate of cornmeal cookies. Marisa had eaten two crab *tramezzini* at the airport—a snack, not dinner. She took two biscuits.

Signora Mazzolin talked on. She had suffered when her son had emigrated to Canada. He'd finally come back to her, and now he had been taken away forever.

"Did you ask him why he would fly to Sicily, without his wife, when he had just returned to Venice?" Marisa bit down to break off a fragment of the hard biscuit.

"It's obvious, for her—that witch."

"He said that?"

Mrs. Mazzolin grimaced. "Why else?"

"He didn't mention business? A deal?"

The old woman's face contracted into a spasm, as if she'd tasted something bitter. Marisa continued to ask about the trip south. The woman answered with accusations against her daughter-in-law and her family. "They are bad people," she said.

"Enough, mother." A middle-aged woman had emerged from the dark hallway and was watching. Marisa stood and identified herself. "Luisa Taviani," the new arrival said. "Samuele's sister."

"The witch is not even coming to his funeral," Mrs. Mazzolin interjected. The witch was her daughter-in-law.

"Don't listen to her. She's hysterical with grief," Luisa said, as she gave her mother's shoulder an affectionate

126

squeeze.

"Perhaps you can help me," Marisa said to Luisa.

"You are here to interrogate us, instead of her." The old woman's chin was trembling.

"No. I'm here to express my and my officers' condolences and to reassure you that we are investigating."

"Murder," Mrs. Mazzolin said.

"It helps if I can understand who your Samuele was and what he was doing when it happened."

"Naturally." Luisa had her mother's prominent nose and hooded eyes, but her expression was calm, pleasant.

"For example, I don't have a picture of Samuele."

"Ohhh, the album." Mrs. Mazzolin was immediately up and off down the corridor.

"Your mother is hostile to your sister-in-law."

"Mamma has had a difficult life, full of disappointments. Her children are everything to her. None of our spouses are good enough. And Sam was the baby, and a son. She would have disliked anyone he married, but Mamma blamed Fulvia specifically for Sam staying in Canada."

"The two of them met and married there?"

"They did. He always intended to come back, when he had enough of a nest egg. Sam found it took much longer than he expected. He said it was a black hole, that city, Edmonton. You fell in and couldn't climb out."

"But he did return, without his family."

"He had a very good job waiting." Mrs. Mazzolin answered from the doorway. She held a large leather-bound album. "Finally, he had a chance to live the life he wanted."

"A friend, an old girlfriend actually, helped him get a position in the Office of Restorations," Luisa Taviani said.

"Samuele couldn't wait." Mrs. Mazzolin's voice was suddenly as loud and as penetrating as the sound of breaking plates.

"Fulvia wanted to stay there," Luisa said.

"Samuele expected the girls and his wife to come, when the school year was over."

"He told me when Fulvia was finished her treatment," Luisa said.

"She's ill?" Marisa said. Had Buonaiuto mentioned this during the phone call? Her notes were in Alcamo. When he would call back with the information on the Mazzolin's finances, she must ask about the wife's health.

The daughter nodded: "A tiny tumour, Sam said. That's why she can't come to the funeral."

"So she says." Mrs. Mazzolin touched her nose to signal her skepticism. "I don't think she can face us. She's guilty."

"Mother, please."

Mrs Mazzolin pushed the album at Marisa. "Look at my poor boy."

"Could you lend this to me?" Marisa stood up. "I'll return it tomorrow, before I leave."

"I left in the wedding pictures, though I wanted to tear them into a thousand pieces."

Marisa's reflection in the hotel mirror startled her; her face was lined and tense. Yoga time: she slipped off her sober work clothes and pulled on an oversized T-shirt. She didn't have a mat but made do with a strip of hardwood floor beside the bed. She bent, twisted, and stretched herself into the prescribed sequence of poses. Breathing in, expanding from her centre, breathing out, aligning mind to body.

She brought the photo album with her to bed. The early pictures were of the formal, studio type: a baby in baptismal clothes, a mother with fat infant on her lap, a boy at prayer with a white first-communion ribbon around his arm, an adolescent with a guitar and dreamy expression, all sepia-coloured on hard matte paper. There were two class pictures: the first from elementary school, the second identified as first year of technical high school, and a few pages of black and white snapshots, some with rippled edges. These were of poorer quality, often a little blurred, but they looked just as posed as the ones taken in the studio. Boy with older sister. Boy dressed as a pirate for carnival. Boy on a dinghy, in a canoe, and on a motorboat. In each picture, Sam sported a smile on the edge of becoming a sneer. A cocky boy, she guessed, confident, difficult. Or had his stance been only bravado? A cover for a sweeter, gentler self?

Sam must have been at least ten years older than Marisa, but his type was universal. He could have been a schoolmate playing soccer with her and her girlfriends in the piazza, peering over her shoulder to copy her answers on a history test, pulling her hair or making strange faces so she'd look at him. He could have been the one who stole a kiss on a dare or flipped her skirt up on the playground.

Marisa continued turning the pages of the album. Young man with friends in the mountains, then at the beach. Although a couple of the photos were overexposed, facial features bleached into imprecision, these were clearer than the earlier ones. Now he radiated coolness, his shirt collar turned up, hair slicked up and back, then long and shaggy. Sam and a pretty brunette with backcombed hair and thick eyeliner. Sam and two friends crewing a sailboat: he was caught in profile, staring at the horizon.

He could have been her first boyfriend winning her with Lucio Battisti and Mina records, with marijuana joints and Baci chocolates. Or her second, whose name and face she had forgotten, though not their make-out sessions in his cramped Fiat 500.

There were three newspaper clippings. One, dated October 7, 1969, declared that three thousand had marched in Trento. In the accompanying photo, Sam was in the front line, waving a placard: *MORTE AI PADRONI.* Death to the bosses. Marisa couldn't find him in the photo of the second clipping, although he must have been one of the dark forms marching in downtown Milan. Only the banners were clear: *SERVIRE IL POPOLO* and *TUTTO SUBITO.* Serve the people, and everything right now. The third was dated December 3, 1969, and was headlined "University Strike Continues." It featured Sam behind a microphone, his mouth open, addressing a sea of students.

So he had been a student leader too, another Roberto Valente abuzz with energy and ideas, riffing with words, improvising a revolution. He could have been the one she lied to and tricked, the one she helped trap and convict. For the greater good, she was still convinced, because words had eventually become kneecappings, then assassinations. But Sam went another way. He stopped trying to change his country, and left.

The next photos were less familiar. Black and white was replaced by colour: four postcards of mountain wilderness and one labelled Edmonton, showing a can-can girl and a log fort. The towering peaks and turquoise lakes reoccurred in the background in subsequent photos. In this Canadian landscape, Sam looked shorter, slighter.

He was a handsome man: on his face, his mother's strong cheekbones, nose, and chin were in better proportion. And when his wife, Fulvia Arcuri, began to appear, she was stunning: a mass of hair, a full mouth, and large, dark, almond-shaped eyes. The wedding pictures looked more spontaneous than those that came before, as if the photographer had taken them without the couple knowing. They radiated a private joy. True love, Marisa thought, at least then.

The last photos were of Sam and Fulvia's children. Baby, toddler, baby and toddler. Sam and Fulvia were pushed into corners and backgrounds.

The next morning, Marisa ate her room-service breakfast, hardboiled egg, rolls, and *caffè e latte*, while again flipping through the album. Her mind went back to a semiotics class at university. She'd been studying law; the class hadn't even been an elective. But she'd decided to audit, for the challenge and the stimulus. The professor was an intellectual star, a master of the startling paradox. He walked the campus trailed by acolytes. And he easily held the attention of the almost four hundred students squeezed into the lecture hall, despite his soft voice and slight stutter. *The photo is an imprint of what is gone.* Of course, Marisa thought, staring at Sam's young face. The photo is an elegy.

Marisa met up with the Sam's former girlfriend, Daniela Bonvicini, at the Lido vaporetto stop. "I have to go to one of those superstores in Mestre," Daniela had said when Marisa phoned her. "Accompany me as far as you want."

Daniela was easy to spot. She was in head-to-toe black, with a face painted almost as white as a geisha's. "I'm in mourning for my Samuele," she said, dabbing at her eyes with a cotton handkerchief.

Marisa waited until they were on the waterbus and settled in the only seats that offered any privacy, the outdoor ones at the back. "I understand Mr. Mazzolin returned to Venice in anticipation of a good job." Marisa spoke loudly to be heard over the noise of the engine. "A job you had arranged for him."

"I did no such thing." Daniela had a deep voice. "I heard of an opening in restorations, I have some friends, I put in a good word. Last fall, Sam flew over for the competition. He won, fair and square."

"You wanted him back here with you."

Daniela made an arching gesture with her right hand. "He was miserable. He had studied architecture, yet for years he laid tiles. Imagine. Eventually he opened his own renovation firm, but still."

The wind blew Marisa's hair about, covering and uncovering her face. Daniela's layered hair must have been sprayed into place. "So this new job you found for Mr. Mazzolin, it paid well?"

"Moderately."

"He made some big promises, including a new apartment for his mother and another for him and his family. And he mentioned a boat. Do you know where all that money was coming from?"

The Arsenale stop, the vaporetto bumped against the quay. "Sam left to make his America, his nest egg." Daniela dabbed her eyes again. "He planned on coming back to me."

"You are both married."

"I'm separated," Daniela said. "Sam and I reconnected when he came home on holiday."

"After he heard about the job?"

"A number of years ago."

"He came with his family?"

With the kids and *la Siciliana*." Daniela stood up. "Enough." She pushed past a cluster of teenage tourists, and though they were at the Zattere rather than her destination, the bus terminal at Piazzale Roma, Daniela strode off the boat. Marisa rushed after her.

"Mrs. Bonvicini, please, wait. I do want to hear your story, yours and his."

Daniela continued walking down the *riva*. Marisa had to half-walk, half-run, to keep up. "You must have been young."

Daniela's pace slowed. "Young. Autumn of 1969. My first year at the university here, Ca' Foscari. Though we actually met in Padua. Venice, as always, was dead politically, and we went up for a so-called strategy meeting. Which turned into a long, boring lecture by a Maoist. I fell asleep, and my head hit Sam's shoulder. Destiny."

"What was Samuele like then?"

"Like?" Daniela looked startled. She pulled a cigarette package out of her purse. "Can I offer you one? Good for you. My husband always lectured me, but then nagging was his specialty." Daniela held a gold lighter up to the cigarette between her shiny, coral lips. She breathed in and out slowly. "Where were we?"

"Sam in 1969."

"He was charismatic, a leader, a real working-class hero." Daniela came to a stop in the middle of an intersection of two *calli*. She stared one way, the other, took a long pull of her cigarette, turned and headed back in the direction in which they'd come. A bit breathless—she needed more cardio than yoga was providing—Marisa followed Daniela across a *campiello* into a café.

After they settled with espressos and mineral water, Marisa said, "It attracted you—his being from a lower-class family."

"He wasn't like his parents. You met his mother. He was educated. But he did seem more authentic than most of the guys I knew."

"Mrs. Mazzolin insisted he was unfairly treated."

"She's right. He was one of a group arrested for wrecking this Fascist of a professor's office. It hadn't been his idea. He left before the real damage was done. One idiot set fire to some papers. Another urinated on some books. But the others had rich daddies and good lawyers. The charges against Sam were eventually dropped, but by that time, he'd been held for two months. After that, he started thinking of emigration. It took a while for the papers and all."

"You didn't think of going with him?"

"Leave my family and friends?" Daniela made a face.

"He didn't ask?"

"He knew I would have turned him down. I'm a Venetian. Can you imagine me in the wilderness with the bears and the red Indians?"

"Oh, I don't think it's like that."

"Whatever. It didn't end up being the right place for him." With a finger, she drew an oval, the outline of his journey, in the air in front of her. "He went and he came back. I thought we might work this time. Instead, he's gone for good."

12   Sicily

SPRING 1973

Our day is at hand, Alex wrote in English across the open page of Fulvia's scribbler.

Fabulous.

Prepare yourself for ecstasy.

Fulvia searched for a hip, English response. She reverted to writing in Italian. *I'm ready for anything.*

"My sister Chiara and her family are going to Florence," Alex explained later at their new favourite spot for lunch. "For Easter, but they leave on Monday."

"You have a key?"

Alex grinned. "Happy days," he said in English.

They were at the century-old Bar Mazzara, a café too formal, expensive and far from the university for their student friends. They didn't worry about being recognized; the café drew an upper-crust crowd. Maestro, Your Excellency, Principessa, the waiters called out to the latest arrivals. They barely glanced at Alex and Fulvia. The couple sat in the last of the wooden booths. They felt free to talk, laugh, and touch. They ordered *arancine*, crispy rice balls with mozzarella or ragù stuffing. They licked their own, and each other's, fingers. Today, Alex savoured two of these "little oranges." Fulvia enjoyed a brioche filled with chocolate gelato and whipping cream. "Give me a taste," he said. She held out the confection; he went for her mouth, sucking the sweetness from her tongue.

Surfacing, Fulvia sensed someone was watching. Over by the counter, a woman holding a cellophane-wrapped tray of Mazzaro goodies. A young woman in a pink shantung suit. With teased hair and a familiar face. Her childhood friend Veronica, her green eyes telegraphing *gotcha*.

Fulvia dropped the brioche. As she slid out of the booth, she wiped her fingers, grabbed her stuff.

"What's happening?"

Fulvia pointed at Veronica, who was heading for the front door. "Have to stop her. She'll tell." Outside, Fulvia hesitated, then plunged into the pelting rain. By the time she caught up to Veronica, halfway down the street, she was wet and cold, her hair straggly.

Veronica, comfortable under her mauve umbrella, flashed a condescending smile. "Calm down. Breathe."

"We have to talk."

"Can't. I'm in a rush." Veronica trotted off to a row of parked cars.

"Veronica, wait."

"Must be in Alcamo by three o'clock." Veronica stopped at a red Fiat 500. She handed her umbrella to

Fulvia. "Can you hold it over me?" Veronica unlocked her door, leaned in, and lay the pastry package on the tiny bench of a backseat. As she got in herself, she took back the umbrella, leaving Fulvia standing, the rain stinging her face, weighing down her wool coat.

Fulvia ran to the other side of the car and rapped on the window. "Veronica." She pulled uselessly on the door handle. "Let me in." Fulvia rapped again. "Please, listen to me."

Veronica held out for what seemed like a minute but was probably ten seconds.

"Who's the *barbone*?" she asked, when Fulvia was in and sitting.

"No one, no one you'd know. A friend."

"Oh sure, a friend. You would go for a hippie."

"You can't tell anyone, please."

"This is good. Can't-smell-her-own-shit Fulvia begging."

For a long moment, only the sounds of rain on the tin roof and a distant growl of traffic. Fulvia cast about for something, anything, she could use. "I saw you and Enzo in the cantina." Enzo's hand up Veronica's skirt, his head at her breasts. "I kept quiet, as any old friend would." More to protect Enzo than Veronica.

"So what? I've moved on."

How to muzzle the little witch? An appeal to her mercenary heart? A bribe could work, but nothing too overt. Veronica might view cash as demeaning. Fulvia untangled her wet ringlets from her thick hoop earrings. "Here, take these," she said. "Solid gold. An early present for your birthday next month."

Veronica made a show of not accepting. The earrings were too big and showy. "I like refined." Still, she tried them on, smiled at her reflection in the rearview mirror.

Fulvia was shivering; she needed to dry off. "They suit you. I want you to have them."

Veronica nodded. "I wouldn't have told anyway. I'm not a gossip."

"A memento of our friendship." Fulvia leaned toward Veronica, and they awkwardly bussed each other on the cheeks. Fulvia's hand was on the handle of the car door.

"Fulvia, wait." Veronica burned with self-importance. "Take a friend's advice. Give him up, before you find yourself in real danger."

"What are you suggesting? That my family would have me hurt?"

"You know they might. That's why you're so desperate."

Fulvia's teeth began to chatter. "You're exaggerating."

"The hippie for sure. And probably you, too."

"Not my father." He loves me. "Or my mother."

"What about your cousin Mara?"

"What about her? She's in Milan. Her lover did desert her, but she started a new life."

"Bullshit. They are both in the ground."

"No."

"You know what happened to that Rita from Partinico." Veronica listed four more dishonoured girls, four more maimed or dead.

Fulvia wished she could slap the smug expression off Veronica's face. "Not us, not the Arcuri."

That evening, Fulvia searched out her father and uncharacteristically gave him a hug. "My daughter the family lawyer," he said and kissed the top of her head. Her anxiety was soothed. *He loves me, no matter what.*

Alex came to their assignation prepared. He brought a beach and a hand towel, a strip of condoms, and a lubricant with the brand name *Passione*. He also brought sandwiches and oranges for them to eat. Fulvia was about to step out beyond the castle walls, into the world with all its challenges. She couldn't eat. She had had only a few sips of coffee that morning.

They chose an ascetic spare room with a low bed. Fulvia wanted to open the window shutters: she craved light. "Someone could see in," Alex said. "From that building opposite." He partly opened the slats, so when they undressed, when, for the first time, they faced each other naked, their skin was streaked light and dark.

Alex lingered, smelled, tasted, appreciated, and revelled in her body. He was gentle, patient, everything she could have wanted for in a first lover. She was prepared for some blood, a little pain, but when the moment came, there was no blood and much too much pain. He couldn't enter. He pushed. He shifted her legs. He spread more lubricant on his penis. He gained a centimetre, then two. "Go on," she said. He thrust: she ground her teeth. He wilted. Again, he stroked her, then tongued first one, then the other crease between her leg and her vulva. He tried again. Despite herself, she shrieked. *Santa Maria*. He pulled back, collapsed on the bed beside her.

"It feels like I'm being torn apart."

"And I'm battering a brick wall."

"Is it supposed to hurt like this?"

"Of course not."

"You've done this before?"

"I confess. You're my first virgin."

"Maybe you're too big for me."

"That's not the damn problem." He rolled away and sat up on the side of the bed.

"Come on Alex, one more try. I'll gag myself with my T-shirt."

"I'm supposed to pluck your flower, not blast through a steel door."

Fulvia pressed her front against his back. "*Chiavami*." Fuck me.

"It's not a turn-on, hurting you."

"Thank goodness, but in this case, it's a means to an end."

He leaned over to plant a kiss on her right nipple. "Not today."

What was wrong with her? In the books she read, when a man took a woman into his arms, they melted into one. Easy-peasy. She must be a freak. Who could she talk to? Mamma—no, the family doctor—double no, he would tell in a second. She could have asked Dorina for advice if she were still in Alcamo rather than Naples.

Was Fulvia deformed? Two sleepless nights and she again met Alex at his sister's empty apartment. This time, along with the protection and the gel, he laid out a fat cigarette, a lighter, and a notepad.

They sat facing each other, cross-legged on the bed. Alex stuck the joint in his mouth. "I should have thought of this before. We're always in such a rush." He flicked the lighter, breathed in, and held out the joint.

Fulvia hesitated.

"You're too uptight."

And she was, she was, tight, tight. She pursed her lips around the joint.

"It's called *vaginimus*," Alex told her. "It's a reflex, let me get this right." He peered at the notepad. "A reflex of the pubococcygeus muscle. It causes a chain reaction of spasms in the adjoining muscles all the way through your pelvis. I phoned my brother in Siena."

"Isn't he a psychiatrist?"

"He was a regular doctor first. Giancarlo says the cause could be an infection or an inflammation."

She sucked in the smoke, coughed, gasped. "How is this shit going to help?"

"Giancarlo said it is probably psychological."

"No, I want this, us."

"Consciously, you do, but unconsciously?"

"Does he have any advice?"

Alex's pupils were dilated. "Advice." He was stroking one of her feet. "He got angry, called me crazy. Told me never to touch you again."

A half hour of slow, stoned caresses did no good. He couldn't penetrate her with even a finger. "I need to be far away. We need to be far away," she said.

Alex pulled out another joint. "We are. We're in our very own tropical hut. Can't you hear the sea? Feel the damp heat?"

She couldn't. Instead of relaxing her, the dope unleashed her fear. She had fooled herself, thinking they were safe, undetected. She and Alex were making a spectacle of themselves, and her own Argus, the hundred-eyed monster, was watching.

Fulvia was leaving the apartment house when she noticed the man loitering outside the *fruttivendolo*'s opposite. A cold prickling sensation between her shoulder blades. She'd seen that lumpy face, the flattened nose before. Where? Despite the distance, their glances met. Of course, with Zio Antonio and once with Papà. She broke into a half-run. This couldn't be the first time she was shadowed. Had she been wilfully blind? A quick glance showed him following a few metres behind. A blundering spy, this one. They must have used different *picciotti*, more skilled and more anonymous. A hundred, a thousand eyes. But if so, why had no one said anything? Why didn't they put a stop to her and Alex? Maybe her mind had conjured up the man. Back at the faculty, standing at the bottom of the main staircase, waiting for the car to take her back to Alcamo, she couldn't see him anywhere.

Once home, Fulvia took a long shower. She sat at her desk, her wet hair wrapped in a towel. She opened a textbook, but the letters swam across the page. She heard footsteps in the hall; her stomach dropped into her toes. Without a knock, Papà and Mamma barrelled in.

"You stupid, stupid girl," Mamma said. She pushed aside some of the strewn clothes on the bed, clearing a space to sit. Papà took the armchair.

"I'm busy. I have to study," Fulvia said in a semi-whisper.

Her mother continued to berate her: thoughtless, irresponsible, stupid.

Papà held up his hand. "Enough." Papà sounded calm. "We have been waiting patiently for this boy to demonstrate his good intentions. Waiting for him to come to me and ask for my permission to court you."

Was that all it took? Asking for permission? Fulvia doubted it. "If you knew all along, why today? Why didn't you say something earlier?"

"I trusted you. I told your mother: she's headstrong, but she's got the right stuff."

"And I agreed. The times are changing. But then." Mamma shook her head. "You started on the path to ruin."

They had let the leash go slack, so she'd forget she was tethered. "I hate that you had me followed."

"For your protection. I'm your father: it's my job."

For your honour, for your name, Fulvia thought. "I don't need protection from Alex."

Her father contracted his right shoulder up and back. "I wanted a real man for you, not a dope-smoking *barbuto*."

"Now you're compromised," Mamma said. "Alex's family will be contacted and made to understand he has no choice.

Fulvia wanted Alex, but only if he wanted her. "Don't humiliate me, please," Fulvia said.

The next morning, another shock, another dose of reality: Nonna fell in the hallway that led to Fulvia's room. Fulvia found her and yelled till the rest of the family came running. Fulvia cried; Papà crouched to take Nonna's pulse, then went off to call the ambulance. Davide tried to lift Nonna, who groaned and lapsed back into unconsciousness. Fulvia screamed at Davide, and her mother screamed at her. "You've killed her. It's your fault."

Patience, Fulvia told herself, *coraggio*. The insults and abuse were bound to get worse. That evening, Davide said smiling, "I always knew you were a little whore." As ordered, Fulvia was serving her brother his supper. He sprinkled the Parmesan on his minestrone and elaborated on her disgrace. She stifled the impulse to pour a ladle of hot soup over his head. He'd love an excuse to deliver a few more kicks to the ribs.

She was not going to sit across from her smirking brother. She couldn't eat. Besides, this was her chance, while her parents were still at the hospital, to phone Alex and warn him. Tureen in hand, she was at the door when something

Davide said penetrated her defences, something about Alex's muckety-muck family, the Zaccos. She dropped into the closest chair. "What do you think you know?"

"What would you do without me to open your eyes? Tell you what's what?"

I'd have to find someone else to bludgeon me with the cold, hard facts, she thought.

Alex's family was old, aristocratic, and though reduced in circumstances, still in control of a sizable estate. "Enough land for a cluster of apartment buildings," Davide said. Their father was angry, of course, about Fulvia's sneaking around, but he would accept Alex as her fiancé. "He understands the need for new alliances."

Fulvia was nothing more than a chip to be wagered. The narrow passage to the kitchen lengthened before her; the walls tilted inwards. The tureen grew heavy, and her feet became blocks. But she shuffled on, until she reached the kitchen and deposited the soup.

Her thoughts veered one way and then the other. Even a house with barred doors and bricked-up windows must have a way out. A marriage was an obvious means of escape. And Alex might agree, for he was true to her and she to him, despite the falseness that surrounded them. Together, they could plot a different life. She envisioned them in Paris: she an art director and Alex a film critic for a chic and intellectual magazine.

Heartened by her daydream, she phoned Alex to warn him that her parents knew. "Don't worry," she said. "They aren't opposed to us as a couple."

"You're joking."

"We'll have to finesse a few things. Make some plans."
She suggested they meet tomorrow after her first exam.
"By the bulletin board in the lobby of the law building."

"I'll be there," he said.

"It's important. The term's ending. It might be one of
our last chances to talk freely."

"I do love you," he said, for the first time.

The next day, as she expected, students were called up
alphabetically. Fulvia Arcuri was the second to undergo
questioning by the three-professor committee. Although
she had barely studied, she had a good memory, and her
answers were articulate and correct. By twenty after nine,
she was standing, waiting, by the student bulletin board
in the lobby. Alex was nowhere to be seen.

For years, she would relive this hour of waiting so
doggedly for Alex. He will come. He won't come. Her
mind produced a hundred scenarios. He is ill. Detained.
In an accident. He will send a friend, a note, a word—
soon, soon. And the minutes and the seconds crawled by.
Had he been frightened off by her telling him that her
parents knew? Was he that weak and inconstant? Or was
Davide wrong about her father welcoming a dynastic
connection? Had Alex been shot? Kidnapped? Was he being punished for loving her? The hippie for sure, Veronica
had said. No, not her Papà.

Her classmates came out of the examining theatre one
by one. A few waved, others paused to chat or compare
performances. She responded minimally. After the hour,

she sought out the claustrophobic booth that contained the faculty's only public phone. "The *Signore* is out," a woman said.

"Has he gone to the university?"

"I said he isn't here."

Fulvia didn't give up. They needed to talk, to work it out, the two of them. Alex would find a way to contact her, to explain why he didn't turn up. One, two, three days and no word.

The first time Fulvia took a turn sitting vigil at Nonna's bedside, she searched out a public phone and dialled Alex's number. It was past nine on a weekday evening; he should be home. She asked politely: Alex, please. "*Strega e puttana*," the man who answered the phone hissed. "You're never going to get your hands on our son." Alex's father accused her of conspiring with the rest of her sinister family, *assassini*, to trap Alex.

Alex, the free spirit, had talked to his parents about her and about them. Worse, he had allowed them to misjudge the entire relationship. What was also clear was that she must stop expecting Alex somehow to pop up; he was no longer in Palermo. His family, not hers, had spirited him away. She could call his brother the psychiatrist in Siena. He'd know, and he might be more reasonable than the venomous father. Or she could ask a trusted friend like Dorina to approach Alex's close friends: Mimmi or Franco.

But her will wavered Nothing she could do would make any difference. She was worthless, immaterial, even as a bargaining chip. This time the reputation of the Arcuri had produced revulsion rather than the usual compliance.

Her mother arranged a meeting with Alex's family. The Zaccos were superficially polite. Alex's father did not insult Fulvia's mother the way he had Fulvia. Mamma reported that *Ingegnere* Zacco blamed modern youth, Marxism, drugs, and Fulvia's misinterpretation of his son's true feelings. Yet Mamma sensed their condescension and disdain, which infuriated her. "Snotty bastards. I blame you." Mamma cuffed Fulvia on the head. "If you'd waited until we chose the right man instead of freelancing." She grabbed a hunk of Fulvia's hair and gave it a sharp tug. "We'll take you to the doctor for an examination. He can testify you're ruined."

"Won't work, Mamma."

"They'll regret this," Papà said, his voice sombre and his right shoulder twitching up and back.

"I'm intact."

"That boy in particular," Papà said.

"I won't have anyone forced to take me. I want love."

"*You* want?" Papà too was angry with Fulvia for her lies, her disobedience, her rebelliousness. She had failed. Worse, she had failed him. He ordered her locked in her room. Alone, alone, alone. "You're allowed out to visit your grandmother, that's all."

She flipped pages, stared at the ceiling, and refused to eat. She was going to die if she didn't get out. Two days in, her body betrayed her again. She tried to stand up, and her legs gave way.

Paralysis.

13   Venice/Sicily
JUNE 1989

Marisa De Luca allowed herself an extra day in Venice to
wander and gaze. At sunset, over a glass of prosecco, she
gave herself a pep talk: stay strong and in control. Yet, on
Tuesday morning, five minutes after she walked into the
Alcamo station, she found herself yelling at Brusca. He
had not led a search of the Inzerillo villa or the surrounding area. "I ordered you." Her voice was too high.

"Easy." Brusca made a show of covering his ears. "I'm
sure you didn't."

She took a breath and dropped her register. "Fine. I'll
put Lo Verde in charge." The impulse was a good one.
Brusca hated being demoted. And a day later, Lo Verde
and Roselli found the stash that Carnevale and Mazzolin
had hidden. The cottage where the men had stayed was
on a promontory, two thirds of the way down the eastern
side of the sparsely populated peninsula. Lo Verde had the
idea of borrowing a cruiser from the *Guardia di Finanza*

and, with Roselli's help, he combed the adjacent seashore.

As he later told Marisa when she came to see for herself, a cave not more than half a kilometre from the cottage seemed likely. An anchored boat would be partly hidden by the overhang of the cliff. And to enter the cave, even at low tide, one had to wade through water.

"That explains the pants stiffened by sea water in the villa," Marisa said.

"We found the crate of marijuana behind that rock," Lo Verde said. "And the two blocks of hashish farther in."

Marisa squinted at the shore, but she could make out nothing. She took off her sunglasses. The bright sun bounced off the sea into her eyes: the cave was a dark blotch. "Good work, Inspector." She looked over at their haul, a large plastic box and the two smaller blocks, all three wrapped in layers of plastic. "As I thought, the hash in the car was a sample. How much?"

"I'd guess about fifty kilos each," Roselli said. "Worth a pot of gold."

But when divided in two, Marisa thought, not enough to fulfill Sam's fantasies of a sailing yacht and a spacious apartment in the historic centre of Venice, as well as a new place for his mother on the Lido. "Maybe Inzerillo and Mazzolin thought this was a start of a profitable business, the poor bastards," Marisa said. She flashed to the dark basement flat and the older Mrs. Mazzolin's tremulous voice: *mio figliolo.*

Back at the station house, Marisa phoned Lanza. "I was right."

"*Brava.*" Lanza's voice was a little bored. "Though I'm not sure of where it takes us."

"I've sent the evidence to your office to hold and weigh," she said. He said nothing. "Are you preoccupied?"

"There is something you should know. It will be in the papers tomorrow." He lowered his voice to a whisper. "There is some new evidence, a misplaced toxicology test. It seems that Roberto Valente's death was not a suicide."

"He was drugged and then strung up," Marisa said.

"You are still agitated about that bastard's death. The fact that he was murdered should make you feel better."

"Do you have any idea who and why?"

"Some prison feud, I was told. He always was an arrogant son of a bitch."

"We put him in that prison."

"No, Marisa. He put himself there. Don't go all soft and sentimental. You performed brilliantly in his case."

"And it was necessary? What we did?"

"You saved your country from a great evil."

Had she fought the forces of chaos? She was no longer so sure.

Marisa stared at Alex's profile. "I'm glad you called."

They were in his noisy old Fiat, speeding along the almost empty highway between Alcamo and Segesta.

"And I'm glad you want to see the other Sicily, underneath all the shit." His right hand held a cigarette; his left was on the wheel. The tight interior was filling with smoke. "The stones of *Magna Græcia*, not just the ruins, but what remains of the culture." He inhaled.

Marisa smiled. "I've seen no sign of the Golden Mean since I've been here. None." She was tempted to add something about his having smoked three cigarettes already.

"True enough. I was thinking of the spirit of the stories, both myths and tragedies."

"Inexorable destiny," she said, referring to the conversation at Ivana's.

"Let's not start that again." He tossed his cigarette stub out the window.

"I have been to Agrigento, to the valley of the temples. The yellow earth, the blooming almond trees."

"Most of the ancient city hasn't been unearthed, but you can still sense what Empedocles's sacred city used to be: powerful and beautiful."

"I went with my landlady and her daughter, who was mostly interested in the souvenir stalls. I looked for the temple of Demeter, but all that was left was the foundation of a ruined church. Close by, I did find a mossy grotto and a deep crack that led into a dark cave." Marisa stopped, suddenly embarrassed.

"Why the temple of Demeter? Why not the temple of Zeus? Or Hera?"

"I had a friend who was a devotee of the Great Goddess." Fierce Carla. "She said ancient Sicily was a centre of goddess worship, and if I was ever on the island, I should visit the sites."

"Your friend passed away?"

"No. We drifted apart." Impossible to explain that she'd met Carla when she was undercover, and though Carla had broken off with the Sempre Guerra group, denouncing Roberto as a chauvinist pig and the group as part of the patriarchal hegemony and pawns of the state, Marisa could have no easy contact with those she'd been close to then. "Time, geography. She lives in Torino, runs a women's bookstore."

"So we'll go to the lake of Peguso, where Persephone was taken, and Erice, the city of Aphrodite. I also used to have a friend who was interested in the Great Mother and the early age of innocence. *When the altars did not reek with bull's blood*. That's also Empedocles."

"I would like that... very much."

"You need regular outings to withstand your work," he said. "Because in twentieth-century Sicily, the streets do reek with blood."

"Clever," she said. She controlled the impulse to touch him, to feel the joint of his shoulder beneath his rough wool sweater, the curve of his cheekbone beneath the tight, lightly lined skin. "You studied classics?"

"Philosophy. Then some art classes in London."

"I did law."

Alex didn't respond. He stared straight ahead at the road with an occasional glance out of his side window at the rolling hills. His mind seemed to have slipped off to somewhere else or someone else.

Maybe that was why she began, without naming any

names, telling him about the Inzerillo/Mazzolin case, describing the crash, the fire, and the drugs in the cave. Alex said nothing. Was he listening? "We don't know if they were planning on selling the hash and weed here on the island or moving it to the mainland." It occurred to her: could she ask him outright about the availability of soft drugs in the area? Might he take it the wrong way? As an accusation?

"We wonder if the local *cosca* somehow found out and, well, punished the encroachment on their territory," she said.

"That's the way things work here."

"But there's a complication. One of the victims was related by marriage to the boss. So maybe he was working with their permission. Or—"

Alex turned his head and gave her a searching look. "Related to the Arcuri?"

"So even you in Palermo have heard of them. Another odd thing, the man was visiting from Canada."

"And his wife?"

"Antonio Arcuri's niece."

"Was she visiting too?"

"She stayed home."

Marisa was going to channel the conversation back toward drugs when the car crested a hill; the view silenced her. Before them, a long and wide valley marked by cliffs and ravines and rolling hills. And cradled in the untamed landscape, the temple of Segesta, its stones glowing and golden in the sun. The road curved, and it was gone. Two more curves, and they were at a parking lot, empty except for a tour bus.

Out of the car, Marisa turned eagerly to Alex. "What a vision."

Alex didn't speak or look in her direction. He started toward a stone path up the hill.

She tried again, "Nature and art, wilderness and civilization."

"An enthusiast." His voice was odd, distant. Where had he gone?

"Aren't you?" Marisa broke off a stem from the broom lining the path. The scent was sweet and heady. The hill was a riot of colours and perfumes: yellow broom, purple borage, and red poppies, punctuated by clumps of wild fennel and prickly pear.

"I do like ruins," he said.

Marisa picked up her speed until she passed Alex and felt as if she were approaching the temple alone. As she drew closer, it evolved from apparition to reality, solid, imposing, yet ideal in its measure and proportion. She mounted the three steps and followed the line of columns. At the sixth, she reached out and rested her hand on the rough, pocked stone. Under her sandalled feet, an uneven mossy floor. The age of the place pressed down on her shoulders, her head. Milleniums of time. The ravages of wind and water. The blinding sun.

In Sicily, you could touch the past, taste it.

Or it could shape you, bake you, into another sightless statue.

From behind her, a booming voice. "The marvel before you is the best-preserved Greek temple anywhere. Yet it was built in 450 BC not by the Greeks, but the Elymians, who came from Asia Minor. Although it hasn't been proven definitively, it has long been accepted they were Aeneas's people, refugees from the city of Troy." The guide was trying to lead and instruct a swarm of children, who were buzzing with high spirits and ignoring him and the two female teachers. The man wasn't giving up. "The temple was never finished," the man yelled. "The columns were left unfluted. There never was a roof."

Marisa looked up at the column-bracketed sky; the children didn't.

"Segesta was at war and appealed to Carthage and then Athens for support. The city started the temple to demonstrate her wealth and culture. Once she had Athens's support, she stopped building."

"The Sicilians have a long history of deceit," Alex said as they walked away from the school group. His voice, his mood, had changed again.

They walked in silence around the outside of the temple, then back up the steps into the main concourse. "You can see why classical form, particularly the Doric, has lasted. It feels right and reassuring," Marisa said. "Because it is based on human proportions."

"Man is the measure and all that," Alex said.

The children were leaving. Their whoops and screeches bounced off the stones. "Finally," he said into her ear. She resisted looking into his eyes, keeping her head turned. His breath on her cheek, his smell, a mixture of spice, musk and tobacco, blocked the aroma of broom and rosemary.

He slid his hand under her skirt and up, lightly stroking first her buttocks, then more firmly her thighs. She was startled, unsure. He was working with a practised swiftness and dexterity, pulling aside her panties, laying claim with busy fingers. She took half a step back. He held on, two fingers pushed into her vagina. "Alex, what are you—"

"Shush," he said. His deep, dark eyes monitored each of her facial expressions. "It's been a while for you." And she was embarrassed with how intensely, how obviously, her body was welcoming his touch. A heavy knot at the base of her skull, legs, feet, hands weak and shaking, she was launched on the slippery stream, sailing. He was kissing her neck. Her hands were on his shoulders; he pushed a leg between hers.

Lulu, she thought, prostitute, needles. And she jerked away "Stop this, now." She gave him a fierce push for emphasis. "I don't like being jumped. Besides, someone could see us."

"They're all gone," Alex said.

"This isn't the place."

"So you are interested."

"This is too sudden."

"We can drive somewhere. Your apartment?"

"Are you kidding? All Alcamo would know."

"Mine then. It's a long drive, but." He made a half-lunge, hand out.

"Alex, I don't know you."

"Who can ever say he truly knows another?"

"Stop that. I don't have a sense of what sort of man you are."

"But you want to know. I'm offering a way to find out."

"No, I mean, I don't know what experiences you've had, whom you've associated with."

This time, he was the one who widened the space between them. "You need my life history first?"

"These days." She struggled for an excuse. "With these new diseases."

"Ironic, your caution. Since I'm the one taking the chance with you, *Commissario*. I don't know whom you've betrayed."

"What?"

"What." Alex mimicked her. He must know something. How much? None of the details, she hoped. She had spoken of a time undercover to Ivana, but she hadn't given any details.

"I've done my job. That's all."

"Of course. Your job." He pulled back and began to walk away. She followed, though her heart was beating at twice its usual rate. They were halfway to the car before he spoke. "You have an unorthodox way of attracting informants."

"What do you mean?"

"You want intel. That's why you came on to me."

"No, that's not true. Not at all. And I did not come on to you."

"What? You don't want to know if I am or have been a junkie? You don't want to know about my connections in that community? And all I know about the soft drug trade? Ivana told me, but I didn't believe her. Not Marisa, I thought. There's something real between us. But then you start telling me about your latest murder case and the drugs, oh yes, the drugs."

"I thought it would interest you."

"Ah, a nice story. An entertainment."

"I have no master plan."

"You have no questions?"

"It's my work. It's on my mind."

"Tell me another one. So you have no questions for me?"

Marisa was about to protest her innocence, but why not get something out of the outing? She'd accepted his invitation in good faith. She'd made an effort. He'd been moody and presumptuous. Manipulative. "I do have questions—about supply and demand."

"Of course."

"Did you hear anything about a shipment of hashish and marijuana? Anything about a new source?"

They had reached the car. He unlocked the passenger door, but did not open it. "No, I've heard nothing." He was back to his slow, pause-punctuated style. "But I wouldn't. I don't partake anymore." His mouth twisted.

"Alex, I believe you. But do you know anyone who would know what was in the air? Could you give me a name?"

"No, I couldn't." His gaze was direct, but it took rather than gave.

"I saw you talking to LuLu." Marisa trailed off.

"Who? I don't know anyone called Lulu."

Was he lying? LuLu could be her whore name. Should she press on?

Alex slid into the driver's seat and fumbled with the cigarette pack on the dashboard. He wasn't going to tell her anything.

"I'll take a rain check on visiting the amphitheatre," she said. "All of a sudden, I'm exhausted," she said, though that wasn't quite it.

On the drive back, Marisa tried to figure out what caused the change in Alex. He had turned cold before he even touched her, so it wasn't her rebuffing him. His advances had felt aggressive and angry. As if he meant to humiliate her.

Marisa stole glances at his profile. He put on a blues tape, much too loud. Now and then he half-sang, half recited a line or two. The ride seemed endless. When they finally arrived in Alcamo, all the parking spots in front of Marisa's building were taken. Alex stopped in the traffic lane. "Thank you for the informative afternoon," she said. He replied with a lifted eyebrow and an ambiguous smile.

That morning Marisa had planned to invite Alex in for dinner. She'd bought ham, asparagus, pasta, and wine. Now she wanted only comfort food: bread soaked in hot milk and sprinkled with sugar.

She locked the door, drew the deadbolt, hung up

her jacket, and took a few steps toward the closet-sized kitchen hidden behind a folding red door. She stopped, turned toward the living room. Something was wrong. A mess, and not one made by her. Someone had been here while she was away. He—they—had pulled her books off their shelves, upended her desk drawers. Scattered on the floor and sofa, files, bills, even some money, coins and two 50,000 lire notes. So not a robbery. In the bedroom, her underwear, everyday cottons and special-occasion silks were spread on the bed. Her flacon of Hermès cologne was uncorked and on its side; a pool of scent had blistered the polished finish of the bureau. Her Lancôme night cream was smeared on a pillow sham and an edge of the headboard. Minor damage. Not a threat so much as a reminder that she was a woman and vulnerable. Then Marisa saw the words sprayed on the blank wall across from the bed. In red paint: *PORCA TROIA*. Pig of a whore.

She felt her heart pound in her ears. Should she call the station? Have one of the constables come and dust for fingerprints? Why bother? There would be no prints. And she did not want any of the men to see her in this weak position. Worse, she could imagine a few of them gossiping, snickering over the words on the wall. "Someone's got her number."

Porca troia, Valente had yelled at her, his toadies hissing and whistling. Most of them must be out by now. Had they tracked her down? Or was the threat more local, springing not from her past but her present activities? And what was next?

162

Her landlady, Gelsomina, ever present and vigilant, had been out that afternoon. "At my daughter's, looking after my grandson." Predictably, Gelsomina was not surprised that an intruder or intruders had managed to enter the apartment building and then Marisa's apartment, despite the iron bars, the security system, and Marisa's deadbolt. The expression on her broad, brown face was almost proud. "They go where they want," Gelsomina said.

"Who?"

"You're asking me? You're the police." Gelsomina nodded three, four times. "The other three apartments weren't touched."

"I can't think of any reason to warn me off."

"If you were being warned, you'd have found more than spilled perfume." Gelsomina lowered her barrel of a body into the only armchair.

"How could the other renters—*Signore* Giacomo just across the hall—how could they not have heard a thing?"

"Remember that house on Libertà? The robbers cut the hole in the cement wall, still no one heard a thing." Again, she looked more amused than indignant.

"See no evil, hear no evil," Marisa said.

"Not necessarily. And don't start thinking your neighbours here are lying. The concrete cutters on Libertà were skilful and quiet. The guy or guys today are probably just as talented."

After Gelsomina left, Marisa contemplated calling Roselli. He'd keep quiet. She should report to Lanza. He might have some advice. But instead of dialling, Marisa

14 Sicily

Falling through the bright air, falling into the smack of the sea, a sudden plunge into coldness, greenness, into liquidity. Her arms and legs flailed. She gulped the bitter water, her lungs ripped. Dark and light, water and air struggled, burned, a fire in her chest.

Fulvia was three years old. Without warning, as they stood in the sun on the Mondello pier, Papà had slipped his hands under her armpits. He swung her back and forth in an ever higher arc. She was shrieking with delight. He swung her past the railing and, when she was over the sea, he let go. Sink or swim, Papà said after she was rescued by a passing swimmer. Sink or swim, he later told her angry mother: best way to learn.

Would he have let her drown? Of course not. The sea around the pier was shallow, though over her three-year-old head. And on that summer day there must have been a sprinkling of bathers, all potential rescuers. He might even have stationed a couple of his flunkies in the water by the end of the pier, including the man who scooped her up and carried her back to the beach. Over the years, Papà would recount the incident as an object lesson: Fulvia is a great swimmer, he'd say. Then he'd claim she had fought like a tiger cub: surfacing, gasping, and gulping, then starting to paddle. Fulvia couldn't remember such details, but the plunge into darkness, the panic, and the pain were etched into her flesh.

Would he have let her drown? Of course not. He had tested her toddler self, tossing her to the elements, and she passed. *Birichina*, he used to call her, imp, toughie. This time she flunked. She had failed to ensnare Alex. She let herself be seduced and abandoned. She had been felled by love. After Fulvia had passed out, her legs didn't work, and the doctors could find no physical cause. Papà's blue eyes darkened each time he saw her in the wheelchair. "You're being ridiculous," he said. She agreed that her legs, at least, were ridiculous. She willed them to move. They buckled and folded. At least, shut away as she was, no one beyond the family would see her in this pitiful state.

Ridiculous, too, the lingering physical pain. Get over it, she told herself ten times a day. Get over him. She stacked her law texts in a corner of her wardrobe. She confined her reading to the books she had loved as a child, *Anne of Green Gables*, *Little Women*, and her volume of folk tales, all stories that encouraged persistence and hope, and even hope lasted only a few minutes at a time. Her wrists quickly tired, her eyes burned, she fell asleep. She slept and slept. When she awoke, she had a metallic taste in her mouth and a churning in her stomach.

Her mother checked up on her once or twice a day. "How's the miserable Miss?"

Mamma plonked herself down on Fulvia's bed, forcing her to shift her legs. She lit a cigarette. "I'm blaming you for this relapse. I hadn't smoked in six years."

"What about last Christmas?"

"One here or there, doesn't count. Six—okay, five years of rectitude. Then you decide to go crazy, and I'm lost."

"You blame me for everything."

"You didn't use to whine." Mamma blew smoke at Fulvia's face.

"My life is over."

"What now, you're Eleonora Duse? Cut the melodrama. Get back on your feet. Then your father and I might introduce you to a splendid young man. Not a degenerate like that *fesso* you're pining for. One of us."

"Spare me." Fulvia's mind flipped through a list of possible candidates and shuddered. "I refuse." Though as she pronounced the words, she realized that refusing could only mean that her confinement would continue.

Her mother was staring at her own image in the mirror on an opposite wall. She lifted her chin and angled her head slightly. "A bit early perhaps. But a couple of more weeks of moping and you'll be fine. Your father and I can make plans." Mamma rotated to check out her other profile. "The boy and his family will pay."

Fulvia bolted into a sitting position. Her legs moved, jerking a few inches to the left. "Mamma, no, never, no, please."

The hours she spent at Nonna's bedside every day were her only distraction. Nonna's anguish dwarfed Fulvia's and gave her some perspective. Nonna's mind and flesh were melting away, leaving skin and vein and bone. Her eyes still spoke, especially to her granddaughter: *enough* and *why* and sometimes *help*. Once a day or so, Nonna managed a word or a phrase. "Your Papà," she whispered. Or "The carriage is taking too long." Or, "More olives."

Watching her grandmother struggle to die helped stiffen Fulvia's resolve. *I will get out.* Her legs were stirring, waves of pins and needles. Concentrating, sweating, she was able to move two centimetres to one side, four back.

One late afternoon, she wheeled herself down the corridors of Bagna in search of her father. She found him alone in the salon with a glass of scotch and a book of Roman history. "Promise me, you'll leave Alex and his family alone," she said.

He denied that he would, that he could, even if he wanted to, touch the Zaccos. His right shoulder lifted up and back in a nervous tick. "But it hurts me to see you like this. So I'm convinced they should be approached again, persuaded."

To have Alex back: her heart leapt. Still she screeched *no*.

Papà's mouth was tight, his voice raspy. "How could you so lose your self-respect? Your honour?"

"They are still here," Fulvia said "in my heart and my resolve. I won't allow myself to be imposed on Alex like a punishment. Papà, don't confirm his family's prejudices." Her own words emboldened her. "Besides, it's not just

Alex who hurt me. It's all of you. First keeping me on a leash. Now confining me here at Bagna. You're taking the breath from my mouth."

"Stop it. I've allowed you too much." He spoke calmly, but his face was revealed the tension he was feeling. "Your Uncle Antonio warned me, women don't belong in university."

"Papà, you of all people should understand. You've been to prison."

"Don't you dare." He paused. "You should be grateful you have a father who defends and protects you."

"How much will it cost me? Your protection? Do I have to pay monthly? Like the shops in town?"

Papà's eyes blazed, and he lunged. He landed on her with his full weight, pushing her back into the sofa. His hands were around her throat, choking off her words, her breath. His face blocked out the room, the light. Black spots in her eyes, fire in her lungs.

A stinging pain on one cheek, then the other. Papà was slapping her hard to bring her back to consciousness. "Fulvietta, *ma sei squaldrina*." Little slut. Now his eyes were gentle, concerned. "It's your fault. You go too far. And often pain is necessary in order to learn."

For nearly a week, her legs were again numb, and she played up her helplessness. She pulled her hair up into a ponytail to better display the necklace of purple bruises. Everyone pretended not to notice, except Nonna, whose eyes locked on Fulvia's throat. She gestured at Fulvia to

169

come closer, and when Fulvia bent over to kiss her withered cheek, Nonna managed to lift an arm with its plastic IV tube a few inches off the sheet. Fulvia grasped the trembling hand and guided it to the ring of bruises. One hooked finger pushed into the skin. Fulvia winced and two fingertips brushed sideways, the trace of a caress. "Papà tried to strangle me," Fulvia said. Nonna's face was a yellow-tinged mask. She dropped her arm and let out a sound: half-sigh, half-grunt.

Back when Nonna had run the house, Fulvia often heard her say, particularly to Papà, "*Non essiri duce sinno ti manciani.*" Don't be sweet lest you be eaten. The proverb was never aimed at Fulvia. She was *femmina* and must be dutiful and accommodating. But now the remembered words spoke to her, suggesting a new tactic. She would be sour, even if it led to her shunning.

For she had to escape. She imagined fantastic scenarios: cruising off in a hot air balloon, while her mother and father called up to her, begging that she return. Goodbye. Bluffing her way out with a machine gun, aiming it menacingly at anyone who tried to stop her. So long. Sneaking out during a police raid. Seeking sanctuary in a church, though not the local church, whose priest was in thrall to the Arcuri. *Addio.*

Papà would hunt her down, no matter what or where. Unless he agreed to let her go.

She mastered her argument. She was everything they said she was. And sooner or later she would embarrass him and not just within the family. *I won't give up.* So far, the gossips were quiet, but eventually she would transgress, and it would get out, and the Arcuri name would be besmirched. And Papà could keep her locked up, but soon people would gossip and say she must have done something terrible. And he couldn't marry her off, because she'd make an endless fuss. *I'll play the madwoman.* She'd tear out her hair, rip her clothes. *I won't give in.* In church, at the altar, she would spit in the supposed groom's face.

Let me go, let me go, let me go. She sought out her father and her mother daily. *Let me go, let me go, let me go.*

They ignored or berated her. She wouldn't give up or give in, she told them, ever. She didn't threaten to go to the police; that tactic would ensure her doom. Instead Fulvia repeated endlessly that she didn't belong here, she wanted no part of this life, their life. Her mother slapped her. Fulvia used a small kitchen knife to cut a ladder of thin lines on her inner thigh. Mamma slapped her again. She had many of Fulvia's possessions removed from her room: books, jewellery, most of her clothes and shoes.

Davide returned from who knows where. "Heyyy," he said to Fulvia. "Enough with the long face." He hovered, smirking, on the lookout for an excuse to pummel her. "You look like a dirty rag, ready for the bin." One day, he pulled her right arm behind her back and twisted. The next he aimed a punch at her shoulder. The family enforcer.

She hadn't seen her father in days. Fulvia began to write notes, slipping them under the door to his study or her parents' bedroom. *Let me go.* And *Call off the bully.* And *I can't live this life.* When Fulvia's and Papà's paths did

15   Alcamo/Edmonton
WINTER/SPRING 1974

When Fulvia was a child, *la conserva*, the tomato sauce for the household, was still made in the old way, once a year. Nonna was in charge, as she was of most of the farm rituals, not the pressing of the olives for oil or the crushing of grapes for wine, but of the meals for the farm workers, the preserving of apricot and quince jam, the pickling of hot peppers, making the sausages, curing the salami. Above all, she supervised the marathon that produced the sauce. Crates and crates of ripe oval tomatoes were sorted, rinsed, and chopped, and simmered for hours in old iron pots, like witches' cauldrons, hung over wood fires. To avoid the August heat, the long reduction of the tomatoes into sauce took place at night, and the darkness of the field beside the house would be streaked and spotted by the flickering orange light of the scattered fires. The women drank wine, gossiped, and joked. Often their words, accompanied by certain gestures, had a double meaning that little Fulvia could not follow. "Never you mind," Mamma said when Fulvia asked for an explanation. Sometimes Nonna recited one of the old tales she usually shared only with Fulvia: stories of curses and enchantments, empty stomachs and misery, mountains made of pastry, and rooms of solid gold. Stories that always taught the need for caution, courage, and cunning.

Would Nonna, the embodiment of the old ways in the family, have been upset to know that she had facilitated Fulvia's escape? Perhaps. Probably. Yet she stipulated in her will that Fulvia should receive more than the token amount she left the other grandchildren, Davide and Antonio's boys, *perche è femmina*, because she was female. Twenty million lire and not from Arcuri sources: Nonna's dowry passed down for Fulvia's dowry. Meanwhile, Nonna's youngest sister had flown in from Canada for the funeral, and Zia Dolores herself suggested that it might do Fulvia good to visit her in the new world. "She's skin and bones," the aunt said. "And she'd still be with family."

In the five years since Dolores's last visit, her nephew Don Fulvio had become more powerful and his home more opulent: gold faucets, Persian carpets, and eighteenth-century antiques. Useful to have such a man grateful and in your debt. "Let me help," she said.

Though Fulvia's parents found Zia Dolores vulgar and pushy, Fulvia had worn them down. They agreed to let her visit Canada, ostensibly to work on her English.

Fulvia landed in Edmonton in late January, and that first

month she was disoriented and disheartened. Where was she? On the far side of the moon? At least that far. She bought a down parka and big boots, and she might as well have been clad in a space suit. The winter gear stiffened her movements. It insulated and isolated her from the elements, the wind. She saw no earth, no green, no colours but grey, black, and white, white, white. The only sounds were mechanical, the only smell that of exhaust. To her surprise, she missed her parents, the friends she hadn't seen in months, the spacious house and the lush, fecund land.

She missed her old bedroom, her cage and refuge. Her new space felt cramped and dark in comparison. The hours of daylight were too brief, plus she was stuck below ground: a basement suite, her great-aunt called it. A cave, maybe a tunnel. She hated the knobbly mauve bedspread, the bulky furniture with ineffective knobs and glued-on swirls, and the pink bathroom with a floral shower curtain. She took down the ugly pictures—the Sicilian peasant with a cart, the little girl and her dog, both with exaggerated, sad eyes, and the Christ holding His burning heart in His extended hand—and stacked them in a corner. She didn't intend to stay long in this stale-smelling place with her aunt and bachelor cousin, who thought they could monitor and control her.

"You're a spoiled brat," said Zia Dolores.

"Snobby, stuck up," said her cousin Joe.

"You don't fool me with your prissy ways," Dolores told her, grabbing Fulvia by the arm. "You threw your honour away on the first boy that crossed your path." Dolores's breath stank of garlic and fatty meat. "Now you want to live alone, so you can have as many men as you want. Spread your legs wide and invite them in."

Fulvia jerked her arm away, suppressing the urge to elbow the woman in the belly. "I'm beginning a new life."

Sink or swim. Zia Dolores screamed and threw plates at Fulvia. She threatened to lock Fulvia in, to ship her back, to go to the government and have her visa revoked.

Fulvia countered with her own threats. She would phone the police and tell them she was being held hostage. After all, her aunt had no legal hold over her. She would tell them her aunt physically abused her. She would tell them she was brought in to be a slave, not a student. Dolores had no *piccotti* to follow Fulvia or keep her locked in. "You have no power over me," Fulvia said.

Zia Dolores grew tired of "setting Fulvia right."

"I'm not staying here," Fulvia repeated day after day. "I'll run away to Calgary, Vancouver, somewhere you'll never find me."

Dolores and Joe were already fed up with Fulvia and her ways. They must have been relieved to work out a deal. Zia Dolores would drop in on Fulvia not less than twice a month. Fulvia would come for dinner on alternate weeks and report honestly on the details of her life. She would respectfully listen and even take direction from her aunt and cousin.

Forget that, she thought. I can pretend, she thought.

Sink or swim. Cruise on the wind or plummet to earth. Fulvia's will had lifted her up and out of Sicily. Escaping this basement was a paltry matter.

On her own, she obtained an extension on her visa. When she was supposed to be at English class, she searched for a job, any job. I work hard, she said, and after three days she was hired to waitress in a downtown coffee shop. She did work hard, before and after English and art, she worked until her feet and arms and back ached. I can support myself, she told herself with wonder, even without Nonna's money. She found an apartment on the fifteenth floor of a newly finished high-rise. The search, like the one for a job, was easy and clean. She used the classified ads, the telephone, and buses. She needed no special connections, and she didn't pay a bribe.

The day she moved into the apartment, not the day she landed in Edmonton, was the first day of her life in Canada.

Fulvia was the first to live in these rooms. The walls were unblemished white, the sinks shiny, the carpet almost untrodden. The smells testified to the newness: paint, freshly sawn lumber, plastic, glue. The place was small and bare, the kitchen a galley. Each time she neatly placed a package or can in a previously empty cupboard or a carton or milk or some plastic-bagged carrots inside the refrigerator, she felt pleased, in control. Even the vegetables were clean here, as if they were grown in air rather than earth. Fulvia cooked casually, in one pot, or one pan. No fuss. No fires, cauldrons, hens, sheep, or pigs. The result was blander, easier to swallow, more innocent in its anonymity than the meals at Bagna Serena.

The sitting room contained a beanbag chair, an orange crate, a pile of books, and three large, bright pillows. One wall was a floor-to-ceiling window, and even standing in the kitchen, she could see the curving, treed river valley and the line of high rises on the opposite bank. Everything seemed untouched by anything but light. A wonderful, slanted light.

Alex should be here with her. In this light and space.

The first couple of months in the apartment, each time Fulvia unlocked her narrow metal mailbox in the lobby, she hoped, fantasized Alex had breached the parental iron curtain, through effort and imagination, and found her. That he had written a letter to explain why he didn't stand up to his family, why he didn't fight for her. Impossible, of course. She decided to reach out to him. It would help her calm down, get over him, if she understood what had happened, where he was. Easy to get the central number of the hospital in Siena where the psychiatrist brother worked. Why hadn't she thought of this earlier? She used an international operator, person to person, and gave a false name.

Giancarlo Zacco was silent for a good thirty seconds after she asked about Alex. "He's in India," Giancarlo said. There was an echo, so each word repeated. India.

She insisted he take her address and phone number. "Everything's all right now." Her voice bounced back at her, pathetic. "Tell Alex I got away."

Now she expected a call or a letter. Neither came. Still, as gentle green months of summer passed, her spirit was buoyed by the sense she was evolving into a new self. She had shed the past, shed the family, like a snake wiggling out of its old skin. She applied to the faculty of fine arts at the university. She bought a new set of clothes, jeans and casual shirts, so she would fit in with other twenty-year-olds. And though she found the jeans stiff and constricting and the colours of the tops brash or muddy, she put away the tailor-made suits and hand-sewn silk blouses, the gossamer-light dresses, and cashmere sweaters she had brought from Sicily.

She had begun to make friends. Frannie, who also waitressed at the café, invited her to join a group going to the bar. "Which bar?" Fulvia asked.

Frannie laughed. The bar was an abstraction. "We might hit several. We'll teach you to bend an elbow."

"Bend an elbow?" Like so many other idiomatic phrases, this one was not taught in the English class at the *liceo*.

"You'll learn to relax, take it easy. Have a few laughs."

Like the jeans and the plaid shirts, relaxation was alien to Fulvia. But she was determined to change. Once a week, she went out with Frannie and her friends to a disco club or a tavern, and she did laugh and chat and dance. She could imagine her parents' horror if they saw her in any one of these places, particularly the beer parlours: enormous, shabby rooms with rows of small round tables topped with terrycloth and glasses of beer, twenty at a time. She soon tired of the seedy atmosphere and the too-frequent drunkenness. She'd never seen anyone drunk in Alcamo. Fulvia herself was intoxicated by the freedom from rules and reprimands. She could go wherever she wanted.

She bought a radio, a television, and then a stereo. Another friend from art class had introduced her to Canadian songwriters: Ian & Sylvia, Gordon Lightfoot, Joni Mitchell, Neil Young, and Leonard Cohen. The music brought her the rhythms of her new home, the dreams, the disappointments, and the melancholy of the land.

Frannie, who had been baptized Francesca, persuaded Fulvia to accompany her to a university Italian club meeting, promising films and house parties. At the first meeting, Ralph, the president of the club, asked, "Aren't you *Signora* Grignoli's niece?"

"Not her niece. We are only distantly related," Fulvia said, making it so.

Her parents expected her to return. They believed this sojourn would help her get over Alex. They also believed trying to support herself in a place with no help from family would wear her down, even defeat her. They did not understand everything was different here because of the distance between here and there, because of the gap in time, which was more than one of eight hours, of the earth rotating on its axis. Hundreds of years lie between Alcamo, *Il Mezzogiorno*—midday, as the south is called— and Edmonton, true north, where the moment is clearly morning.

Fulvia explained all this in a letter addressed to Alex but in care of his brother. Here the sun was never harsh and direct; the houses, trees, and even the rocks had long shadows, but her name was clear-edged without shadow.

Arcuri identified her as a foreigner but nothing more. And she was herself and nothing more.

She stood alone on the small balcony. Ahead, above, around was the endless delight of the sky, so close she felt as if she could touch it, so far that she was overwhelmed by the size, the spread, the urge to see beyond the blue. Her spirit was caught by the wind. She flew, swooped, soared. No limits beyond those of possibility.

III
Water

It takes faith to plant an olive tree.

—Sicilian proverb

I wept and mourned when I discovered myself
in this unfamiliar land.

—Empedocles

16   Edmonton
MAY 1989

When John Buonaiuto left the police station, he was convinced that visiting his soon-to-be ex-wife to gather some background information on Fulvia Mazzolin was a smart idea. Janet knew everyone in the fashion business in Edmonton; she'd have a fix on Mrs. Mazzolin, her reputation, as well as any current gossip or innuendos. But once at West Edmonton Mall, he began to question himself. Was this meeting just an excuse to see Janet? A way of testing himself? To measure how much pain she still provoked? And how much he could stoically withstand?

The giant mall put him in a bad mood. Walking through the noise, the lights, the crowds, John was reminded of the crime that went on in front of and behind the false fronts: the bribery and corruption that had built this disproportionate place. John saw the runaway youths, the shoplifters, and the gangs. He saw the ghosts, the Vietnamese kid cut up outside that nightclub, the tourists tossed from the roller coaster, the sweet child lured away from the food court to be raped and slaughtered. "Does anyone actually shop in that hellhole?" he'd once asked Janet, trying to convince her that West Ed was the wrong location for her second shop. She hadn't bothered to answer, which was typical; instead of responding, she'd become inert, unmoving. She was a stone, and he ended up with a boulder in his stomach.

Janet's store, Threads, was thronged with young women, clucking over nightgowns, holding up corsets, or wrapping themselves in boas. Janet stood by a cash register, conspicuous in vibrant red and yellow, a big-shouldered jacket, egg-sized earrings, ankle socks, and sparkly high heels.

"Trying out the elf costumes?" John said.

She blinked and then smiled. "You've made detective, and you're still in a uniform." She gave his khakis and polo shirt a disdainful look. "Boring."

"I'm not working undercover."

"I can't interest you in an aquamarine T-shirt? Give you a discount."

"As I said, I don't need to look like an idiot."

Janet laughed. "You sure this is a police matter?"

At the coffee spot, she said: "You drink espresso now?"

"I'm a new man."

"So what do you want to know, new man?"

"I'm gathering background information on Fulvia Mazzolin."

"The owner of Persephone in LeMarchand Mansion?

Wow, I wouldn't have pegged her as being an object of police interest."

"Have you heard any gossip about her? Or her husband, Sam Mazzolin?"

"Oh, I never met him. Unless— Wait. I did see him at the launch of her new store. Short, dark, and handsome. An eye for the ladies."

"Stared down your dress?"

"You would have been with me and met him yourself except, as usual, you were on duty that night."

"And her?"

"Standoffish. She's got a terrific eye. I'll say that for her. Taste and talent. We worked together on a number of shows years ago when I was with Holts, and she was sales manager at Moda."

"You don't like her?"

"I don't think she likes me. A question of different styles. Back then, she made it clear that she thought her style was better than mine."

John restrained himself from delivering an easy zinger. "But no question of anything shady? Illegal?"

"Like what? Fake designer bags? Not Miss Fulvia."

"Drugs? Like that exercise gear store that sold cocaine out of the backroom."

"Typical of you to think I'd know."

"You don't?"

Janet shot him a look. "There used to be a few rumours about Moda when Sandra Rossi owned it. Jokes about dustings of white powder. But about six months after Fulvia took over, she changed everything, the name, the place, the type of fashion. People predicted she'd soon go broke."

"Because she stopped the coke?"

"Because she features avant-garde designers. Too fashion-forward for Edmonton. Anyway, the scuttlebutt was wrong. Persephone may not be making money hand over fist, but it's doing okay. Five years now. So someone must buy the stuff."

"Edmonton women don't go for avant-garde?"

"Not at those prices. Ladies here like the Escada look, bright colours and gold trim. Fulvia's merchandise is subtle, unusual. Last year, she started her own line. Recently picked up by an exclusive store in Vancouver. The woman has talent. The clothes are elegant, lots of draping, sort of ancient Greek in chiffon or cashmere.

"Not your kind of stuff." John closed his notebook.

Janet smiled her thousand-watt smile. "I don't know. They suit my secret self. I might surprise everyone."

Persephone's sun-filled backroom was startlingly bare: white walls and beams, one corner mirror, a black metal table, and two metal runners of hanging clothes so light and spare they seemed to float in the air. John flipped over a price tag and did a double take.

"Can I help you?" He'd stopped in for a quick impression, but the salesgirl's skceptical look pushed him into identifying himself. "You'll want to talk to Mrs. Belmondo," she said and led him to a side workroom and the store seamstress.

John placed Mrs. Belmondo in her late fifties, crow's feet and a slackening jaw line, but a pleasant face, thick hair, and light-grey eyes. She had a straightforward, earnest manner and a subtle but definite accent. "Such terrible news. Sam was one of our boys, as I called them. He lived with us when he first came to Canada. We took in boarders when our children were small and I was stuck at home. That way I could contribute, too, and we had company. But they were all gone when Sam arrived. We welcomed him because Sam's father was a friend of my father-in-law."

She and John were sitting on folding chairs, almost next to each other, in front of a long high table with a pile of fabric bolts at one end. "He wasn't married then?" John said. "No, no. This was about seventeen years ago. But still a different time from when we came in the fifties. He was another generation, one that had more back there and expected more here."

"More financially?" John was taking notes.

"He may have dreamed he would make a fortune. But I meant opportunities. Sam had a diploma as a *geometra*, an architectural draftsman. He'd been told by the embassy staff that Canada needed skilled and educated workers. But when he got here, none of his credentials counted. He had to take hard jobs, hard on his back and his pride. We got tired of his complaining. Patience, my husband would tell him. But Sam never had much of that."

"He met his wife after a year?"

She'd turned away from John and was staring at a silvery grey fabric. "A bit longer. He was starting to find himself. Had a job with a tiling company. He'd been seeing lots of women. Said they were introducing him to Canada. But once he met Fulvia, that was it. We warned him. He was still young. He had no savings." She stretched out her right hand and began to run two fingers back and forth on a corner of the material.

"You didn't approve of Mrs. Mazzolin?"

"We didn't know her. Now she's my friend, and I respect her. She's a good woman. But then she was just a young girl in the community, a girl who came to Canada alone, and we didn't know why. And probably we had foolish ideas, prejudices, about Sicilians. One of the proverbs of our region says *wives and cows should be from your hometown*."

"I've heard that one."

"It's about customs and attitudes. Besides her Aunt Dolores and her cousin Joe, the Grignoli, had a bad reputation. So we wondered. Not that she saw them much."

"They were separated at the time of his death. Maybe you were right in the first place."

Mrs. Belmondo shifted her head, so she was facing John full-on again. "I blame him for that. He became obsessed with the idea of moving back to Italy. It had always been our plan too. And once we had our nest egg, we sold our house and everything. We returned home, but it didn't work. Home was no longer home. It had changed, and so had we. And the children were miserable. We told him: it happened to so many of us, but Samuele never listened to anyone, not even his wife. *Testa dura*. They tried for a few months some years ago. It didn't go well. When they came back, she bought Moda, and a year or so later, he started Goodfellas Construction.

"He called his company Goodfellas?"

"Sam's sense of humour. Fulvia hated the name." Had the man been tone deaf? Or was he trying to provoke?

"You say she stayed away from the great-aunt?"

"Fulvia didn't respect her. They weren't close."

"I'm asking because when we went to speak to her yesterday, Mrs. Grignoli arrived, and she seemed at home."

Mrs. Belmondo shook her head. "Not so strange. Fulvia is ill and has lost her husband. Who else does she have here? For family? I always suspected that *la Grignoli* kept an eye on Fulvia for the family in Sicily. Now they must be extra worried. Need extra reassurance."

"Were you working at Moda when Mrs. Mazzolin took charge?"

"I began then. She knew I'd trained as a dressmaker before I was married. I need your help, she said. She was so excited."

"Do you know why she bought the store and then after a few months changed the name and location? Seems like a waste."

Mrs. Belmondo looked embarrassed. "You must ask her that."

"I intend to. You didn't notice anything? You didn't speculate?"

The woman's very pale skin flushed pink. For a long moment she said nothing. "Once, sometime before she closed that shop, I arrived at work to find chaos in the backroom. A new shipment was scattered all over, the clothes and shoes thrown about. And some of the boxes were hacked up. I asked Fulvia what had happened. She claimed the order got mixed up, and she lost her temper."

"She has a quick temper?"

"Just the opposite. Even when she has cause, she stays calm."

"So you didn't believe it was a question of some extra dresses?"

Mrs. Belmondo waited a few beats. She shook her head. "That day she fired the manager, the woman who'd taken Fulvia's job when she went off to Italy. Made her leave immediately. And after that, she started to talk about starting again with a clean slate."

"And how did you interpret that?"

"I didn't." Seconds passed. John let the silence build. Finally she said: "It wasn't the best decision business-wise. She had to sell everything off at bargain prices and break the lease. So there must have been something going on, some arrangement from before, with the previous owner, that Fulvia couldn't accept. "

"I'm doing some work for a chief of police in Sicily." John regretted his words as soon as he said them. He was having lunch downtown with Sophie, an old friend and a defence lawyer. He didn't want her to think that he was boasting. The case was simply on his mind.

He had spent the morning going over Mazzolin's financial records and his varied employment history. In his first year in Alberta, Mazzolin had worked laying subfloors, pouring basements, and fixing railroad tracks. In the next few years, the man had been a tiler, a framer, a painter, a surveyor, a draftsman, and a property assessor, until four years before, when he had started Goodfellas Construction.

"Wow," said Sophie. "And you such a newly hatched detective. What does it involve?"

"Murder, drugs."

"What kind of drugs? There isn't too much action between Italy and Western Canada. Most of it comes through the States."

"I know that." Good old Sophie and her lectures. "The drugs were being smuggled into Italy, not out of Italy. The *Commissario*, that's what she's called, contacted us because one of the two victims was from Edmonton."

"A female chief of police? In Sicily? Good for her."

"In Alcamo. I don't think it's a big place."

"But this could be a big case?"

John shrugged. "I haven't heard any good stories about the police over there. The RCMP sent them some super-useful info. They'd got it bugging one of the Montreal wise guys. Then no one looked at the transcript for ten years. Incompetence and arrogance."

"And there's none of that here?"

"We're all good guys."

Sophie let out a bark of a laugh. "And I'm helping all the bad ones?"

"You said it. And you were such a goody-goody in

high school."

John bit into his sandwich. Sophie leaned over the table and touched his arm. "You okay? You're not still brooding?"

He chewed and swallowed. "I'm great."

"You should get out more. I've heard about this new play at the Phoenix."

Janet had warned him about Sophie. "She's crazy about you, and you lead her on." Of course, he denied it, and Janet looked superior in that maddening way of hers, accusing him of being dishonest, even with himself. He said the pot was calling the kettle black, and she was a big flirt and worse. And they didn't speak to each other for two whole days. Now he couldn't avoid seeing the hope in Sophie's face, but it left him uncomfortable, not smug.

"I can get the tickets. Does Friday work for you?"

"I'm on duty," he lied.

Sophie's face froze. "Don't turn around," she whispered. "Oh, dear."

He didn't have to. Janet walked right by the table, her head up, not a glance in his direction. With her bright hair and shiny dress, she was a shaft of light bisecting the dim room. Bathed in her glow, a man followed, tall and tanned with blond streaks in his hair.

"I didn't think we'd run into Janet here," Sophie said. "Not trendy enough,"

"She's always liked variety." John put down his sandwich. He'd been ambushed by the memory of Janet on their wedding day: picture perfect, a golden river of hair, luminous skin, and eyes full of light as she recited her vows. *Forsaking all others*. What a joke. She had cheated a mere two months after the ceremony. And continued to cheat for the next three years of their marriage. She'd told him so when she asked for a divorce. "It's not fair to you," she said, after sandbagging him with the details.

"It's not a proper wedding," his mother had complained at the time, a Justice of the Peace at a country club instead of a church, and hors d'oeuvres and champagne instead of a full dinner and dance. "Cheap and boring," his mother had said then. "Doomed," she said now.

John couldn't stop himself from glancing over at the booth where Janet and friend were sitting. She wasn't batting her eyes at the guy but looking in John's direction. She waved and made a slight gesture with her head. Meet me at the bar.

"It still hurts, doesn't it?" Sophie was leaning over the table. She was about to grab his hand.

"Excuse me a minute." John stood and self-consciously squared his shoulders.

Janet was already perched on a stool. "Fancy meeting you here." Her smile was uncertain.

John mumbled a hello.

"Still having lunch with your chubby friend, I see."

"What's up?"

"I asked around. You know, I think I have a talent for detective work."

"Janet, cut to the chase."

"It's about Fulvia Mazzolin. Well, about that shop she

bought, Moda." Janet leaned over, lowering her voice to a whisper. "Cocaine was one of the available accessories." Her mouth was close to his ear, her lemony sweet scent fogging his brain. "If you were on the right list. This was just for a short time. Not long after Fulvia took over, she put a stop to it. And she made those changes, name, place etc."

"I figured."

"You knew this already?" Janet was disappointed.

"You have been helpful."

"Anytime. It's good that we can still talk like civilized people."

"Thank you."

"Take care." She spoke over her shoulder on her way back to her friend.

"Mrs. Mazzolin is clean," John told *Commissario* De Luca five minutes into an extended international phone call. "Self-righteously so."

"Well, I never suspected her, despite his mother's claims." De Luca's accented English was formal, her voice low and melodious. "Did you?"

"At first, I found it odd she didn't declare him missing, but once I figured out they were estranged—"

"Were you able to obtain a copy of her recent phone bills?"

"I was. Two calls to Alcamo in March, one on the 19th and one on the 28th." John read the two numbers out slowly, so she could write them down. "The first was 42 minutes long, the second 38."

"Bravo. It would have taken maybe a year to get the equivalent here."

John summarized Sam's restless work history. "I know the type," Marisa said.

He went on to the Mazzolins' financial situation. Sam's company had gone bankrupt; Fulvia's was flourishing, but she was carrying a large line of credit. Marisa told him about her discovery of the blocks of weed and hash. John was impressed.

"He made all these promises in Venice, a yacht, apartments. Importing from Tunisia must have been his money-making scheme."

"Wouldn't bringing drugs into Sicily be like bringing coal to Newcastle?"

"Pardon?"

"Doesn't the Mafia have it covered?"

"Only the hard stuff. They discourage the softer drugs."

"So the two men would be challenging the control of the local mob. No wonder they were killed," John said.

De Luca sighed. "I won't be able to prove it. It's often like this, not much evidence. Unless someone on the inside confesses, and you can imagine how often that happens. Besides, some things don't fit. If it were simply a case of these men encroaching on established territory, why try to disguise the murders as an accident? Killings are used as examples. This is what happens if you try to muscle in. And the arson? For a while, it hid their identities. Maybe the Arcuri did agree to the smuggling, branching out into new endeavours, but another *cosca* was against it."

John had the sense De Luca would talk for another hour if he let her. "It must be late over there." Then he said, "We'll be in touch."

But she was not finished. "Wait, Buonaiuto, I wanted to tell you: a few days ago, my apartment was vandalized, and then this morning, my office. All the drawers in my desk were jumbled. In the cabinet, the files were mixed up."

"Anything missing?"

"Not as far as I can tell."

"Did you have some sort of classified or sensitive information?"

"Nothing out of the ordinary, notes and a few personal things. At my home too. I think both searches were symbolic. There was a drawing too—of me—an obscene one."

"Do you suspect anyone?"

"A few of my colleagues. At least for the mess in the office."

John was shocked by her disloyalty. He would never air doubts about his fellow officers to an outsider. "You should find out."

"How do I do this?" Her question did not sound rhetorical. "I'm new to Alcamo."

"There must be someone who can help you. Are you telling me all this because you think it has something to do with this case?"

For a few seconds De Luca was silent. The static on the line emphasized the distance between them. "I am uncertain, surrounded by fog."

17 Alcamo/Edmonton
MAY 1989

The riffling of Marisa's office came two days after the break-in at her apartment. The words *porca troia* were still flashing hot and red on her inner screen. And now, in her inbox, a crude drawing: a woman on her hands and knees, or rather an amalgam of cunt, tits, and mouth before a bodiless phallus, and "I need to suck cock" printed in box letters over what passed for the head. Marisa was under attack, but she was careful to act unfazed, unthreatened. She gave a short, firm lecture to the men on duty. "No more impudent jokes, no more disrespect. You will be sorry."

She did not mention the drawing; she didn't want to acknowledge its existence. But she suppressed her impulse to burn it. She dated it and placed it in a folder she labelled "future ammunition."

Who was responsible? Brusca, for sure. He'd been on duty that evening. One or two of his usual sidekicks? Arcangelo? Surely not the mournful-eyed Lo Verde. Unless those who cooperated with her, like Roselli, were actually plotting against her.

Stop it, she told herself. Paranoia won't help. An hour of yoga, a long hot bath, and a glass of wine might. She could announce an outside appointment and leave early without looking like she was fleeing the scene. A sudden explosion of laughter catapulted Marisa out of her chair. "What's so funny, boys?"

"It's me, Chief," Arcangelo said. "You remember Dalia Rimi? Last week, that poor girl nearly beaten to death?"

Marisa could see Dalia in the hospital bed, arms in plaster, head bandaged and swollen. "Thirteen years old. And if that doctor hadn't called to alert us we'd never have known. Hardly a source of mirth."

"Not at all. The mother wouldn't talk, the girl couldn't. You sent us to harass the father."

"From the outside, his house looks small, rundown," said Brusca, who was perched on Arcangelo's desk. "But when we get in, the floors are made of mother-of-pearl."

"For real?" Marisa said. "Classic."

"Welcome to Sicily," said Brusca.

"So we can presume this Rimi is involved in something illegal. Besides assaulting a child."

"Bet he's a *picciotto* in the Arcuri gang," Brusca said.

Inspired by her general state of anger, Marisa ordered Rimi followed. She then called Patrizia Tuzzo, an *assistente sociale* in Partinico, and asked her to visit Dalia while she was still in the hospital. "The little girl needs help."

At the Edmonton police headquarters, Fulvia Mazzolin sat in a chair John had drawn up next to his desk. She was dressed completely in black. Even her face was without light.

"Thank you for coming in," John said.

A ghost of a smile. "I didn't want you in my house again."

"You sure you won't have some coffee?"

Mrs. Mazzolin answered with a short, impatient shake of the head.

She had arrived only a few minutes before, but John had been at his desk all morning. He stood and unobtrusively stretched his legs. "Lloyd?" he asked.

"Sure. Fill 'er up." His partner handed over his mug, which had *I like it wet and warm* printed on the outside. He also gave him a look, a how-about-this-broad look. When John returned, two hot cups in hand, Lloyd was staring at Mrs. Mazzolin. She was looking off into space, a dark statue under the fluorescent lights.

"What can you tell us about the drug deal your husband was involved in?"

"Pardon?"

"Come on. Hashish was found in the wreck of the car."

"That doesn't prove it was his."

"We have other evidence."

"Then you know more than I do," she said.

"He never mentioned a plan to make some quick money?" John said.

"Sam always had plans. Before he left, he said he had a way to solve everything. That's all."

John wasn't going to give in. "You didn't question him?"

She shrugged *no*, paused. "He'd suffered some financial setbacks lately."

"He, not we? Are you legally separated?"

"Our finances are independent, because of our respective businesses. He had a stake in my shop, but he wouldn't have been able to sell it without my permission."

"It must have been tough, your husband not confiding in you." Lloyd was trying sympathy.

"Usually he confided too much."

"I would have been furious if my wife took off for another continent just when I needed her," Lloyd said.

She shot him a go-fuck-yourself look.

"Did your family in Sicily invite him to visit?" John said.

"I don't know. I doubt it."

"We know you've been in contact. You phoned Alcamo twice in March."

"I've been ill. It's natural."

"He was in your family's territory when he was murdered."

"I don't believe that. There's another explanation. The roads are treacherous. Sam could be careless. He had a bad accident a few years ago on Groat Road. Got a concussion, spent a few days in the hospital. You can check." Her tone remained neutral, her large eyes clouded.

"Your uncle, Antonio Arcuri, is a boss of bosses, as your father was before him."

"What the hell do you know?" She sounded more tired than angry. "So my family has a reputation. That doesn't mean they had anything to do with Sam's death. Or that I did." She paused, closing her eyes for five, ten seconds. "I keep my hands clean. I always have. That's why Sam would never confide in me about an illegal scheme. He knew how I'd react."

"We're not accusing you of anything," John began. But Fulvia Mazzolin had gotten up and was walking out, his words rolling off her sallow skin, her black robes, like rain on a slicker.

John Buonaiuto was standing with his brother Mike at the Italian Cultural Centre, worrying about the speech he was about to deliver, when Mrs. Grignoli, in shiny purple, appeared at his elbow and muttered, "Filthy, rotten pig."

He looked down at her amazed. "Pardon?" But she was already off, waddling through the crowd gathered to honour the departing Italian vice-consul. John usually avoided such ethnic occasions: he was a resolutely non-hyphenated Canadian, scornful of a heritage represented by, and reduced to, pasta or spicy sausage, to children dancing the steps of folk dances that had no connection either to their own lives or those of any child in Italy. But today he was stuck representing his soccer team, the Ital-Canadians, which he had joined because they were the best team in town. The ethnic bit was beside the point.

"Everyone else bailed out on me," he explained to his brother. "I had to come."

"As if you had anything else to do," said Mike, who was attending for the Italian-Canadian Businessmen's Association. A waiter handed them each a glass of red wine. They edged toward the long buffet table.

"I could have been working out. This is disrupting my routine." As John picked a plate off the pile, he saw Mrs. Grignoli staring balefully at him from the other side of the table. He chose some slices of pear wrapped in prosciutto, a couple of cheese cubes, and a miniature pizza. He was feeling the old hunger for a cigarette. He needed something in his mouth, quick.

Mrs. Grignoli was still giving him the evil eye. *Cazzone*, she hissed as he bit into the pizza. "Bothering a sick woman."

Mike leaned over and asked in a low voice, "What's going on?"

The speeches were starting. The Italian ambassador, in an upper-class British accent and in an attempt at humour, compared Consul Tintoretto first to a snake in the grass and then to other, as he put it, zoological phenomena. None of the audience laughed.

"She claims I'm harassing her niece," John whispered. "Which I'm not."

The ambassador thanked Tintoretto, faithful as the family dog, solid as a gorilla, for his service to Italy and to the Italians of Alberta.

"She's tough, that one," Mike said.

"I didn't expect someone like her to be invited. You know her?" John said.

"I know of her. And you must know her newspaper, *The Italo-Albertan*? It carries your team's game schedule. It's a bit of a mess: mostly stories from press agencies, but oddly cut up and laid out, and the occasional editorial praising Italian industriousness in Canada. Lately, she has been featuring immigrant success stories: the entrepreneur and his millions. She has piles of ads; shit, I've taken a few out myself for the salon."

John was not listening to the provincial Minister of Finance on the podium. He had seen him so often on the TV news that the sight of his face conjured the words *necessary cutbacks*.

"*Cornuto!*" John nearly dropped his dish. The old woman had somehow got behind him without his noticing. "Cuckold!" she said louder in case he or someone around hadn't got it. "Cuckold!" John glanced at Mike.

"Arrest her," Mike said with a relaxed smile.

"Shush, we're trying to listen here," a young woman in a tight black dress said to Mrs. Grignoli. The leader of the provincial Liberal Party had taken the podium. He was testifying to his personal love of Pavarotti and pizza. The audience did not seem as overwhelmed with gratitude as he expected them to be; they clapped politely. Italy was great; Canada was great. Hooray for diversity and tolerance, triple hooray for multiculturalism, bring on the pasta. And the votes.

Mrs. Grignoli was poking John, pushing her heavily laden dish into his right kidney. He took a step forward. She followed. "*Cornuto!*" John could feel everyone around him turning, watching. The witch couldn't know about Janet; she was improvising.

"Control yourself," he said quietly, trying not to show he was perturbed.

The speaker from the New Democratic Party was repeating a few of his predecessors' phrases about community and friendship. Italian immigrants had helped make Edmonton what it was today. "Brick by brick," Mike said.

John moved to the front. It was his turn. The woman's voice followed him, a loud whisper. "Dirty pig, bothering innocent people." He took a deep breath and rattled off his lines, mostly in English but with a few appropriate Italian phrases. As he shook Tintoretto's hand, after having presented him with the rather ugly bronze statue the club president had chosen, three flashbulbs went off. Partly blinded, John stumbled a bit on his way off the platform.

A day and a half after Marisa had ordered surveillance on the child-beating Rimi, the man was judged and sentenced, though not by the servants of the law. Working as a tag team with two cars, Arcangelo and Mancuso had tailed Rimi through the streets of Alcamo, along the state highway and into the small seaside village of Balestrate, where the man met with a known soldier in the Arcuri family. Rimi and the enforcer, Bibi Valle, had talked for maybe five minutes, each knocking back a double shot of Scotch whisky. After that, on his way back to town, Rimi must have been aware he was being followed. "He evaded us," said Arcangelo.

Late that night, Rimi was dumped, covered in blood and unconscious, in front of the main entrance of the Alcamo hospital. Arcangelo interpreted the beating as just punishment. "And we didn't have to twist ourselves into a knot convicting him."

"But we don't know if Rimi was punished for beating his daughter or for making himself conspicuous to us," Marisa said. "We are not going to ease up. Let's find out what's paying for the mother-of-pearl floors." She assigned three separate teams to Bibi Valle, the man who had met with Rimi in Balestrate. "Who is meeting with whom? What are the Arcuri up to? As before, no police cars and no uniforms." It felt good, formulating a plan, giving orders. "If we get nothing, we throw up a roadblock, brandish the machine guns."

A few minutes later, Brusca appeared at her office door. "*Commissaria*, feeling unwell today?"

"You're a slow learner, Brusca. Address me as *Commissario*. Please."

"The disruption in your office upset you?"

"It takes more than that. Are you a little off today?"

"What? No. My liver has been acting up, but that is a long-term irritation. No, this idea of a roadblock, most unusual. And it ties up manpower."

"The men are often idle. Actually, *Capitano*, it's you who inspired me. Sometimes we need to flex our muscles."

Valle spent the next two days in his narrow three-storey house on the Balestrate seafront or in the bar two streets down, watching soccer games, exchanging the usual loud commentary, and knocking back shots of whisky. On Thursday, before dawn, he managed to slip away. He turned up three hours later, strolling around the walls of the castle in Alcamo, chatting with a town councillor.

Marisa ordered Roselli and Mancuso to mount the roadblock on the narrow side road between Alcamo and Balestrate. They waved cars through until Valle drove up in an Alfa. "He was all relaxed and confident when I told him to get out of the car," Roselli said. "But his eyes changed when we told him to open the trunk." They found a plastic-wrapped white brick at the bottom of a crate of oranges. Heroin, barely hidden.

This time *Questore* Lanza phoned Marisa. His congratulations sounded genuine. Still, Marisa felt compelled to half-apologize. "I didn't expect to find anything. I wanted to make the *picciotto* nervous."

"Never underestimate, *Dottoressa* De Luca, *vero*?"

"Be good to know where he got it."

"I myself had some success last week when my squad discovered a heroin refinery in the backroom of a tailor shop."

"Admirable, sir. I did call to congratulate you, but you weren't in, and you didn't return my call."

"The best tailor in Palermo, unfortunately. The sleeves on his suits were exquisite, hand-sewn to fit perfectly."

"A major bust. Significant."

"The pipeline goes from Turkey to Sicily to America, with the base refined here on the north coast. It's worth a careful survey."

"You're finally giving me the go-ahead to investigate?"

"Only subordinate to our larger offensive."

Valle would admit nothing. "I picked up the oranges for my wife. Nothing like the tarocco. Don't you agree, *Signora Commissaria*? Sweet and red. A couple of squeezes in the morning, and everything's good." Valle had small, dull eyes and a hulking presence.

"Half a kilo of heroin," she said. "You won't wiggle out of this one."

"Someone is setting me up," Valle said in Sicilian.

"Tell me who. You deliver, and something could be worked out."

The man used a handkerchief to wipe the sweat from his neck. "Dream on."

After a morning of trying and failing to extract any information, Marisa followed Lanza's orders and sent Valle, under heavy guard, to police headquarters in Palermo.

The farmhouse where Valle claimed to have picked up the oranges turned out to be deserted. After checking a map, noting where Valle had disappeared and where he had reappeared, and taking into account a week-old report of unusual traffic on a particular country lane in the area, Marisa pinpointed five separate farmhouses. "Use any excuse you can to get in the front door," she ordered Verdura and Arcangelo.

The third house they checked was also deserted, with boarded-up windows. The two junior officers jimmied the locks, forced the door, and stepped into what was obviously a recently abandoned heroin refinery.

Marisa drove out with Roselli to investigate, to view what had been left behind: broken glass, dirty coffee cups, a moka coffee maker, two stained mattresses, a Milan newspaper from the week before, a gleaming new electronic pressure pump and, stuffed into a wooden crate, eighteen empty jute bags, each labelled with Cyrillic letters. The entire house stank: a curdled, burnt, acidic smell that coated her tongue and pushed up her nose. The gang must have cleared out Monday, as soon as they heard Valle had been caught.

"Slippery turds," Roselli said, giving voice to Marisa's frustration.

Marisa was sorry they hadn't caught the gang in action, but she was exhilarated by the size of the discovery. The pressure pump gave the refinery the capacity to produce eight kilos of pure heroin a week, four-and-a-half tons a year; this was according to the hard-drug expert Lanza had sent from the city. "Wow, major, colossal, terrific. They weren't up to speed yet. Thank God. This is our biggest breakthrough yet," the man said.

Lanza took the glory and the responsibility for her sake, or so he claimed. "I mean the *cosca* knows, and your superiors know. All in your records, a big plus. But if you choose the spotlight, you'll make yourself even more of a target."

Lanza announced the bust on television, praising his "exceptional team of dedicated men and women." He drove out from the city with his entourage and met with a covey of journalists at the farmhouse. He posed for the cameras at the front door and took the opportunity to lecture on the extent of the heroin addiction problem in Italy. "This is big business. Organized and ruthless, locally and internationally."

Unsung though she was, Marisa decided to dwell on the positive. Let the bad guys take note: she wasn't going to sit around and wait for them to fall into her hands like ripe figs from a tree. Don Antonio Arcuri, for example: she was going to pay him a get-acquainted visit, without telling Lanza or anyone at the station of her plan. "It's not done," they'd say, emphasizing her foolishness. But she could and would act. The drug lab was in Arcuri territory and Valle a known Arcuri soldier. Besides, she intended to question the Don about the murder of Inzerillo and Mazzolin.

Marisa couldn't worry about raising the Don's enmity. She had a duty to the two dead men. In particular, she felt as if Sam Mazzolin was a man she'd once known but forgotten. She owed him an acknowledgement, a reckoning.

18 Edmonton
SPRING/SUMMER 1975

Sam Mazzolin first seduced Fulvia with words, with stories of rebellion and bravado.

When they were introduced at an Italian club outing, Fulvia paid him no heed. Her heart was still wrapped up, tied up, given away. She resisted all the young men who showed interest. And there were a number; at twenty, Fulvia was disruptively beautiful. In her mind, she was meant to be without a mate or a family. For company, besides placid Frannie, feminist Mary, and Libero, a white fluffball of a cat, she had a surprising number of acquaintances, at least a few of whom might turn into friends. But no love, no protection: that was the price of her freedom.

At first she hoped she could pull Alex's heart back just by wishing it. Finally, ten months after she arrived in Canada, the number of times a day Alex's image floated through her brain began to diminish. And though her stomach still lurched at the sound of a Bob Dylan song or the scent of patchouli, hurt had morphed into anger. She got rid of the last of his tokens: cracking the George Harrison and Ravi Shankar albums, ripping up three scrawled notes. She took a ring box containing a wisp of his hair and a package of salt to a picnic in a park by the river. When her friends were distracted, munching on grilled hot dogs, Fulvia edged closer to the fire pit.

Every January, Nonna used to have a fire lit in one of the pits, not to cook a sauce but for one of her nameless rituals. *Throw the salt into the fire.* The fire would rear up, a green dragon, hissing and crackling, muffling Nonna's incantations. Fulvia strained to remember. She tossed the box with the hair into the flames. She poured the granules into her left hand. *It is not this salt I wish to burn.* She threw one handful, two. *But his heart.* The flames exploded— bright orange. She was improvising. *Let him burn for me.*

She should have used sea salt. Was it essential the light be green?

"What did you do?" A male voice in her right ear.

Fulvia stepped away. "Nothing." She registered that the bearded man was Sam Mazzolin.

"You are extraordinary."

"Stop it." She turned away.

The following week, Sam aroused her interest. The Italian club had convened at a pizza parlour to drink sour red wine and nibble on slices of rubbery pie. Someone brought up the movie *Billy Jack*; was it manipulative or inspiring? In the middle of the debate, Sam described the police rousting of the occupiers of the Institute of Architecture in Venice five years earlier. "Sometimes you have to throw rocks."

"I wish I'd been there." Fulvia recounted her running away at fourteen. "I almost made it to the battle of Valle Giulia in Rome."

"We wanted to overturn everything." Sam had opposed professors, administrators, the police, the politicians, and the capitalist bosses. He had been kicked out of university, beaten by a club-wielding policeman, arrested and blacklisted "I couldn't find any work, not as a draftsman." The worst of all were those he looked up to—the leaders of the movement in the Veneto. They decided one of the Marghera chemical factories should be torched, which led to the release of poisonous fumes.

"I read about that. The fumes spread through the area, and people got sick."

"Those guys didn't know what they were doing. Never imagined toxins could be released," Sam said. "They ended up harming workers and their families, the very people they were championing. Then, instead of reflecting and regrouping, they chose their next target, the manager of the Dow Chemical plant."

"Kneecapped?"

"Machine-gunned outside his front gate."

He had principles, Fulvia decided, integrity. He was brave and enterprising enough to leave the corruption of Italy behind. He hadn't let his mother or friends and their sticky sentimental appeals dissuade him.

Fulvia did not shape her account of her coming to Canada into a story. She said, "My parents are stuck in another century. I couldn't take the useless rules and re-strictions." Or "I came for the freedom and the opportunity." She didn't describe the castle-like Bagna Serena. She didn't allude to her father's power, to its depth and reach. Eventually, she told Sam she'd had a romance that finished badly. "His parents didn't approve of me and sent him away to Bologna."

"What's not to approve?"

"I wasn't good enough for their boy."

"Rich snobs?"

"Rich snobs."

"Fools."

Sam laid siege. He employed all the usual weapons: words and caresses, flowers and wine, fast drives, long walks, all fuelled by his coiled energy.

"You said you were finished with men," Frannie said to Fulvia as they jogged along a path in the river valley.

"I thought I was." The light was dappled green. "I don't know. I'm confused." They were both breathing hard.

Frannie stopped and bent to help catch her breath. "He's got you."

He had her. Sam unwrapped Fulvia's heart as smooth-ly, as unobtrusively as he peeled off her clothes. She was undone. He had skilled hands; he could reach up under a shirt and, with one economical movement, unhook her bra. He could slip a hand past a waistband and unfurl his fingers in a caress as light as a butterfly's wings.

"You've had a lot of practice at this," she said.

"What? I'm no Casanova." He smiled. "I did start young. Though my talent is inborn, of course." And honed, she later learned, on the bodies of young foreign tourists. "This is new to you," he said.

"I've had some experience." Fulvia was determined to go all the way. To be freed of what her mother called her precious possession. The first two times, she stopped Sam at the last minute. Then the difficulty that existed with Alex was gone. Her body opened to Sam, welcoming him with a sudden, sweet pleasure. This must be it, she thought. The real thing.

In the first months, Sam was wary of commitment. Still, even then, he recognized Fulvia was gold in a landscape of lead.

Sam had made a mistake coming to Canada. He expected opportunity and found none. The only jobs he was offered were menial. He quit the first, pick and shovelling for the railroad, because his back was breaking. He was fired from several subsequent jobs, all in construction, for incompetence. He lasted two months on an itinerant work gang, pouring concrete foundations for fourteen hours a day. "I'm not suited to this kind of employment," he had told the woman at the employment centre. "I have talents."

"Your diplomas and experience mean nothing here," the woman said. "You have to be re-educated and re-examined."

He could not go back to Venice defeated, a failure, a fool in the eyes of his family and his friends. He had to have something to show for his sojourn in this Wild West, not just money but accomplishment.

Sam rediscovered hope when he began working for a company run by an Italian architect. But Peruzzi preferred to hire Italians, because he got away with paying them below the going rate. And before the arrogant bastard allowed Sam to work as a draftsman, he had him toil for months cleaning up a building site and then assembling mobile homes.

This place where Sam had landed was a simulacrum, an image without substance; real life was somewhere else. This place was no place, at least for Sam. He clung to the one connection he did feel, his link to Fulvia. He showered her with extravagant declarations, such clichés, and meant them. Still Samuele was who he was, prey to flickers of resentment.

"We are special together," Fulvia said as they lay together.

"Not bad. You've still got a lot to learn. You haven't been taught. The woman isn't supposed to just lie there and take it."

Her satisfied glow vanished; her eyes filled with tears.

Years later, Sam would mock Fulvia, calling her a princess. Yet it was the way she radiated class that first drew him to her: the way she moved, dressed, and spoke. Her Italian was cultured, even overly correct, with no trace of a Sicilian accent. He fantasized a return to Venice with her on his arm; all the snobs who had humiliated him would be impressed. And she was an asset, he had to admit, even in Edmonton. She calmed him down when Peruzzi offended him, which the dickhead did regularly. Her advice was solid; her support never wavered. Where would he be if she left him? Things came so easily for her: jobs, friends, speaking good English. Of course, she had had private tutors for years. Of course. How could he stop her from turning away? Sam considered himself anti-marriage. He used to say a couple shouldn't need a piece of paper. Now he saw the advantage. "It would be cheaper to live together," he said as an opening salvo.

Fulvia wanted a lover, not a husband. She revelled in living alone, except for Libero, without rules or constraints. "*Che femmina*," what a woman, Sam said. And not ten minutes later: "You are an uptight bitch." He could lift her up, free her from self, then, with a word or two, plunge her back into the depths of separateness. The flashes of pain highlighted the intensity of the pleasure. Fulvia accepted Sam's power over her not as a warning, but as a sign he was the one for her.

19   Alcamo
JUNE 1989

Marisa sat in her car outside the eight-foot electric fence surrounding Don Antonio Arcuri's villa, her right leg quivering. She took two deep belly-expanding breaths. *Forza*. She had an appointment, but the guard would not let her in.

"Can't be," he snapped when she introduced herself and her purpose. He didn't use the two-way radio on his belt to check. He simply stepped back and began staring at her through the windshield, a leering, sneering stare.

Marisa stuck her head out the open window. "Enough. You let me in, or I'll come back with a police unit."

As she spoke, someone got in beside her: a man with a narrow, frowning face and large hands. He nodded to the guard. The tall metal gates swung open.

"Don Antonio is waiting for you," he said, as if she were the cause of the delay.

And he was, when Marisa finally reached him, after a

curving road, a winding path, and a pause at the front door, after corridor and room, room and corridor, after light to dark to dim. Don Antonio, her very own Minotaur, was lying in wait in a book-lined room behind a large, antique desk. Marisa had studied a number of surveillance photos, but they had been taken years before, and he had aged. The oversized head, pale features, and bulky shoulders were the same, but his hairline had retreated, and his dark moustache had grown into a white goatee. His cheekbones were knobs beneath the creased skin. And the photos hadn't shown his stoop or the force in his dark, shrewd eyes; they had given no hint of his carnal authority.

"*Brava*," Arcuri said. "You came alone." He motioned her to a carved wooden chair. "What can I offer you? A coffee? A glass of white wine? A *granita*? Such a hot day." Though it was almost chilly in his air-conditioned office.

Marisa gave in to the charade of hospitality. For a good five minutes, until the coffee arrived, Antonio Arcuri and Marisa De Luca chatted about the weather. She complained about the airlessness of her apartment and the inefficiency of her two small fans. He lamented that his vineyards were burning up in the heat wave, one literally so. A woman with bleached hair and a blunt peasant face brought in the coffee and water on a gilded tray. She sugared the espresso, two teaspoons for Marisa, and handed her the gold-trimmed demitasse and saucer. After placing a tall crystal glass on a coaster in front of Marisa, she repeated her actions on Arcuri's side of the desk.

Once the door was closed, Marisa emptied her cup in

two gulps. "I'm here to ask you some questions."

"If I can be of service."

"We have arrested an employee of yours, one Carlo Valle, for the possession of heroin with the purpose of trafficking."

"This Valle is not my employee."

"He admits he has worked for you."

"He did, past tense. As a field hand." Arcuri took a sip of water.

"Your lawyer, Barbaccia, is representing him."

"He asked for my help. And I helped. I'm made that way." Sip.

"He had picked up the drug at a refinery just outside town."

"I know nothing about a refinery or about drugs." Sip.

Marisa kept pushing. Don Antonio dodged and denied. "You slander me," he said. The more she questioned, the more bored he looked and sounded. "You're wasting my time," he said.

"And you mine. The play-acting is unnecessary, *Signore* Arcuri. We know what you are." He stared at her without blinking. The expression in his eyes, the attentiveness leaked away until his gaze was empty. She could feel the weight of him on the back of her neck.

Forza. "What can you tell me about the car crash of April sixth that killed Silvio Inzerillo and Sam Mazzolin?"

"What bad luck. *Poveracci.*" There was a glint of emotion in the leaden weariness.

"Did you meet with Mr. Mazzolin before the crash?"

220

"Certainly, at the home of his mother-in-law. He was her guest for a couple of nights in the last week of March. We thought he had gone back to Venice."

"Did he explain why he was in Sicily?"

"He said he came to pay his respects to his wife's family."

"Did you think that was odd?"

"Why? It was the proper thing for him to do. At least, we think so. Respect and tradition still matter here. In Cremona, obviously you view things differently. Or Trento. The customs there are quite Germanic."

He let it drop so casually, his knowledge both of Marisa's hometown and the site of her undercover work. Marisa had not told anyone in Alcamo where she was from. She had mentioned that she was in Rome before her transfer and that she'd gone to university in Bologna, but that was it. His knowing about Trento was even more troubling. Had it been a couple of his men who had broken into her apartment? And not just pawed through her things but read her papers? And fingered the medal and commendation from the President of the Republic for her "contribution to the war against terror"?

"But odd when he had recently abandoned his wife while she was seriously ill."

"I understood he was preparing the way for the family. Fulvia and the girls would join him at the end of the school year. I am shocked."

Marisa kept her back straight and her face expressionless. "Come on, Mazzolin was not here for a courtesy visit.

221

We have found the kilos of hashish and marijuana he and his friend were smuggling into the country." Had Mazzolin and Arcuri plotted and planned here in his room? Hard to imagine: irony and gravity, wind and rock.

"Hashish? I never would have guessed he'd be that stupid."

Marisa continued with the leading questions, and Arcuri blocked each one. He had only heard about the accident last week. He was shocked to hear about the arson, shocked it was considered a double homicide. "Are you sure?" Shocked *Signorina De Luca* would suggest the men were being punished for presuming to horn in on the action or, worse, for betraying his niece. No, he didn't know there was another woman in Venice.

"*Ché cazzata.*" The words slipped out of her mouth. What a pile of shit.

"What right do you have to come into my house to insult me?" He was speaking softly, almost whispering, and slowly, so each word seemed emphasized. "None. You are a stranger here."

"I represent the law in this place. It is my duty to investigate, particularly such a grievous crime."

Arcuri let out a strangled laugh. "Now that is *una cazzata.*"

Marisa felt herself flush. "I believe a society needs to be ruled by impersonal and impartial justice." How pointed should she be? "Or it will be run by influence, corruption, and violence."

He looked amused. "And you've found your ideal in

the police force? Or in the courts? So slow and bureaucratic? I suspect you haven't seen even the shadow of your ideal justice flickering on the cave wall. Oh, the stories I could tell."

"We aspire. We strive."

"We all strive, my dear *Signorina*." Now he sounded professorial. "In Sicily, we have a saying: *Cu tuttu ca sugnu uorbu, la viu niura*. Do you understand? No? It is attributed to a blind man in 1940, when Mussolini declared war on England. 'I may be blind, but I see it black.' No illusions, no hopes. Still, I understand the necessity of authority, of order." Arcuri was stroking his goatee. "Even if you and I would differ on how to achieve it. I am a man of the old order: a traditionalist. Authority and justice should be based on history, tradition, the custom and habits of the people. Their needs and emotions. It must be rooted, not imposed from the outside."

"You are old-fashioned: resorting to an eighteenth-century thinker. A rather discredited one."

"Joseph De Maistre may be temporarily unfashionable, because he opposed the French revolution. I would say he was right."

"That's not the only reason. Didn't he call war divine?"

"What a pleasure to debate with such a well-read and charming woman. In my day, police chiefs were never female."

Marisa hadn't expected to make progress with Arcuri. She had come to let him know she could stand up to him, at least symbolically. She wasn't cowed, like too many of her colleagues. But she never imagined she would feel this physical oppression from his mere presence. The weight of him pressing on the back of her neck, behind her knees, and increasingly on her chest. Her will leapt up in resistance. *I won't be ground down.* Her other self had gone languorous, content to remain longer in that cool room lined with leather-bound books, debating in the half light. Marisa stood up. "You're being evasive, and I have a busy afternoon."

He also stood. "Crime, like the poor, will be always with us."

She turned, took a step toward the door; Arcuri was beside her, his large hand around her upper arm. "Wait. Stay a little longer. It will be worth your while."

"Are you offering a bribe?" She smiled to show she was half joking.

"Humour me. We'll have a little debate. I so seldom get the chance with a worthy opponent."

He let go of her arm. Curious, Marisa sat back down. Arcuri went around the desk and reclaimed his chair.

"In Sicily, we've learned over the millennia that our rulers are never interested in righting our wrongs."

"I've heard this argument before. Rome is impotent. Blah, blah. You are forced to avenge yourselves."

"A man destroys another's livelihood. A man mistreats his wife. Sometimes the victim or the family must turn to someone stronger, an individual or an association of like-minded individuals."

"Must turn? It would be tempting if one had a *cosca.*" Marisa paused. "Spiky and close."

With an open-handed, circular gesture Arcuri managed to evoke the literal meaning of the word for clan—artichoke. "Inward looking, yes, tight and protective. That is how a group, a society survives."

"But at whose expense? You are defending vigilantism based not on people's customs, but too often on their basest emotions."

"No, on their beliefs, on their passions."

"Justice must be rational."

"But there is a barbarism also of reason." Now he was quoting Vico. Could he be trying to impress her?

"Invalid reference," Marisa said. "Giambattista Vico believed in the state and its institutions."

"But also, my dear lady, in tradition. The ancient wisdoms of Italy. In the lessons of Greek and Roman literature and philosophy."

"Justice can't be subject to impulse or to personal whims. We have rules of evidence, checks and balances, appeals. And what can be done if your vigilantes make a mistake? Who will right it?" She was warming to her argument.

"De Maistre's *Ode to the Hangman*: the spectre of punishment is behind all justice. Man needs the threat of hell to strive for heaven."

"I don't follow."

"Another hypothetical case. The director of a chemical plant that continually spews toxins into the air and the water, let us say, of a lagoon that is the lifeblood of an extraordinary city." This was no random dialogue. Don Big Head was setting something up. A trap? Humiliation. "The man knows that he is poisoning the environment. A high percentage of his workers and the people in the immediate area are stricken with cancer. The number of miscarriages and deformed babies rises. He is responsible for numerous deaths, but he is untouchable. He is powerful and the state's laws on pollution are toothless." Arcuri was describing Monteverde. Roberto Valente had been connected to his assassination as well. Marisa opened her mouth, but no words came out. Arcuri sailed on: "So a young man plots the CEO's demise, in retribution and as a warning to others. Some might call him a hero, a servant of justice, but you would condemn him."

Arcuri's gaze was intense. Did he expect her to confess she was responsible for the state's case against Roberto? "If we allow each individual or little group to function as judge and executioner, we'll be overtaken by chaos and anarchy," Marisa said. "Blood will run in the streets."

"In public instead of behind prison doors."

"It comes down to whom you trust to investigate, as well as to apply the law."

"Exactly. Who do you trust?" Arcuri was checking his wristwatch. It had a thick gold band, and a diamond-studded face. "The people you work with and for?"

Marisa made a small face. No use lying. He knew everything. "Not the men here in Alcamo. I'm new, there are some problems."

"Your previous superiors? In the domestic terrorism section?"

A rash of goosebumps down her right arm. "Yes, of course."

"You worked for Giorgio Lanza in the past, and you

are in his jurisdiction again. You trust him?"

Not so much anymore, but she said fervently, "With my life."

"Stupid of you."

So that was Arcuri's purpose: to plant the seeds of doubt. "Why? I should trust you instead?"

The man was wallowing in secret knowledge. "Listen." He stood up again and began to pace. "The kidnapping and murder of Prime Minister Aldo Moro was a set-up. The state, Moro's *democristiani*, and the supposed servants of the law in the department of justice—they were all guiltier than the Brigades."

"That's your secret? An old and discredited rumour?" Marisa stood up too, wiping the sweat of her palms on her linen skirt, leaving stains she hoped were faint enough that Arcuri wouldn't see. "I was told—at a dinner party— that the whole thing was set up by the CIA to stop Moro from allying with the Communists."

"The Americans could have been part of it. I don't know. I do know that the Brigades couldn't understand why the government refused to negotiate. One element in the Brigades was ready to release Moro. I also know that one of my associates, who happened to be in the Regina Coeli, learned where Moro was being held. I personally carried the message to the police."

"Why would you do that?"

"Ah, dear lady, that involves another secret that I'm not willing to tell. Let us say, there are certain agreements in effect. Certain signed treaties. The point is I spoke to that man, Lanza. Moro could have been saved. But those in charge wanted a martyr."

Arcuri continued to talk, but Marisa did not hear him. She'd been figuratively punched in the head. Moro's execution had been the catalyst for the war on terror. "Our nation is in grave danger," Lanza had said. He'd persuaded her that Valente and his Sempre Guerra Group were involved in the kidnapping. "I'm sending you to the front lines," Lanza said. To spy. To entrap. It turned out Valente was only peripherally connected; he'd helped one of the so-called masterminds to get away to Canada. He was convicted as an accessory to the assassination of Aldo Moro. Only at a subsequent trial, where Marisa also testified, was he found guilty of murder—that of a director of a Dow Chemical plant near Venice. And even then Valente had neither pulled the trigger nor plotted the ambush. He had initiated the idea, provided the justification, the theory of action. He had promoted, pushed, and insisted. Conspired.

And what had she gone along with? Because of naïveté, because of ignorance.

Arcuri had a hand on her elbow. He was guiding her out of the study. Ridiculous to believe this gangster. "Come again," he was saying, "my dear lady."

He had lied from beginning to end. But why the last revelation? To teach her a lesson for daring to question him. He hadn't made up the story of the collusion of the police on the spot. It wouldn't have had such an effect if it were just another rumour. She'd handed the beast a chance to deliver a significant blow.

20

Alcamo

Fulvia prepared for her father's funeral. She smoothed out her hair and twisted it into a bun. She pulled on a black skirt and left the waistband undone. She was five months pregnant. Her breasts were swollen, which was why the blouse she was buttoning was her mother's, black crepe from Armani's latest collection.

Straight back, her grandmother used to say. Still mind, and you can withstand anything. Fulvia fought the urge to slump, to weaken. She was bone-tired, queasy, and light-headed from the trip. Three, or was it four days ago, the phone had rung in the middle of the night. Fulvia scrambled out of bed, before Sam had turned over. Her heart banging in her chest, she knew even before she heard Davide say, "*Papà.*"

"You couldn't have waited till morning?" she said. No one at Bagna Serena seemed able to calculate time differences. Not an hour later, her mother called sobbing. "You must come. Your ticket is at the airport."

For years Fulvia resisted and stayed away, impervious to calls, letters, and Aunt Dolores's rants. When Fulvia married Sam, she and her family had not made peace but called a ceasefire. She could stay in Canada for the foreseeable future. They sent $10,000 in cash as a wedding present or dowry. Aunt Dolores had been visiting Alcamo again, and she acted as the mule. Without consulting Samuele, who back then didn't know his in-laws' true identity, Fulvia rejected the money, which he would have argued they needed. She managed to send it back. Thanks, but no thanks.

Since then, her parents called at Christmas and on her birthday, and they exchanged courteous greetings. "Give Samuele our best wishes," Papà would say. "How's Enzo/ Davide/Zio Antonio?" Fulvia would ask. Also twice a year, the family couriered them a small crate of fruit, the only offering Fulvia would accept. The note would read "Remember Sicily." And in the dead of an Edmonton winter, the sweet, red-streaked pulp of the Tarocco oranges did evoke the best of her childhood: the Eden of the garden, the sanctuary of her imaginary world cobbled together from myths and folk tales, and the matchless beauty of the landscape punctuated with antiquities. The prickly pears arrived in September when the leaves were turning yellow and the days growing short. The cactus fruit spoke of the Sicilian summer, parched, unrelenting, and long. "Watch out for the thorns." She taught Sam how to peel the hard, spiky skin to uncover the deep purple, crisp flesh, though one of them always ended up with a barb embedded in a finger.

Her mother stuttered, "They've slaughtered your father. You must come." And Fulvia did not hesitate. Why? So that her absence would not be ammunition in the hands of her father's enemies.

Even his daughter deserted him, they would say, victorious.

Her father had been betrayed, Davide explained on the way home from the airport. Papà had been shot soon after leaving a business meeting in Palermo. Salvatore, after twenty-five years of Papà's favour, played Judas for the Corleone gang. "He's gonna get his." Papà's car had only gone a few hundred metres when a car pulled across the road, blocking the way. The centre of a busy neighbourhood, fishmonger, deli, bread and tobacco shops. People everywhere, but no one saw a thing. The killers drew up on motorcycles, Kalashnikovs in hand. Using a concentrated spray of bullets, they shattered the bulletproof glass of the new Mercedes and blasted the driver in the chest. Half of Father's head was blown off and splattered through the car. "And the police don't give a shit."

Open warfare. The same day that Don Fulvio and his driver were hit, handsome Enzo, Fulvia's first crush, was found stuffed into a garbage bin in the main piazza of nearby Castellamare. He had been strangled, his body bearing the marks of torture. The next day, two other *picciotti* fell to the white *lupara*, the so-called shotgun that left no trace. Eight hours later, in New Jersey, a cousin was decapitated, his head left on the seat of his parked car. The same hour, in Istanbul, the city police announced the discovery of a dismembered corpse in a green garbage bag. The identity of the dead man had not yet been confirmed, but they all suspected he was another cousin, since the bag was found behind his rented villa.

"And who's next?" Fulvia's mother asked. "Which one of us?" Lela had lost her husband, her work, and her position in the community. In the past, women and children were safe, but who knew these days? And with these monsters? One moment, she was noisy and turbulent with grief. "I have been cursed." The next, she turned in on herself, opaque and silent.

At their reunion, Lela hugged Fulvia long and hard. She landed kisses on her hair and cheeks. "Welcome home. Welcome home." The next morning, Fulvia heard her mother's keening. She followed the eerie sound to find Lela rocking back and forth on a kitchen chair, her hands over her face. Fulvia offered the usual meaningless soothing phrases. When she leaned over, to embrace her, Mamma shoved her away. "Get me Veronica," Lela screamed. "I don't want you."

Fulvia's childhood playmate had married Davide and turned into a plump matron with red-purple hair. She was bedecked with diamonds and gold, rings, earrings, necklace, and clanging bangles. But her most important accessory was three-year-old Fulvietto, the heir apparent, who clung to her skirts or rested on her right hip, his chubby hand clutching the material over her right breast, his mouth working a bright red soother. Veronica bustled, even when she was loaded down with her boy. She bustled into the kitchen and over to her mother-in-law, who had gone back to keening. "Not now, Mamma," she said, plopping her whining son onto Lela's knees. "See, you're scaring Fulvietto." The boy shrieked and tried to scramble down. His grandmother held him by the shoulders, Veronica by a leg. He couldn't escape.

"*Bello mio.*" Lela kissed her grandson's cheeks and hands. She and the boy were both crying.

Veronica took Fulvia by the arm. "I need you to phone the printers and see if the holy cards are ready. You could pick them up? I have so much to do."

Lela deferred to Veronica. Should Lela wear a hat to the service? A veil? Or was that *démodé*? And what about Fulvia? She needed a bigger top, maybe a jacket? "What would I do without you, Veronica," she said. But when she and Fulvia were alone, she whispered, "She trapped your poor brother. Got herself pregnant. He tried to get out of it. He'd fallen for someone else."

"Davide, really? Who?"

"A sweet American girl. Belinda, daughter of cousin Menico."

"The one in New Jersey?"

"Unfortunately. Poor girl. Belinda was here for an entire summer. Davide was bowled over."

"They are related."

"Second cousins, so what. Veronica's also a cousin—

even if further removed."

"But he was seeing Veronica for a long time, wasn't he? Before Belinda arrived."

"Your father said he had to be a man, no shirking. Poor Davide was stuck."

No one came to the funeral at Saint Agatha's. The immediate family, of course, a grim Zio Antonio, with wife, two daughters, and his fifteen-year-old son, who was still young enough to be safe. A few of the cousins. Peppe and three of Don Fulvio's men, now unofficial bodyguards. Five of Uncle Antonio's soldiers, Veronica's parents, but not her brothers. Sara and Vita, the housemaids. In the back pew, four policemen, representing different forces. But none of the many who had relied on his protection or sought his favours, none of those who fawned and swore their loyalty, none of the thousands who had inclined their heads as he had been driven through the town. They were afraid, each one of them, afraid of being caught on the losing side.

O Lord, do not bring Thy servant to trial.

The church was crammed not with mourners but flowers. Truckloads of wreaths. Thousands of blooms sacrificed to commemorate Don Fulvio Arcuri. Fulvia stood beside her mother, providing a supporting arm. Lela was sedated and dazed. She daubed at her eyes with a lace-trimmed handkerchief. Veronica, ever the show-off, let the tears run down her cheeks unchecked. Fulvia's emotions did not flow; like gallstones, they were hard and spiky, crystallized in bitterness, calculi of anger and shame and grief. She did not grieve for her father, for the man he had been, though she wished that she could. She grieved for the father she should have had, the father she had needed, the father that Sam would be with their baby, tender, careful.

I am in fear and trembling at the judgment and the wrath that is to come.

The scent of the flowers was sickly sweet, suffocating. In a flickering montage, Fulvia saw her wrist sliced open, the blood seeping out, saw her father's hands stained with blood, the Alfa soaked in blood, saw Enzo's terror-filled eyes. She bit the inside of her mouth to keep from swooning. The pain in her cheek, the salty taste of her blood, beat back the blackness at the edges of her vision.

Deliver us from the lion's mouth, that hell swallows us not up That we fall not into darkness.

Long ago, her father had told her, it was believed killing a man was not enough. You had to neutralize your victim's power by either washing your hands in his blood or drinking it. Otherwise, you would fall to the vengeance of the dead. Otherwise, blood called for blood.

Vengeance. Did it call out to Zio Antonio? Did it call out to Davide? As they stood before the altar and the coffin, were they listening to the chant of the priest or to that deadly song? And the killers, were they answering an earlier call of their blood?

Eternal rest grant unto him.

She wouldn't listen. With her ears blocked, she could hear more clearly the pulse of blood in her own veins and the flutter of the new life she carried.

This was the riddle of blood: it nourished and destroyed. It was life and death.

The next day, Zio Antonio left for Venezuela, Davide for Montreal. The men were forging alliances, seeking support. The women were meant to stay home to tend the hearth fires, to wait and worry, with strength and dignity. Qualities Lela either lost or never had. She moaned and howled and pulled her hair.

"Calm yourself," Fulvia said to her mother several times a day.

"Your father adored me," Lela said, which was an exaggeration. "Your father was a paragon, a marvelous husband, and an exceptional father."

Fulvia couldn't stop herself from saying, "*Dai*, Mamma. Papà was no saint. Far from it."

"And your Venetian, he's a knight in shining armour?"

Veronica butted in: "Made of tin. He can't even support you. You have to work, a shop girl. I'd be humiliated."

"I want to work," Fulvia said. "I like earning my own money. I'm happy with my life and my marriage." She called up the clean-musky presence of Sam and gave him a mental hug. She would never admit to these two that Sam had any flaws. "He's the right man for me," she said. "I'm lucky."

Lela made the face she used in the market to suggest the vendor was trying to palm off shoddy goods on her. "We don't know the man. Your father kept waiting for the day you'd realize that you needed your family, that you didn't belong over there. But no. You broke his heart. Let that be on your conscience. You self-righteous bitch. Your day will come."

Fulvia clung to the fact that she was no longer an Arcuri or even a Sicilian, that she had made a life for herself, untouched by darkness and safe from the spiral of hysteria and need in her mother's eyes. In this house, Fulvia's wedding ring was a talisman, like the *cornicello*, the curved gold horns the others wore to ward off the evil eye. Veronica wore a particularly ostentatious one on her chest, next to a crucifix. What a joke: if anyone had an envious eye, it was Veronica.

Fulvia felt as if she were eight again. She wanted to slap her mother. She needed to pull Veronica's purple hair. You're a grown-up, she told herself. Another ten days and she could fly away.

Fulvia decided to fill the hours by putting the house in order. Not the business wing, of course, not her father's office or the cantinas. There was more than enough work in the rest of the house, even with Sara and Vita helping her. Fulvia now understood the benefits of Nonna's strict regime, the mania for cleaning, the intolerance of waste and extravagance. Her mother had filled Bagna Serena with stuff: silver, linen, china, crystal, paintings, and statues. Where had it all come from? Fulvia hauled out Nonna's old standbys, bleach and rubbing alcohol. Too much was stained, tarnished, dusty. "Everything must be spotless," she told Sara and Vita, "even after I'm gone."

Lela's closet was a jumble Fulvia didn't dare untangle. Eighty-five pairs of shoes and forty-nine purses, five of them Chanel. Fulvia entered only to examine the cut and seams of the designer clothes. She had begun to sketch a fashion line.

Fulvia stripped her bedroom, which had been left the way it was when she fled at nineteen. She threw out the junk: fashion magazines, scratched 45s, a turntable, textbooks, scribblers, psychedelic posters, and curlers. Expired lipsticks, nail polish, and girlish colognes. In a desk drawer, she found some of the old notes that she and Alex exchanged during university lectures—out. Of the classic works she had studied in school, she kept only a survey of Italian poetry. Several romance novels, *libri rosa*, out. A framed picture of Fulvia at ten holding Fedele, a small photo album, an old sketchbook full of her early drawings, keep, keep, keep.

She would also take home two volumes of Sicilian folk tales, to read to the baby, and because she still carried these stories in her heart: tales of empty stomachs and mountains made of pastry, misery, and rooms of solid gold, reversals of fortune and the possibilities of transformation. The lessons were basic, but worth passing on: be cunning, be wise, always be kind to the old, the humble, the poor, and all the animals. But as Fulvia flipped through, pausing to read one favourite, then another, she noticed what she had missed when she was younger: another, more ambiguous thread. Vengeance. The evil were hanged, skinned, thrown into boiling oil, chopped to pieces, cooked, eaten.

She would have to change the endings, make them new and Canadian.

To her surprise, for she was not grieving, part of Fulvia couldn't accept her father was gone. She expected him to appear any moment, in the doorway, at the head of the table, in the salon sitting next to her on the velvet sofa. And the day before she was to leave, he visited her. She was sitting under her oak tree, revelling in the early spring. She was eager to get home to Sam, but in Edmonton it was still the dead of winter. Here the earth was stirring; the early spring sun was warm on her legs, and the breeze wafted the sweet woody scent of almond flowers. On the branches overhead, the leaves were unfurling. Before her, the line of almond trees was a riot of white and pale pink blossoms.

A bird materialized about a metre away. Large, but not fully grown, dark grey except for chestnut belly, red claws and beak. (Back home in Canada, she searched through a book on birds of prey and found its species, a male red-footed falcon.) It flapped open its long, pointed wings, and the baby moved, leapt in her womb. The bird hopped, screeched, and folded its wings in again. A tight band squeezed her heart. What if it flew at her, attacked? Instead, it stayed still, moving only its head in little mechanical jerks. For a long moment, Fulvia was convinced it was not a living creature but a sinister clockwork creation. The band tightened; she couldn't catch her breath. But she heard no ticking. And its red-ringed, black-bead eyes were watching her, not just aimed in her direction.

A raptor's gaze. Papà, waiting for her acknowledgement. She knew this to her very core: Papà was here, present. The world was spinning, only she and he were still. Like when she was little, and he'd lift her up and flip her upside down, up and down. What a spin. She heard his voice in her head.

You loved it when I carried you on my shoulders.

She smiled. Her father was not standing in fear and trembling at the judgment.

She said aloud, I wanted to see you again, Papà. Now her heart was pounding with excitement.

A current, a charged wave, linked Fulvia and the falcon. *You were always my special girl.*

Three years old and you dropped me off the end of the pier.

You grew up resourceful.

I couldn't be an Arcuri. Do you understand now? I had to make a separate life.

A red-banded eye. *I don't forgive you.*

Likewise. Another flash, Papà, red-faced and yelling. His fingers bruising her arm.

The red-topped beak pecked the air, click click. The red claws scratched the dirt. *You mutilated yourself. You are no longer whole.*

She had said in a moment of teenage despair: I'll cut off my arm if I have to. Again the flutter of the baby in her womb. I am complete. A good life, a good husband. She was suspended over a sea of sadness.

The falcon moved closer. Its feathers glowed with

light. *Another baby girl, another special girl*, he said. From an almond tree, the piercing cry of another falcon, this one rusty orange.

My daughter will never be an Arcuri.

The orange bird swooped down and wings flapping, pulled up. It shrieked over and over, as if it were calling Fulvia's falcon. Fulvia was standing now, her back pressed against the twisted tree trunk.

Her father lifted his wings. *Time to go.* His grey head jerked right, left, yet the red-banded eyes still held her. *Blood will out.*

She felt herself falling through the air, plunging into a sea of sadness She must swim to the light or drown.

Blood will out.

A root poked into her back, her right foot throbbed. The grey falcon was in the air, spiralling upwards. A keening cry to salute her, to haunt her. And he was gone into the white sky.

21

Alcamo

Marisa couldn't go back to work after her confrontation with Antonio Arcuri. She barely made it to her apartment before throwing up in the toilet. For a few hours, her digestive system was in as much turmoil as the time she got food poisoning from some raw clams in Rome. She shouldn't have gone alone. Arcuri wouldn't have brought up the Moro business if she'd had Brusca there. She'd been stupid, cocky, thinking she could take on the big bad boss one-on-one. He'd shown her: *you can't trust anyone*, blasting the ground from beneath her feet.

Even after her stomach calmed down, Marisa couldn't eat or sleep. By ten o'clock, the temperature had only dropped from forty-two to thirty-three degrees. Her apartment was a suffocating box, the two fans providing little relief. She'd opened the windows, but kept the outdoor shutters latched, thus blocking any hint of a breeze. She didn't want to be visible to the apartment opposite or the street. Even with the sheers drawn or the lights off, someone might discern her shadow. And what about night goggles? Was she being followed, spied on? No sign of it, besides the odd, prickly sensation between her shoulder blades and at the nape of her neck. As if someone were standing behind her, out of sight, watching. The heat was cooking her brains. She took a quick, lukewarm shower; the stall was too confining to linger, and let herself air dry. She held an ice cube to her wrist. She dampened a nightgown and a sheet, squishing them both into the small fridge.

She put a pillow on the floor and sat with her back pressed against her bedroom wall. Her mind tried to focus. Was Arcuri's revelation about the Moro case all bullshit? He was a practised liar, after all. She'd doubted him when he disassociated himself from Valle, and even more so when he claimed ignorance of his niece's abandonment. But Moro's martyrdom had proved useful for the government. And Arcuri's charge that the forces of the law did not save Moro when they could have, that they wanted his death, perhaps even planned it, felt possible, even probable.

Marisa pulled on the icy nightgown, wrapped herself in the sheet. Both fans were aimed at the bed, yet she didn't drift off. Through the window, the rumble of passing trucks, the blare of a car alarm, the stink of exhaust. She began to imagine how she would confront Lanza. Could she goad or trick him into admitting the truth? Unlikely. Her boss ran their meetings according to his agenda, not hers.

The next morning, Marisa was on her way out, pulling on her linen blazer, about to pick up her briefcase when she saw the letter. In the few hours she had slept, someone had pushed the threat under her front door.

Stop putting your nose where it does not belong. Otherwise you will suffer the consequences.

A woman warned is a woman saved.

an anxious friend

This could not have come from Valente's friends. Their note would be more ideological and more obscene. Arcuri? Hadn't he flattened her already?

First thing at work she called Lanza's office; she was told he was in important, top-level meetings all day. Before the station house opened to the public, she had Roselli convene the sixteen men on duty and Grazia, the receptionist, in the squad room. She launched into a short pep talk, stressing the recent successes of the team. "We must continue to act as one." A few smiles. "More roadblocks and more surveillance. Our waters are infested with poisonous fish. All we have to do is lower our nets."

The men muttered, gestured. Only Roselli and Grazia nodded: they were on board.

"These will be random, unexpected blocks. Surveillance of the Arcuri house, as well as the two bars in Alcamo that the *cosca* frequents."

Brusca said "How? We don't have the manpower."

"At random intervals. For the next week. Everyone

must take their turn, including you, Captain." Brusca opened his mouth to protest. Marisa cut in. "You can draw up the duty roster." She pointed at Mancuso and Roselli. "Meanwhile, you two will take the fingerprints of everyone who works here. The squad, cleaning people, everyone. And I'll need it by tomorrow at noon."

"*Dottoressa*," Mancuso said in a shocked voice.

"Call in those on different shifts or on days off." Marisa turned on her heel, closed her office door behind her. Her plan was to take the anonymous letter and its envelope into Forensics in Palermo. If there were any fingerprints on either, she'd send in all the employees' prints. And if there weren't, having the prints could be useful in the future. The usual suspects in the area would already be on file. A woman warned is a woman saved indeed.

In Palermo, they wouldn't get to such a task for months and months, unless Lanza pushed them. His needs were a priority. Maybe it was safer to send everything to headquarters in Rome. There were computers there, which would speed up the process. But again, she'd need Lanza's stamp of approval.

When the phone rang, she thought it might be Lanza or the pleasant Sergeant in Edmonton. Instead, Grazia asked if the *Dottoressa* would accept a call from Alex Zacco.

He and Marisa hadn't spoken since their outing to Segesta. Since he had stuck his fingers up inside her, then gloated at her response. He hadn't acted out of lust; she was sure of that. So why? A need to humiliate? Dominate?

Perhaps he was overcome with remorse. He was going to apologize, explain. He'd been afraid of the strength of his feelings for her. Could they please start again? She indulged in thirty seconds of fantasy before picking up the phone.

"I have something to tell you," he said. "Should I come to the station?"

Alex picked her up in his dusty, rusty Fiat outside a funeral home on the street running behind the station house. "Thank you for coming," he said.

"It's lunch time. I wanted a break."

It was his eyes, Marisa decided: they promised a depth of being. They made you want to dive in. All an illusion, she told herself. You knew pretty quickly he was all wrong. Though it was hard to imagine anyone in her world who would be right. Or even appropriate. And now she was beside him in the car, she again felt a physical pull.

He wore black jeans and a black T-shirt with the white outline of a man's head on the front. His arms were thin yet muscular, and, as far as she could see, without injection scars. He drove impatiently, passing, switching lanes, and now and then grinding the gears.

"I wish I could keep a tape deck in this car," he said. "I've had three stolen. Out of a wreck like this. You police shrug when I report it." Marisa made a show of shrugging. He smiled: "Some background music might make this less awkward."

"Doubtful," she said.

246

Two thirds of the way up Monte Bonifato, Alex pulled off on a wide shoulder cut into the side of the mountain. "*Minchia*—fuck—it's hot." Alex said.

Marisa got out of the car, leaving the door open. She could feel the faintest of breezes moving over the parched fields. Above, the ancient Arab watchtower loomed. Across the road, the hill broke off; Alcamo was below. To her right, there was a row of olive trees and, behind, a stone wall and a crescent of terracotta roof. Alex was watching her through the windshield.

She turned away, into the shade thrown by the wall of earth. Beneath the thin covering of loam, rust-brown faded to tan, to gold, to yellow: layers of dry earth packed against and around pebbles, then stones, then boulders, until all was rock. Lemon-grey rock. Bedrock.

Alex was beside her, rambling on about having wanted to go elsewhere and inevitably quoting Lampedusa. "There is hope for the Sicilian only if he leaves early, before he is twenty. It's too late for me. I missed my chance. Worse, I failed the test."

Was this what he had to tell her? That he had regrets. Who didn't? He was speaking deliberately, as if what he had to say was of great importance. He went on and on about university and a first love, perhaps an only love. Without meaning to, Marisa let out a short grunt of irritation. He didn't stop; now he was explaining how he and the girl were so young, and how both families were opposed to their relationship, to their love. Both the Zaccos and the Arcuris. That woke her up.

"You're kidding. The girlfriend was Fulvia Arcuri?"

"So my brother was right. You didn't know." Alex pulled off his sunglasses, wiped the sweat off his forehead. "I was sure you did. That day we went to Segesta, and you started talking about her husband's murder."

"I had no idea you'd known her. How could I?"

"Ivana might have told you. Not that I ever talked to her about me and Fulvia, but she must have heard—family gossip."

"If I had guessed, I'd never have brought the murder up. Or the Arcuri. Not the way I did, anyway,"

"I thought we got on, you and me. Even if you were a police chief. But when you mentioned the Arcuri, I was hurt, angry. Convinced you had some sort of plan."

"To extract information? Not at all."

"Then, you started asking me questions about drug shipments."

"On an impulse, that's all." Marisa took a step closer to Alex. Was her fantasy coming true? "But you must have suspected you misjudged me. Or why come to me now?"

"My brother the shrink thought it'd be cathartic."

"You said he was sure I didn't know."

"He said even if you did, it would be good for me to acknowledge my past." Marisa felt a flicker of disappointment. "So tell me, what was Fulvia Arcuri like when you knew her?"

"A rare bloom." Alex pulled a wallet from his back pocket. He fished out a small colour picture and handed it to Marisa. Two young, beaming faces cheek to cheek,

Alex with hair to his shoulders and without lines on either side of his mouth. Fulvia: almond-eyes, full mouth, and a mass of hair, but softer, less formed than in the wedding picture Marisa had seen in Venice. They looked delighted with themselves and each other.

"You were children," said Marisa. The snapshot was faded, the bottom edge worn. Alex hadn't placed the picture in his wallet to show her. It lived there.

"She had everything: sweet, smart, beautiful." He took the photo from Marisa and gave it a long look. "She was pure and true." He slipped it into a plastic sleeve and tucked it in amongst the credit cards.

"But rooted in a pile of dung."

He hesitated. "Unfortunately. But she wasn't like them. My family couldn't see that. They deemed her manipulative, dangerous, contaminated, just because her father was who he was."

"Her husband was murdered a half-kilometre up this road."

"If I'd been as strong as she was," he said, "if I'd gone with her, I could have had another life. I failed her and myself."

Marisa pressed Alex to tell her more, to go deeper. Could Fulvia have instigated her husband's death? Could she have wanted to punish him?

Alex dismissed the possibility, never, never. "She was good. I'm sure she still is."

But he had known Fulvia Arcuri for a few months when she was nothing more than a girl. They weren't together long enough for the romantic haze to dissipate. "She may be another person now. Life changes you," Marisa said.

"Then don't ask for my opinion," he said. "I can't believe you suspect her, half a world away. After I just told you... Must be the cop mentality."

"I have to examine all the possibilities."

He was looking at her with distaste. "You can't prove she knew anything. So why sweat it?"

"To uncover the truth, not just the facts. I feel I owe Mazzolin that." Marisa pressed her right hand hard against the wall of earth.

"Even if you can't avenge him? It sounds personal."

She could feel the dirt catching under her nails, settling into the damp creases of her hand. "He does remind me of someone I used to know, who, as it happens, was murdered the same day." Roberto Valente. She saw him, his face disfigured with anger at her. *Porca troia*. Even in the shade, the heat was fierce. "I couldn't do anything about that killing." She felt dazed, yet tense.

Alex was no longer listening. He was walking away, a dark shape against the bright light.

The fan in Marisa's office barely stirred the air. For about a second, she considered commandeering one of the three standing fans from the squad room. She was imagining the squawks when Brusca opened her door without knocking. He stepped in, pulled the door closed. "Enough with the fingerprinting."

What next? Mass disobedience. Marisa stood up. He took four steps and loomed over her. "You don't know what you're doing."

She didn't flinch, kept her voice calm. "You're afraid I'll be able to prove you've been threatening me."

"Afraid? Of you? I've done nothing."

"Brusca, collect yourself."

"You're crazy, you need fucking so bad."

Was he drunk? His breath stank of wine. "Get out."

"I've got the balls." He was unzipping his fly. His bloodshot blue eyes were intent, gleeful. "To do the job." His hand waved the red blob of flesh. His penis hardened. "Hey, look at this big boy."

Later, Marisa would wish she'd come up with a couple of put-downs or managed a mocking laugh. But in that moment, she was without words or thought, disbelieving and overwhelmed. She screamed and lobbed the first thing that came to hand, a fat law book, which plummeted to the ground. Then, a pen holder, papers, a pencil. Brusca was sneering, zipping his fly. Finally he turned. "Hysterical female," he said over his shoulder, then slammed the door behind him.

"Captain Brusca has to go." It was almost the first thing Marisa said to Lanza when she was finally allowed in to see him.

She'd received a call from Silvia, his right-hand woman, the previous evening. The *Questore* could grant her a few minutes at nine thirty. "His schedule is tight. I presume this is a matter of utmost importance?"

"Certainly," Marisa said. She'd first requested the meeting because she wanted to confront Lanza about the Moro kidnapping. Although she instinctively believed Arcuri's accusations, she hoped Lanza could counter them, could reassure her: the forces of order had tried to save Moro. The threat to democracy and the people had been real. The country had not been hoodwinked. She had not been lied to, fooled, used.

By the time she got the call, Marisa's purpose had changed. She needed to secure Lanza's support and cooperation. "Brusca has been insolent, disrespectful, from the day I arrived." Lanza gave no sign of surprise or concern as she explained. "I've suspended him for a week, but I don't want him back at my station. You must arrange for the man to be transferred. Somewhere he'll feel foreign and out of place."

"Marisa, you're overreacting. A little sexual banter, it's natural. You're an attractive woman. You should expect it."

"Banter? Are you kidding? He had his cock out."

"You should be able to handle it. With all the experience you've had."

Was he alluding to her going to bed with Roberto? He, who'd wound her up and sent her off to trap the man? Marisa flushed red in anger, in shame. "What are you insinuating?"

"Nothing, nothing. You're a woman of the world. That's a compliment." He nodded his Roman bust of a head. "You could probably benefit from some management workshops. Learn the latest techniques for obtaining consensus, inspiring your group. How to lead."

"I'm not the one who needs workshops."

"You've been under stress. Valente's death upset you. You've felt isolated. You could use more than a weekend away, a real change. There's a course on art theft, all expenses paid. Two months in Florence, relaxing and useful."

"Brusca had been drinking while on duty."

"It was after lunch, no?"

"I'm surprised you're not taking this more seriously." She handed Lanza the anonymous letter. "And I think he had something to do with this. I was trying to make the connection when he decided to put me in my place."

As he read, Lanza's expression turned grave. "Why do you think I told you no investigations? I was afraid of this." He wagged his finger at her. "If you had followed orders, it wouldn't have happened."

"It's Brusca and some of his cohorts. They want me out."

Lanza was staring at the piece of paper. "I don't think so. This came from the outside. It is a serious warning. You need to leave."

"You want me to run away?"

"De Luca, these people do away with anyone they judge to be a threat." A long list of names began to unroll in Marisa's head. "They don't hesitate. They shot down Monreale's chief of police at the town fair while he was holding his three-year-old son."

"I know, *Questore*." Was his concern genuine?

"No one was ever charged. Not for most of the other assassinations either. And now you have placed yourself in grave danger."

"Because they get rid of those who have no protectors. And I am isolated." *Alone.* Her voice quavered. She breathed deep, held on. "Sir, you told me that when the general heard one of his captains had received threats, he immediately drove to the village where the man was stationed."

Lanza nodded. "The general walked arm-in-arm with the man to demonstrate to everyone the captain had powerful friends."

"He saved his officer. But when the General's turn came, no one stood with him. He was left in a vacuum."

"May he rest in peace."

"*Questore*, please come to Alcamo. If you make a show of your support, both my police and the criminals will get the message." Then, quickly so the words almost ran into each other: "You do still support me?" Lanza stood up, leaned forward and patted her hand. "Of course."

Her throat was so tight she had to force the words out. "I've served you well. Please come."

"I wish I could. I'm leaving tonight on vacation." He made a rueful face. "You should do the same. Escape the heat. Make everybody think you are retreating, so they all calm down." His broad hand on her back guiding her out the door. "Believe me, I have your best interests at heart."

22

Edmonton
JUNE 1989

When Marisa told John about the anonymous letter, he laughed. She'd called, she said, to bring him up to date on the investigation, though she didn't have that much to report: a talk that went nowhere with Fulvia Mazzolin's uncle, the local boss, and a conference call that yielded little more with the police in Tunisia. "They think the two victims could have bought the hash in the resort town of Sidi Bon Said." John was about to wrap up the exchange, when Marisa mentioned the letter. And he laughed. "I expected some sympathy and, as you say, moral support." Her voice, until now so impersonal and matter-of-fact, was reproachful.

John turned his rotating seat so that he was facing away from Lloyd's inquiring eyes. "I'm sorry. It's like a cheesy movie."

"Cheesy?"

"Showy, cliché. A threat in cut-out letters. You think

it's a genuine threat?"

"My *Questore* in Palermo does. Or he says he does. I suspect my captain is trying to frighten me into leaving."

"One of your men, wow, that's tough. But if you're right, you aren't in danger."

"Not mortal danger. Still, it's common enough here. Officers of the law, successful ones, are eliminated."

"You've been successful?"

"Relatively. Increased the number of arrests for break-ins, assault, manslaughter, the usual. Found a major heroin refinery."

"Congratulations."

"My chief claims I've been too proactive. I'm supposed to concentrate on paperwork. Probably thinks I deserve whatever I get. "

"Nice boss."

"You're being ironic, yes? He says he is worried about my safety. Told me to take a vacation. Then yesterday one of my guys observed a government bigwig, a minister, visiting the Arcuri."

"That's not illegal?"

"No, but significant. This morning, the *Questore* phones me. He is more insistent about my leaving. And what on earth was I thinking ordering surveillance?"

When John hung up the phone, Lloyd said: "Your Sicilian friend is pretty persistent with the calls."

"She's been threatened. She's in danger."

"I'm not surprised. What were the Italians thinking putting her in charge of a Sicilian station? It's not a post for a woman. Around here, we've had more sense."

"She seems first-rate: smart and gutsy. And she's getting done what the guys before her didn't do." Though, John admitted to himself, having a female boss would take some getting used to.

"I don't doubt it. But she's more vulnerable than a man would be."

"I'm with you there," John said. "She's coming here for a visit."

Lloyd was smiling. "Whoohoo, smart and gutsy. What about her looks? Has she sent you a picture?"

"Of course not." He did wonder what Marisa looked like. Hot, if her face matched her voice.

"You figure she's your type?"

"We're working on a case together, that's all," John said. And he thought: she's a woman of substance and principle, nothing like Janet.

A few hours later, Janet materialized at his weekly soccer game, which she had never attended when they were married. It was an evening in early June, the air fresh, green, the sun still bright. The beginning of the second half, no score, and the other team was hogging the ball. John cut in from the side, a deft move, and he had it. A short kick, then a long one, the ball soared. Buoyant, solid, he ran down the field toward Belmac's goal. The IC fans were cheering. He glanced over and was caught by a flash of red hair. His stomach flipped. Janet. What the hell?

The ball bounced, landed a metre away. With a hook

of his foot, he guided it into position and kicked. A sound, half pop, half crack, from his hamstring. A sharp pain and he was down, sure he'd been hit: a kick or a rock. Peter and one of the Belmacs were standing over him. "You okay?"

"Who threw the rock?" John hauled himself up. He couldn't move the injured leg. He hobbled on the other.

"What rock? Action getting a bit too hot, eh?" Peter was smiling.

"Can you stretch it?" from William, the coach.

William palpated the back of John's leg. "Torn tendon? It'll fix itself. Anyway, we're starting. Nerio, in you go."

"I'll take care of him." It was Janet. She was hovering solicitously. She leaned in; he was engulfed in her perfume. "Do you want to stay for the rest of the game or go now?"

John awoke the next morning to a throb in his leg and Janet in his bed. The warmth and weight of her pressed against his back. Her morning scent green and bitter. He remembered not each step but enough, too much, of the dance of seduction. She'd come prepared; the woman, who hated to cook, had two bottles of California red and a bag of groceries in the trunk of her car. "I'll make us some dinner."

What would she have done if he hadn't snapped his tendon? Or if he'd refused her help? Moved on to some other poor bastard? He almost asked, but he hadn't seen her this way, charm at full throttle, in so long. He didn't mind if she put on Frank Sinatra, did he? She missed so many of his records. Would he let her come over and tape them some time? How about some Advil? Chocolate cake? Brandy and a leg massage?

He knew he should brush off her fingers, get off the sofa, get away from her. If his injured leg hadn't made him awkward and slow——. Wait, she'd whispered. If he hadn't kissed her and she hadn't answered, long and lasciviously. Let's pretend, she whispered, when he broke away. Her tone was ironic, conspiratorial. She'd come dressed for her part, black silk underthings, a lace garter and stockings, a condom in her wallet. Inventive in her touch and responsive to his. She played it. She played it. Goooaaaal!

Wasn't that a party, trick *and* treat, Halloween apples, tootsie rolls, jaw breakers and one sucker—him. His lungs ached for a cigarette, one sweet, acrid drag. He suppressed his cough so as not to wake her. If they hadn't been in his apartment, he'd have snuck out, without a word. They had fucked impersonally, a kind of fancy undress, and the pleasure of it had rattled him to the fillings in his teeth, to the end of his toenails.

It would help, breathing the smoke in, pushing it out. He had a grassy taste on his tongue; he was rock-hard. Janet stirred, exposing her shoulder and breast, her skin creamy, her nipple the palest of pinks. He coughed, and she groaned. "What time is it?"

"Early."

"I need coffee."

"Room service coming up." But he didn't move. The

spectre of other mornings, other nights hovered in the air.

Fool. He'd watched Janet at parties, flashing breasts and eyes and teeth. *Remember*. In the weight room of their sports club. *Remember*. He was on his back, doing bench presses, eighty-two kilos. He sat up, between repetitions, to tell Janet that he was almost done, half an hour to a cappuccino. *Remember*. She was halfway across the room on a leg machine, smiling up at Paul, a college kid. And he was leaning down, touching her face, caressing her face. *Right in front of me*.

"So what?" she said. "So I'm a flirt. Big deal."

He would question and cross-question her. Where were you? It took you four hours? He'd check out her body for new marks, sniff her underwear for alien smells. If he could uncover one fact, one hard fact, he could confront her. He had to know, and he dreaded knowing.

"So I like to party," she said.

"I used to do a bit of coke," she told him. "Before you." Her face sullen, her ass up in the air. She was lying sideways across the white-canopied, king-sized bed they had bought before they were married. "I'm sick of you policing me," she said. "Treating me like one of your suspects." Janet then, a year ago. John sat up and looked over his shoulder at Janet now, splayed out, but this time on his minimalist double, his bachelor bed.

"Breakfast can wait," she said. And he fell back, fell to her fingers, her tongue, her expert mouth. In the months of doubt he had made love to her, fucked her, two, three, four times a day. His appetite was endless. *Fuck*. As if sex could unlock her mystery. *Fuck*. As if penetrating her physically laid her open mentally, *fuck*, as if he could batter through to the very quick of her.

She was untouchable. Then and now.

When he brought her coffee and toast, she was wrapped in the top sheet. "You were rough." She pointed to two red marks on her right arm.

He settled the tray on her knees. "What's going on?"

She had dark shadows under her eyes. "It wasn't make-up sex, if that's what you're thinking."

"You were trying to prove that you could still play me." She has met a new guy, he thought, and she needs me to keep her detached.

Janet shook her head. "You were hot for revenge sex. And I'm a generous woman, delivering what you need."

The day after her conversation with John, Marisa cancelled the heightened measures. "Back to our routines." She also announced she was leaving Friday on vacation. "I have several weeks coming to me, and we can't all be away in August." At the bank, she made a show of purchasing traveller's cheques in Canadian dollars. At the dairy, she asked for her usual, an *etto* of ricotta, but added, I'm going away.

She walked slowly back to her apartment. Midday, and the sun was a blow to the head. Under the weight of heat and light, colour and detail were crushed, solidity sucked away. The piazza shrank into a sepia etching. Reaching a narrow, shaded side street, she paused to wipe the sweat from her face and neck with a tissue. Beside her, a wooden door bestrewn with pieces of paper and crowned with a picture of a young man barely out of childhood. *In memoriam*: a notice of the loss and grief within.

A few days ago, she had been awakened in the night by the keening, the long prehistoric wail of the women until dawn and again from dusk till dawn the next night. Mournful Lo Verde told her about the accident. Four drunken youths in a *Cinquecento*, on their way home from a disco in Alcamo Marina. "No mystery, an open-and-shut case," Lo Verde said.

Four lives, open and then shut. Four doorways decorated with the badges of mourning: declarations of the departed's virtues and testimonies of sorrow. After the funerals, makeshift altars would be assembled on each threshold, a wreath on the door-handle, cut flowers and candles spilling onto the sidewalk. The flowers might fade, the candles burn out; the pieces of paper, at least, would be left up for years, becoming fixtures in the neighbourhood, like the shrines to *La Bedda Matri*, Mother Mary. The ubiquitous memorials ended up not as commemorations of the dead as much as reminders of death. *Momento mori*, as if anyone in this death-haunted place needed reminding.

Two young girls in sundresses sauntered past, followed, a few metres back, by two young men in jeans. The taller one called out suggestively, insistently. Marisa understood his male cry from the tone and gestures: the words were unintelligible, Sicilian. This was another country, with another language that tightened the mouth and lowered the pitch. A harsh and guttural tongue, dominated by *d*s and *b*s and *u*s, but with its own rhythm and melody.

Another country, *Sicilia martoriata*, tortured, afflicted, Sicily. Stone walls, secret gardens, barred doors, dead-end paths. She was trying to decipher signs and judge mores. She could be misreading everything. Was she being watched? The prickly unease between her shoulder blades was back. The windows all looked shuttered, the street behind and before her empty. The only sound the click of her heels on stone.

Who would mourn her, besides her aunt and three or four old friends? And they, how deeply? A *lupara* could be trained on her at this very moment. If the trigger were pulled, how much difference would it make to anyone?

A two-minute delay saved her. Late Friday morning, Marisa was at the outer door of the station house, her hand on the knob, when she remembered the Mazzolin case notes. She'd photocopied the original pages a week ago, when she first decided to go to Canada, so she could review each detail with John Buonaiuto. She'd put the folder in the bottom drawer of her desk.

Marisa turned to Roselli, who was driving her in the Alfetta to Punta Raisi airport, and handed him her suitcase. "I'll be right there."

Grazia, on her way back to the station from the nearby caffè and carrying a tray of coffees, saw baby-face Roselli put a suitcase and a satchel into the trunk. Roselli unlocked the driver's door, slid in, and inserted the key in the ignition. He did not turn the key. He got out, circled

23   Edmonton
WINTER 1988

Fulvia swam four mornings a week. Water, cool and transparent, was her element: her stroke was clean, efficient, her legs coordinated and strong. She stowed away anxiety and anger in the locker room. She didn't fret about suppliers or sales, about her daughters' schoolwork or her husband's business. She counted off the laps, the numbers often interspersed with nonsense phrases: twenty-one, twenty-two, too blue, touch, turn, true blue, twenty-three, see. Sometimes random images floated in the brightness. Barbara's sweet face contracted into a pout. An aquamarine silk dress on a mannequin. The snow- and slush-clogged road in front of the house.

In the last ten laps, when her pace began to slow, words crackled and fizzed, like firecrackers: *pull yourself together*, *suck it up*. They were always exhortations, sometimes aimed, she suspected, at Sam rather than herself. *Be patient, you can do it. Hang on, hang on, hang on.*

One dark January morning, the phrase she heard was Sicilian: *la viu niura*. Fulvia was thrown off, her forward thrust interrupted. *I see it black*, the blind man says. Of course, she did: daylight was brief in winter this far north. Or was her subconscious warning her about the future? Black? Not likely, the shop was doing well, and even her modest line of separates was starting to attract customers. Daughters—check. Marriage, double check. Sam had his faults, but who didn't? *Non è omu*, the words seemed to bubble up from the bottom of the pool. *Non è omu*, he's not a man. Fulvia's fingers splayed, her legs churned. She lifted her head and heard the phrase booming from the intercom, echoing from the soaring glass walls. Her father's voice, deep and melancholic.

She never—almost never—thought of her father. Why would she channel his voice? Channel his evaluation of her husband? For she had no doubt that was who the *he* was. Sam might not be more of a man than her father had been, but he was a better one. It was Sam's integrity, his refusal to cut corners or build what he considered shoddy and ugly that caused him to lose business. The phrase was unfair. Papà had never met her husband. Zio Antonio knew Sam, and he spoke in such terms: little man, not a man, old woman, cunt. But it was Papà's voice. Fulvia hauled herself out of the pool, four lengths short. Her throat was tight, her skin goose-bumped.

Four years earlier, she, Sam, and the girls had flown down to Alcamo, because Davide insisted that Mamma was dying. "Her last wish is to see the granddaughters she has never met," Davide said. They had already spent three months in Venice, burning through the money Fulvia had saved to start her design line in Edmonton. She'd put her dream aside and agreed to the return for Sam's sake, for the sake of their marriage. He had been so miserable, sick of the crappy jobs, the snow, the cold, the people, and the place. His spirit needed beauty, needed Venice, needed home. The move seemed feasible; he had a good job lined up with a luxury hotel chain. How could she deny him his heart's desire? "You'll find something," he told Fulvia.

When they arrived, the job had evaporated. Sam looked for other work, but jobs that paid well and used his talents were as rare as they had been years earlier, when he'd emigrated. Sam concentrated on winning friends: you couldn't get anywhere without a *padrino*, a protector to recommend you. They rented a *capanna* on the Des Bains beach, the most exclusive on the Lido. He joined a rowing club and, with his new pals, idled away too many afternoons going from bar to *enoteca*, drinking one *ombra* after another. Once a week they'd go out to eat with his old friends. "You never know when you might get a lead," he said. These friends rarely tried to include her; they often slipped into Venetian, and Fulvia would feel shut out. Worse, one of these friends, an overly made up, snotty type, was an old girlfriend. Daniela flirted with Sam in front of her.

Fulvia was happy to get away from her suspicions, from the heavy, sirocco air and the stagnant canal water, from the forced social life and the overspending. "*Facendo una bella figura*," Sam said, making a good impression. Respite too from Sam's family and their hostility. You Sicilians, his mother would say, touching her index finger to her nose. So when Mamma turned out not to be dying, not to have pancreatic cancer, but gall stones, Fulvia hadn't been angry that they'd been lured South on false pretences.

The Arcuri welcomed all four of them. They laid out feasts of food, drink, and for the girls, dolls, smocked dresses, and gold necklaces. They gave the Canadians a sampling of the pleasures of northwest Sicily: beaches, boats, rambles in the countryside. Not that Fulvia was taken in. The beauty of the land, the ancient ruins, and the art, all of it spoke to her, but what about what we're not seeing, not hearing, she thought, the history: the blood, terror, and subjugation. Veronica was the designated keeper/guide, and in each place, she'd say: "You have nothing there that equals this." And though that was partly true, Fulvia would argue using the foothills, the Rockies, the magnificent wilderness.

The excursion to the medieval town of Erice was typical. Davide drove off with Sam in a Ferrari Testarossa; Veronica took the rest of them in a Mercedes. The four children, Anna and Barbara, and Fulvietto and Zaira, sat in the back with no seatbelts. When Fulvia asked, Veronica evoked the inescapability of fate. "If it's your time to go, that's it." Fulvietto took after his father: ten years old and a terror. He mocked Anna, pulled down her bathing suit, kicked her, and twisted her arm. He managed to strike on the sly, Anna said, when the adults weren't around. And Zaira? She'd giggle and tease. "Kids," said Davide with a shrug, when Fulvia complained. "Boys will be boys," said Veronica.

During the ride to Erice, Fulvio pinched Barbara's chubby legs, and when Anna, only seven but already a caregiver, put herself in between him and her sister, he pinched Anna's arms and legs. Anna was as fierce and stoical as Fulvia had been as a child and didn't make a sound.

The men should have been waiting for them in the main piazza, as agreed. With Davide's tendency to speed, they must have arrived first, but there was no sign of them or the car. After a few minutes of standing in the piazza, the children were restless: Fulvio kicked the tires of the Mercedes, and Zaira ripped off Anna's scrunchie, which led to a wrangle and Anna stomping on her cousin's foot. So with Barbara in a stroller, they set off to search the town of grey stone for both the castle and their respective fathers. The tense little group walked around and up and down the maze of narrow streets.

Where were those guys? Fulvia was growing convinced that the Ferrari had crashed; she saw it smashed against a tree, halfway down the mountain slope. Davide had always been too reckless. She should have managed it so Sam drove. Or that they hadn't divided up this way. Every outing she was stuck with Veronica, who on this occasion was delivering one of her lectures, this one on the foundation of Erice in ancient times. "From the beginning it was dedicated to the worship of the love goddess, first called Astarte, then Aphrodite, and in Roman times, Venus. Shall I tell you a story about Venus?" What was she going on about? The children weren't listening, and Fulvia knew the historical details and more.

"Veronica, I was the one who studied classics in high school."

Fulvio and Zaira's whining forced them to stop three times, for gelato, Coca-Cola, and cannoli. Meanwhile, Veronica expounded on how American women—like Fulvia—didn't cook for their families. "Your children eat too much fast food."

"Are you kidding me?" Fulvia said.

Veronica was now an elementary school teacher with thick yellow streaks in her hair, a shelf-like bosom, and a tendency to use an instructing-the-little-ones voice. "*Le Americane* don't know how to eat or dress." She openly pointed at two passing, plump, middle-aged women, both in Bermuda shorts and pastel T-shirts.

"Those women are British," Fulvia said. "I can tell from their accents. Listen, Veronica, you shouldn't generalize."

"And you were planning to go into fashion. What an idea. In the frozen North. Fur coats maybe. I have a chinchilla jacket and a full-length mink myself."

"Rather unnecessary in this climate, I would have thought."

"Davide and I often visit Paris, Rome, the top cities. I am regularly exposed to high fashion. You aren't." They were all growing tired. They stopped at another café, and this time they didn't rush. They bought ham sandwiches, which the mothers ate, and the children shredded.

Veronica continued on: she had a good job, good children, and a good husband. A faithful husband. What was she implying? She couldn't know about Daniela, could she? And Davide's business was doing so well. He was expanding into so many areas, legitimate areas. Fulvia should not think otherwise. Veronica protested too much. Her life couldn't be as good as she said it was. Not with Davide as a husband.

They finally came upon Davide and Sam coming out of a restaurant. While the women and children were searching, the men had been eating *pasta con le sarde* and stuffed swordfish and drinking a bottle of white wine. "Have you been to the castle?" Sam said. "You can see half of Sicily from up there."

"No more outings," Fulvia told Sam that evening. "I might crack and throttle Veronica."

"You're not the only one. Your brother's a damn show-off." To imitate Davide, Sam stiffened his posture and assumed a smug expression. "I am so rich and successful I don't know what to do with all my money." Sam was using an exaggerated southern drawl.

Fulvia laughed, "Rooms, warehouses of gold."

"I'm planning to expand, expand, expand, into wine and fashion."

"He said fashion?" Fulvia said. "*Santa Maria.*"

"Davide said the Arcuri dominated the construction business on the island," Sam said. "He offered me a job. We were standing on the castle ramparts, with half of Sicily below, and he broke out the *all this could be yours* routine."

"The devil. You didn't listen?"

"I felt a flicker of temptation. But I've seen the kind of tacky, unsafe buildings they throw up." Sam shook his head.

Bagna Serena brought Sam back to his irreverent self. Intermittently, he snuck references to things like acid baths, vendettas, and *il pizzo* into his exuberant and extended utterances. "You know *I'm kidding*," he'd say if anyone reacted, which they usually didn't because the words kept coming, each new one cancelling the last. Zio Antonio was almost excessively courteous with Sam; at times he addressed him with the formal and outmoded *voi*, which emphasized that Zio considered Sam an outsider. Had Zio ever said Sam wasn't a real man? In different words: he'd dismissed him as unserious.

Why had she heard her dead father's voice? Four years after her visit to Sicily. *La viu niura.* And in a City of Edmonton swimming pool, of all places. *I see it black.*

Then, under the hot needles of the shower, she remembered flashes of the previous night's dream: the smell of burning olive wood, the crackle of the bonfire, orange and yellow flames sparking up into the night. A cluster of dark figures silhouetted against the light, and a witches' cauldron bubbling red. Talk about seeing it black—the night, the smoke, the mood. Her father's voice was a hangover from an irrelevant dream. And nothing more.

272

Late winter, the days grew longer, but for Fulvia, newly prey to insomnia, the nights still felt endless. She lay awake; Sam breathed deeply, steadily. A riddle from her childhood repeated itself, like a catchy tune, in her head. *Si 'un mi movu, sugnu fimmina.* If I do not move, I am female. *Si mi movu, sugnu masculu.* If I move, I am male. *Who am I?* She extended her leg; Sam's thigh limited her range. Who am I? She turned away. Who am I? His body heat and a new high-pitched whistle as he exhaled followed. *L'aria e il vento.* Air and wind.

It makes no sense in English, where nouns have no gender. *L'aria e il vento.*

They should have bought a bigger bed, king-size. Fulvia needed air, a breeze.

In the end, they remained rich and consoled, while we just sit here and continue to get old.

Two hours earlier, as she and Sam had prepared for bed, she'd asked him to take Anna to her ballet class the next day. Fulvia wanted an afternoon without interruption to work on payroll and refine some design sketches. Sam claimed he had plans and accused her of presuming he had nothing to do. "I'm submitting bids on new projects," he said.

"Shall we go over the figures together?"

"You think I'm incompetent."

"I do not. Two heads are better than one."

"I thought you were drowning in work? But you have time to check on me."

"Sam, stop it. I'm trying to help."

"You blame me when it's the economy."

"I don't. I know. Now if you could get those clients—the ones with the extravagant tastes—to pay their bills."

"I could call on your Cousin Joe to lean on them," Sam said.

"You're joking right? It's never a good idea, asking the family for help."

"Technically, he's not an Arcuri."

"Even worse. He's freelance-crooked. No, you should try phoning and writing to those in arrears. And we could talk to a lawyer."

Sam groaned and pulled the top sheet over his face.

She should get up and move to the family-room sofa. As long as she woke up before the girls, and they didn't catch on. For they worried; her clear-eyed, straight-backed girls worried.

They loved their father; they revelled in his attention.

When Fulvia was very little, her father carried her high up on his shoulders. She would look down at the black and white tiles and shriek and giggle, her middle twisted into a knot of fear and joy. Sometimes, he flipped her over and held her upside down. "Beg for mercy," he would say, "beg." And she would try, she could barely get her breath, Papà please, please, before he eased her onto the floor. How often? Not that often. Don Fulvio Arcuri was a busy man. From one day to the next, he disappeared, and her mother never explained. Don't go, Papà, little Fulvia said the few times she did know he was leaving. Don't go, Papà, please.

After his time in prison, she was too big to be flipped and dangled. He would walk with her through olive trees or the orchard, holding her small hand in his big one. She couldn't remember him ever asking her questions about herself, what she liked or didn't like. And he didn't talk about himself, no childhood tales. Papà liked to sing the old Neapolitan songs or recite rhymes and riddles. *Dil'ucchi mancia carni / d'a vucca mancia pezzi.* He eats flesh with his eyes and cloth with his mouth. Who am I? Scissors. Who am I? Snip, snip.

In her teen years, she rolled her eyes at his rhymes and riddles. Not again. How many times had she heard that one? Papà eats flesh with his eyes and paper with his mouth. Bang, bang. She was beginning to understand who he was, who the family was, and what that meant. And she loathed his attention.

Fulvia never had fun with her father in the easy, egalitarian way Barbara and Anna did with Sam. Just yesterday, the three of them had been sharing giggles and laughter, as they swept in from an afternoon of skiing at Snow Valley, shedding a mountain of toques and boots, mittens and snowsuits.

"Sam Tombà," he said.

"Give me a break," Anna said. "Sam Wipeout's more like it."

"All that stuff, in the closet downstairs," Fulvia said.

"Mom, Mom," Barbara laughed. "It was so funny— "

"You should have seen us."

Fulvia suspected, once they hit their teen years, Anna

and Barbara would become critical of their father. If everything went the way it should, their disenchantment would be ordinary, part of their growing up. Shame would not be tattooed into their skin the way it was into hers.

The four of them sat around the kitchen table with mugs of hot cocoa. "Papi, tell us about when you were little," Barbara said, as if they didn't know all his stories by heart. The fall in the lagoon. The speedboat ride. His sister's disappearance on the night of the Redentore.

"I often remember," Sam began.

Anna, who was watching Fulvia, said: "Mom, you tell one of your stories."

"Okay, I could tell Prince Miser and the Girl who Lived on Wind. Or The Pony Who Would Only Eat Cannoli."

"No," said Barbara, wiping off her chocolate moustache with the back of her hand. "From when you were little."

"Yes," said Sam, "you tell."

Fulvia wiped her daughter's face with a paper napkin. "I don't have the fun kind of stories your Dad does."

"You don't?" said Barbara.

What could she say? I lived in a stone house encircled by a stone wall. They knew that. Anything else appropriate for a family audience? Nonna and the servants? The pickling of her cat Fedele? The murder of numerous family retainers and two of her cousins? Her father's assassination? Not stories but stones that would weigh her daughters down. "My anecdotes are too depressing," Fulvia said. A glass shard in her chest.

"They can't be all bad," Anna said, her face troubled. "I had fun in Alcamo. Well Fulvietto was a total pain, but otherwise. Don't you remember anything happy?"

"I must have forgotten. But have I told you about how your father and I met? Or about the time you smeared your diaper cream all over your bedroom furniture? Never mind the long ago and far away."

Never mind. Fulvia tried to forget more than she tried to remember. Most of the memories from her childhood were involuntary, physiological responses: sensations of sun, light, heat, stone, darkness, enclosure.

"When I first met your mother," Sam said, "she wouldn't give me the time of day."

"Naughty Mommy," the girls said in unison. For this too was a familiar tale.

"She ignored you," said Barbara.

"And she was the most beautiful woman you had ever seen," said Anna.

"A princess," said Sam. "And though I was no prince, I didn't give up, and I won her over."

"Such a fairy tale," Fulvia said. She remembered no acts of daring and courage. She'd unlocked the dungeon door on her own.

"My princess. Little did I know," he said, with a sudden edge in his voice. Fulvia warned Sam with her eyes, not in front of the girls.

Was it this way for others? What drew you to a lover became what repelled you? Certainly for Sam. He turned every cloud inside out looking for the lead lining. Liking and complaining about her initial inexperience, liking and complaining about her family. Was she any better? Drawn to his irreverence, his restlessness, his rebel pose, then frustrated by his inability to find satisfaction or peace. Even before they had gotten married, she reminded herself, even then, his love had been steam heat one day, cool rain the next. Even then, his words caressed and wounded.

In the darkness of their bedroom, she strained to see him. She made out not his face, but a head-shaped mass of deeper blackness. He stirred, shifted. His smell, sweat, pepper, grass, masculinity, teased her.

She could get up for a glass of brandy. But no, she had been doing that too often, drinking to slow and calm her thoughts.

In the early years, Fulvia had been proud she'd pledged herself to Sam, body and soul, he and she, strong, open, adventuresome, together. And she was proud of what she was willing to do for him, proud of the completeness with which she surrendered to Sam's sexual appetite, to his will. On those few times when her desire wavered, she ignored her discomfort, controlled her flinching. Sam's need for experimentation and novelty spoke to her own craving for intensity, her impulse to extremity and oblivion.

Now, the steady rhythm of their lovemaking, the positive heartbeat of their marriage, had grown sporadic, fitful, ten days since the last time. When she wasn't able to climax. She was exhausted: work, the girls, and the lack of prolonged sleep, so her desire was dampened. But not smothered, not snuffed.

Fulvia rolled onto her back. Morning was too far and too close. She touched Samuele's shoulder, his bare velvet skin, and withdrew her hand. She knew each element of his body: the indentation of his spine, the knob at the base of his neck, the pinkish mole below his collarbone, the four white chest hairs whorled with the black, the work-thickened fingers, the muscled buttocks, the cracked right toenail, the feel of him, sandpaper and velvet, soft and hard, the taste of him, tongue, semen, tears, how he looked when he was asleep and when he was pretending to sleep. Each and every element lodged within her, the love and the strife.

24 Edmonton
JULY 1989

Wouldn't you know it, Janet reappeared five minutes before John planned to leave for the airport to pick up Chief De Luca. He was giving himself the once-over in the wall-to-wall bathroom mirror when he heard the sharp knocks. "Hey, Johnny-boy," she was yelling. "It's your honeybun."

"Shuush," he said. "Think of the neighbours." She was wearing a low-cut, lime-green dress and sky-high heels. "How did you get up here? You didn't buzz."

Janet giggled. Her lipstick was smeared, her hair ruffled. "Are you going to let me in?"

"I was just leaving."

"Give me a break." Her pupils were enlarged, glittery.

He let her step into the apartment, but he kept the door open. "I have to go."

She tipped forward, so one hand landed on the back of his neck, and her face was close to his. "Come on, Johnny.

Your mean streak is showing."

"Don't get me started."

"I need you." She pushed out her lips in an exaggerated pout.

She staggered a little when John stepped away from her and closed the door. "Christ Almighty, you're stoned out of your mind."

"Maybe. Maybe not." Janet tilted her head so it rested on the wall. Her eyes closed. "I need help."

"Scram."

"Did you hear me? Help me be good." Blink, blink, Bambi eyes.

"No," he said. "I can't." Janet shifted, so her face was pressed against the wall. "How did you get here? You didn't drive, did you?"

"I'm smarter than you think."

"I'll call you a cab."

"I'll only go if you drive me."

John headed for the phone. "I don't have time. I'm meeting someone."

That brought her back. "A female someone?"

"No one you know." John dialled the taxi company.

"Who?" Janet was on him, her mouth by his ear. "Who, who, who, who, who."

He held her off, reciting the address into the phone.

"Of course," she said, "Mr. Hunk. Mr. Stud. Got a new source of nookie."

He could taste his anger, black-brown and scorched. Smother it, he told himself as he steered her out the door and down the hall, smother it, sensing how easy it would be to push her limpness a little too hard. "Where's the fire?" she said.

In his veins, in his hands, the flames arcing from his fingertips, singeing her milk-white skin. Too easy. He could feel her shoulder bones as he nudged her along to the elevator. He could see her sprawled, marked. "Stay away from me. I mean it."

"Hey, what about your leg?" she said. "You all better?"

He limped through the terminal, out of breath and out of sorts, scanning the milling crowd. "How will I identify you?" he had asked De Luca.

"I'm rather nondescript," she told him. "Brown eyes, brown hair. And you?"

She saw him first. He was still scanning the rush of newly-arrived, when he heard his name. Chief De Luca was right in front of him, her hand already extended. "A pleasure after all this time."

"Sorry, I didn't see." In his embarrassment, he fell back on his broadest smile. Her face remained serious. He lunged for her bag. "Let me," he said.

"I can manage." But she passed him the battered leather carry-on.

"This is it? No suitcase?"

"Blown up. I didn't go back to my place for other things. I picked up a few necessities in Rome."

She was limping as much as he was. "We're quite the pair," he said. "Is it serious?"

"No, no. I can't even decide which leg to favour. One knee is bruised and scraped, and there was a small piece of embedded metal in the other thigh that they had to remove. And you?"

"Pulled hamstring. Soccer."

De Luca, Marisa, as she insisted he call her, was not what he expected. Her voice had promised another type of woman, one you didn't have to look at twice to see what was there, the clear grey eyes and thick shiny hair. She was short, came up to his mid-chest, and narrow, with small breasts and muscular calves. She wore no makeup, not even lipstick, and no jewellery besides a pricey-looking watch. Her clothes were practical, dark blue, and simple.

In the car, she stared out at the green fields. "I needed this," she said.

"Edmonton isn't your usual vacation spot," he said.

"When I was a girl, every year we went to the seaside. Now I have no interest in lying in the sun."

"The Rockies are worth a visit."

"This city of yours is far away from everything."

"Depends on how you define everything. Not from nature."

He'd gotten her attention. "To be sure. I was referring to everything in the subjective sense. My everything."

"Good thing, considering," John said.

"Certainly. Although I'm not here solely for my protection. I am still on the Mazzolin case. I intend to question the wife, Fulvia Arcuri."

"You won't get much out of her."

"Perhaps woman to woman?" Marisa was massaging a spot between her eyebrows. "I will wait until I've recovered from the time change to see her. I must have all my wits."

They'd reached downtown, which must have looked paltry to her, a cluster of undistinguished high-rises. "You'll be comfortable, I think, at this hotel," John said as he pulled up to the Four Seasons on 101 Street. "It's as good as we've got."

Marisa's visit was unofficial, but on John's advice, she had contacted the communications department, and John had been assigned to be her guide and minder. An easy job: Marisa was undemanding, the opposite of a burden. By ten thirty the next morning, when he met her in the lobby to walk her over to police headquarters, she'd found a gym and been to a yoga class. "I was awake at four o'clock," she said. And during the tour of headquarters she was interested and enthusiastic. "Computers," she said. "You are lucky coppers."

"Coppers?" John said. "No, no, you can't say that here. Cops. Where did you learn English?"

"Summer courses at Oxford." That explained her accent: upper-class British softened by Italian.

"I'm going to have to give you some lessons in Canadian." He hadn't meant to sound flirtatious. Luckily she didn't respond.

As Lloyd pointed out, it wasn't John's job to take the Italian woman out for dinner. That evening he did, because he wanted to. He chose the cheap and cheerful Earl's on Whyte, with its big windows and the profusion of rainbow-coloured stuffed parrots, for beer and burgers.

By the time he and Marisa were sitting beneath the flightless birds, her mood had plummeted. She'd stopped asking questions or reacting to his attempts to be amusing. She made a face at the idea of meat and ordered a spinach salad and a half-litre of red wine.

"You must be exhausted."

Marisa picked at the spinach leaves. "I'm all right."

"Are you thinking of the bombing?" Marisa didn't answer, so John added: "Did you get news of your colleague? Back at the hotel?"

"Agent Roselli is out of danger. I spoke to his doctor. They managed to remove most of the embedded metal." She took a sip of wine. "But they don't know the long-term effects. His leg was broken, his hand. And probably he will be scarred, particularly in the face. Which will be a pity because Roselli is a handsome young man." A bigger sip. "A trivial thing to regret, but still. They were after me. I feel responsible."

"Being the target doesn't make you responsible."

"Whoever was behind the bomb knew my habits, which suggests someone inside the station. And the car was in the police parking lot, which has an attendant.

"One of your men? Worse and worse. But maybe you were just being watched?"

"Maybe. I brought down an extremist political cell a few years ago. It could have been one of them, especially

285

since their leader recently died in prison." She paused for a bigger drink of wine. "There's the usual suspect, the local boss, Antonio Arcuri, and of course, one or more of my men. Most of them would love to get rid of me." More wine. "Or most likely, a combination. A few officers on the take. Connected. Eager to be helpful to Arcuri."

John had ordered a crème caramel; she had to eat something. And she did finish it in a few bites. "*Sono brilla*," she said. "I'm a little tipsy." She began complaining about her boss in Palermo and how he'd reprimanded her for being too aggressive. "He thinks it was all my fault. Whoever it was, my fault." She made a face. "I did make some mistakes."

"You were doing your job, catching the bad guy."

"I survived."

"You did. So they—whoever they are—failed."

She drained the end of the wine into her glass. "I wonder if my surviving was part of the plan. If I was just supposed to be warned, roughed up, pushed into leaving. I hate that I retreated."

John had a sudden craving for a cigarette, fresh air and a cigarette. There was a 7-Eleven a couple of blocks away. What was the harm if he gave in to the urge once or twice? A minor relapse. "Are you tired?" he said to Marisa. "You're here to recover, debrief and recover. Give yourself a break." He looked around the crowded room for their waitress.

Marisa didn't look ready to leave. She leaned over the table. "Before I went to Sicily, when I was still in Rome,

I met this Sicilian aristocrat. He said all the usual things about the Mafia being a myth. Doesn't exist, he kept saying. Racist propaganda, he kept saying. But then later when someone mentioned some extraordinary measures of security for the minister of justice, this man laughed and said: if they want to get him, nothing and nobody will be able to protect him."

"Did you call him on it? "

"Call him? Oh, I understand. No, I played the part of the polite party guest. I didn't even identify myself as a policewoman. Now, after these months in Alcamo, it seems so emblematic of my experience—doing battle with a force that is both nowhere and everywhere, both illusion and reality."

This wasn't the way police officers spoke. Where did the difference come from? Her foreignness? Her character? Marisa was waiting for his response, her eyes searching his face. His thoughts were weights balanced on his tongue. Again, the stabbing need for a cigarette.

"Too much," he said. "Totally frustrating," he said, aware of the inadequacy of his words. "Let's get you back to the hotel."

25 Edmonton

By summer, Goodfellas Construction had won three new contracts, but remained in financial difficulty. Sam complained. "*Non me va mai dritto*," it's never straight for me, never right. "We shouldn't have come back to this damn place." His nostalgia for Venice grew and fed his bitterness. The poison thickened his blood, slowed his step and heart.

"Sam, you have to resign yourself. *Basta con i castelli nella aria*. Stop fantasizing. We're never going to be rich enough to live comfortably in Venice."

"A man needs a dream," he said. "You understand nothing," he said.

Fulvia swallowed her retorts. She stopped giving advice. He only ignored it. Instead, she soothed and supported. She was patient, because her daughters loved their father, patient because she loved their father. Patient because she understood Sam felt humiliated. Patient because she had vowed for better or worse. She would be as steadfast as Maruzza, who sat mute on a terrace for seven years, seven days, seven hours and seven minutes to release her prince from an evil spell.

Three months later, Fulvia's resolve wavered. Sam had a new fixed idea. They would ask Lela, Fulvia's mother, to invest in the company. With an infusion of cash, he could be more than a glorified handyman, fixing up shoddy houses. He would have a chance of going big, hiring more and better workers, and creating something beautiful, something significant. "Make my name."

"No, no, and no. I would have to ask—not you. And I won't."

"You're a hard woman."

"Don't be dense." The words fell from her mouth. "You won't ever be your own master. Sam, listen, the Arcuri aren't interested in beautiful buildings."

A smug smile. "I don't buy into the myth of the all-powerful Don Antonio. I'm not afraid."

"You should be."

"I've been trying," Fulvia told her friend Frannie over a lunch at Happy Gardens. "But I'm getting sick of Sam's poor-me attitude. And he's stepped up the propaganda on going back. He's trying to infect the girls. Telling them nothing compares to Venice."

"From what I remember, he has a point."

Fulvia shook her head. "If we were there, he'd go on about here. He'd be complaining about the cronyism, the rich."

"The grass is always greener syndrome," said Frannie.
"You don't know the half of it."

"From what I've noticed, he has too much nostalgia.
And you have none."

"I'm immune."

"Try some of this, Fulvia. It's delicious." The platters
of food exhaled exotic and comforting smells: ginger,
lemongrass, and sesame oil. And when Fulvia took a bite,
the flavours were distinct, sharp, and salty.

"Sam has always had his moods," Frannie said.

"But now it's worse. He thinks the company is on the
edge of bankruptcy."

"Oh, no."

"He needs to make some changes, but he won't listen
to me. He comes up with the craziest solutions. They
aren't solutions. And he gets so angry. Usually with me."

"He's abusive?" Frannie's eyes, behind her gold-
rimmed glasses, were alert, focused. Frannie loved any
kind of emotional revelation. "How do you really feel
about that?" was one of her habitual questions.

"No, not at all. Well, only verbally, sometimes." Fulvia felt a pang of guilt. She and Frannie often discussed
the minutiae of their lives, motherhood, bargains, weight
loss, politics, and whatever issue was flavour of the month.
But the situation with Sam was different, more intimate.
She was being disloyal to her husband.

Still, she was glad she could vent to Frannie. Fulvia
had been at home when Frannie was most career-driven;
now Fulvia had the boutique and her designs, and Frannie

was tied down by twins. But their friendship had survived their differences, mostly because of Frannie. She was the one who cultivated and tended, the one who phoned. And Fulvia was almost always happy to hear from her.

"I'm glad we're friends," Fulvia said.

Frannie beamed. "And I'm glad I pushed you to go for a physical. You and your I'm-too-busy."

Fulvia rolled herself another Mu Shu pancake. Frannie was telling a story Fulvia had heard before, about Frannie's previous GP, who had misdiagnosed her hypothyroidism as depression. And Fulvia had a flash memory of the parish church in Alcamo: Saint Agatha. Why? She looked for a trigger in the cheerful bustle of the restaurant, the noisy patrons, the plate-laden waitresses, the year-round Christmas decorations, shiny balls and silvery garlands. She saw no connection between this modest place and the gloomy excess of the Baroque church.

"You should have filed a complaint," Fulvia said. "I would have."

"I'm sure you would."

"Let's have dessert," Fulvia said. "I feel like stuffing myself today. They must have something disgustingly sweet."

"I crave sugar when I'm tense too," Frannie said. "It's the lump, isn't it? You're worried? About what the mammogram will show? Of course, who wouldn't be?"

Fulvia lifted one shoulder in the smallest of shrugs. "The doctor said it was probably a cyst. Though he did book me for the mammogram right away. I'm still young for something bad."

"You look calm."

Fulvia was falling into a dream: she was with Nonna in the church, standing before the back wall of the secondary altar, a chaotic expanse of hand-written pleas for healing and testimonials of divine interventions, blurred snapshots and hundreds of silver amulets, representing hands, legs, eyes. Breasts. Nonna, a dark presence rather than a face. Bend that head, pray for your protection and that of the family. Pray for salvation from the forces that would destroy us. Pray for the souls burning in Purgatory.

A dream or a memory? What she saw in her mind's eye was less important than the enveloping emotion, a yearning for comfort and consolation.

"Earth to Fulvia, come on, try one," Frannie said. "You insisted on ordering these. You haven't been listening, have you? Don't apologize. I'd be worse. I remember when I got a positive Pap smear. I was rattled, but it was nothing—a yeast infection."

Fulvia bit into the bun, and the sweet, elusive flavour teased her tongue. "*Zuccata*, that's what this tastes like, the preserves Nonna and the maids used to make. Boiled summer squash and jasmine water. Heavenly."

"Maids?" Frannie said. "I never imagined you had maids."

"We rarely made desserts at home. We bought them, mostly from the local convent. And only on special occasions, thank goodness. They were the best sweets ever, so subtle. The nuns must have poured all their blocked sensual appetites into their culinary creations. Take *minni di virgini*: pastry crust of almond flour, then layers of *zuccata* alternating with sponge cake and custard, topped with almond paste, and, on top of the mound, a candied cherry."

"Sounds obscene. Virgin breasts? Really?"

"They commemorate Saint Agatha's mutilation and martyrdom." Fulvia pushed away the dish with the remains of the bun. "Listen to me. I say I'm immune to nostalgia, and five minutes later I'm looking back."

"What's the harm? I now know I had the wrong impression of your childhood"

"Ah, the maids."

"Not that you have ever said much."

"I have. I've told you all sorts of stuff. So I didn't boast about my family's financial status.

"You said your father was a farmer, and I imagined someone like my Nonno. A small plot."

"A big estate. Some prime vineyards. But I left all of that behind."

"I wonder what else you haven't shared with your best friend." Had Frannie guessed the truth? Her cheeks and eyes were glowing with curiosity.

"Not much." For a second, Fulvia considered confessing. *I was born into darkness. I had to fight to reach the light.* A release of sorts. Sam had never blabbed, as far as she knew. But he was ever more drawn to Arcuri power and money. Frannie would be titillated, not tempted. She'd want all the juicy details. But could she resist telling her husband, her brother, or a couple of her many friends? Inevitably, the word would spread. Fulvia would be boxed up, la-belled forever: the Mafia Princess. Worse, much worse, her girls, Barbara and Anna, would be marked too.

"I told you my family was repressive," Fulvia said. "It's all too boring and common." Fulvia gave the plate of half-eaten dessert a shove. "I'll be late for the appoint-ment if I don't get moving."

Frannie waved at the waitress. "This has been good. Let's not wait so long next time. We could do dinner, have more time to talk."

"I'll have to see." Fulvia said, buttoning up her coat.

Outside, Fulvia took a deep breath of the crisp fall air.

"Call me after the mammogram. They tell you right away if you're clear."

"I can feel the lump. I'm going to need a biopsy."

Frannie took a step toward Fulvia and enfolded her in a hug.

Suddenly, Fulvia was afraid. She knew too well what was ahead.

26 Edmonton
JULY 1989

The memory of the bombing kept Marisa untethered. She floated through her days in the cool, green city, whether alone or with John Buonaiuto, floated through the light-filled nights, sleeping on her over-sized hotel bed, airborne, except in her dreams, where she was threatened, chased, about to be caught, trapped, and bound. Where she suffered and resuffered the explosion, the inhuman force sucking her in and slamming her down against the asphalt. The night before she was to meet Fulvia Arcuri—Fulvia Mazzolin—for the first time, Marisa dreamt of Roberto Valente: young again, a head of curls, a smile that split his face in two, Roberto without his Marxist jargon, without his *Death to the Bosses* and *Kill One to Educate a Thousand*. It didn't make much difference, he said. What you did. He was holding her in his arms; they were making love with such tenderness that when she woke up her body ached, screamed, *Don't stop!*

It had taken a few days to fix the appointment with Fulvia. At first, she refused. "I've said everything that needs to be said." When John explained that Chief De Luca had come from Sicily, Fulvia was incredulous— *you're all crazy*—yet she agreed. However, she was busy, she was ill, she couldn't today or tomorrow or the day after. John told her that they would come to her house, and she reacted: "No, I don't want you here. I'll come to the station house."

In the days before the interview, John took Marisa to the sites in and around his city: a giant mall, the fort, and, in the country, a buffalo park. He showed her Italian Edmonton: two cafés, one with billiard tables—both filled with men, no women—an Italian store with long aisles of olive oil and pasta and outdated magazines, two cultural centres, one run by northerners, the other by southerners, neither exhibiting any culture other than bocce lanes. He drove past the church, fronted by a marble statue of its namesake, Santa Maria Goretti, the embodiment of purity, of a pastoral past. The statue was glassed-in, sealed off from the harsh Canadian elements, and it was flanked by a bell tower that contained no bell, only a tape deck and loudspeaker. For Marisa, everything seemed to be behind glass, removed, a reference point out of context, an approximation rather than the real thing.

Even John Buonaiuto was weightless; he had seemed more real when he was only a voice on the phone. This weightlessness made him easy to be with. She didn't feel that she had to be on guard or even alert. Despite her detachment, Marisa registered that John was an attractive man: even features, blue eyes, and dark hair. His body looked strong and hard. "I work out," he said, and she asked, "as opposed to working in?" He laughed, explaining that he meant exercising with weights. He had a casual manner, a Canadian manner, she decided, one moment serious, the next teasing. Polite and deferential, yet clearly amused by the expected courtesies.

Then, he caressed her cheek. They were standing on a street corner waiting for a light to change, when suddenly John turned, hovered, lurched and swept her up. One hand on her back, the other on her cheek. He bent closer, his mouth to her ear. "Sorry. My wife, almost ex-wife. OK?"

Maria understood as soon as she saw the woman, her bright hair, sparkly earrings and white, semi-sheer dress, swooping in. "John, honeybun." She grabbed John's arm, pulling him away from Marisa and out of the pedestrian flow. "You haven't called."

"Called?" John's voice was ice-cold.

"You haven't phoned me. You said you would." She inspected Marisa as she spoke. "So this is who you've been neglecting me for. You naughty boy."

"Can it, Janet," John said. "Marisa De Luca, this is Janet Regan." He took Marisa's hand, linking fingers.

"I'm his wife. He did tell you about me?"

Marisa was happy to play the new girlfriend. When John touched her, she felt a jolt, and she was newly aware of him as both a person with a complex private life and as

297

a man whose body carried a sexual charge. "*Caro*, we're running late." She threw Janet her best *back-off bitch* look.

In the car, on their way to Persephone, Fulvia Mazzolin's shop, John was grateful. "You helped. She's a curse."

"Any time."

Marisa almost asked John about his marriage and what had gone wrong, but he switched the conversation back to their interview with Fulvia. "What are you after?" he said. "I told you, the woman is a brick wall."

"The she-wolf," Marisa said. "That's what her mother-in-law called her." "I don't think she's a predator."

"The fact remains her husband was killed in Arcuri territory."

"You think her uncle needed her permission?" John looked sceptical.

"No. Samuele Mazzolin broke the Cosa Nostra code. You don't abandon your wife, especially not a sick one."

Marisa left John in the car, windows open, reading a murder mystery, when she went into Persephone. She was going to be quick, wander through the shop and form an impression. Two long, white rooms, four customers, one hovering clerk, and no sign of Fulvia. One glance told Marisa the clothes were elegant and expensive. She paused at a rack with a few hanging pieces. These must be Fulvia's designs. Not at all in the current fashion: no shoulder pads, bright colours, or tacked-on decorations. The fabrics were light, the lines soft and curved. Marisa pulled out a one-shouldered black sheath and checked the tag, $199.00, not as pricey as she expected. Why not try it on? When she returned to the car half an hour later, she carried the tunic and a white collarless jacket, both from Fulvia's Demeter Line.

John laughed when he saw the plastic bag. "You women are all the same."

"I never shop," Marisa said. "I was gaining insight into Fulvia Arcuri's character."

"You were?"

"She's contrary, swims against the current. And she has talent, the real thing."

Fulvia Arcuri looked older, thinner, more fragile than in the snapshots Marisa had seen in Venice. The beautiful thick hair was gone, cut into a cap of wispy curls. Still, Fulvia drew the eye with her presence and elegance. She wore a steel-grey suit, the jacket finely pleated and closed by a mother-of-pearl clasp.

Marisa crossed the interview room with an extended hand. "Condolences," she said.

Fulvia answered with a curt nod. Her eyes closed. The wary expression faded from her face.

Marisa and John exchanged looks. Marisa spoke more loudly than usual. "I visited your shop yesterday. Out of curiosity. And I found myself buying a dress and a jacket."

"Which ones?"

Marisa described them. "Everything I saw in your line was original and refined. Fit for Milan or Rome."

Fulvia lowered herself into the chair opposite Marisa,

her face contracted into a fleeting grimace. "So what am I doing here? Miles from nowhere?" The trace of a smile. "I was recently offered the means to go big and wide. I wasn't tempted. Here, I'm in control of my business. I don't owe anyone anything."

Marisa pushed the on button of the tape recorder. In Italian, she listed the time, the place, and the names of those present.

"Marisa De Luca, chief of the Alcamo *Commissariato*," Fulvia repeated, lifting her hand to her temple and arcing it in a circular salute. "Impressive. In my day in Sicily, there were no female cops, let alone a head of a division. I'm glad things are changing."

"As you can imagine, it has been a difficult posting. Most of the men are openly hostile." Marisa made a face.

Fulvia nodded. "I believe you."

Marisa had decided beforehand to try and build rapport with the widow. But Marisa hadn't expected she herself would feel a connection, would like the woman.

Samuele Mazzolin. Remember him, Marisa told herself. The young man with a guitar and a dream expression in the sepia photo in his mother's album. She should have a copy of that picture here, on the table in front of her. Remember his end: his reduction to fire-charred flesh and bone and his abandonment for those long weeks in that steel drawer. She switched back to English: "Mrs. Mazzolin, why didn't you declare your husband missing?"

"As I said to Detective-Sergeant Buonaiuto, my husband left me when I needed him. I didn't care where he was. Besides, I didn't know he was missing."

"We have the phone records," John said from the side. "Since last November you have been in frequent contact with your mother and your uncle, Antonio Arcuri. You spoke to him on January 30, March 15, and on April 1, less than a week before your husband was killed.

"I think I already mentioned we've been in closer contact because of my illness." Fulvia turned her head to face John, and Marisa caught the family resemblance, the trace of Antonio Arcuri in her prominent cheekbones. "They let me know when Sam arrived in Alcamo for a visit and when he left. Nothing sinister. No plotting. We all presumed he had returned to Venice."

"The question is why would your husband visit your family when you two were estranged," John said.

"Why?" Fulvia was silent for a long minute. "I was surprised. I had no idea he'd go south."

"Do you think he might have been looking for your family's blessing? Or their help setting up a smuggling business?" Marisa said. "They must have had an opinion as to why he went to see them."

The shadow of her uncle was not just in her cheekbones and the shape of her mouth. She had his gravity, his immovability. "Chief De Luca, you should have asked my uncle that. You're from there, and you come thousands of miles to ask me what he thought?"

"Your uncle is not the most forthcoming of men, *Signora* Mazzolin."

"Exactly. You think Don Antonio confides in me?"

"So you did know about your husband's plan to smuggle hashish from Tunisia," John said.

"I only know what you told me, Sergeant. Sam knew I'd never accept such—such idiocy."

"Did you know Silvio Inzerillo?" Marisa said.

"I did. We first met him about five years ago on the beach of the Lido. He had a Venetian girlfriend, and her *capanna* was next to ours. He and Sam made an instant connection. I didn't like him much."

"Why?" John said.

"Silvio was a Peter Pan, one inch deep, flying here and there. Sam found him amusing, fun." Fulvia's tone made clear what she thought of *fun*. "They were talking about going into some sort of business together, even then. I never thought it would come to anything. They kept in touch. Silvio phoned from time to time, came to visit once. He seemed to look up to Samuele." Fulvia shrugged. "Called him captain."

"Your husband would have been the instigator, the leader of their expedition?" said Marisa.

Fulvia did not move, but the distance between them widened. When she spoke it was in Italian. "Who gives a shit whose idea it was? Both of them are dead. You've got the drugs. I don't understand why you wasted money and time coming here. These questions." Fulvia gestured at the concrete walls.

"Have patience," Marisa said. She switched to English. "Samuele left you when you needed him. Is it possible that your family decided your husband needed to be punished?"

"Possible? I don't think so. But how would I know? I left Sicily behind. That was at the root of the estrangement between Samuele and me. He was determined to return to Italy. I couldn't do it."

John must have moved his chair closer to the table. "You were abandoned. And you're telling us you didn't want payback?"

Fulvia shook her head. "You think because I was born an Arcuri I must inevitably be guilty of something. Like original sin. With no possibility of redemption. I chose another life in another country."

"You must have fought hard to get away," Marisa said.

"We're finished here?" Fulvia began to push herself up out of the chair.

"Not yet," said Marisa. "Would you like a coffee?" John said. "Tea? A juice?"

Fulvia hesitated. "Tea, black."

After John had closed the door, Marisa said, "I didn't come here to track you down. *Signora*. I am not here officially. I did take a particular interest in the murders of your husband and his friend, perhaps because Samuele was not identified for so many weeks. Then when I did have a name, and I was making a bit of progress, my life was threatened." Marisa paused. "I questioned Antonio Arcuri, and a bomb was placed under my car. I had only a minor injury, but my colleague was more seriously hurt."

This had an effect: Fulvia flushed. And for maybe three seconds, she looked distressed, then embarrassed. "A bomb."

Marisa said. "A bomb. I have to take it personally. And I was advised—ordered—to take a leave, for my own safety."

"I'm sorry," Fulvia said. Marisa waited, but Fulvia did not continue.

John was back. He passed out three cups of tea. When he sat, he pulled his chair over, so he too was at the table. "I heard you've always wanted to stay clean and on the right side of the law."

Fulvia did not react. Marisa decided to take a chance. "Do you remember Alex Zacco? He vouched for your character."

Fulvia looked as if she'd been slapped. "You questioned Alex? Why on earth would you do that? You are on a witch hunt." She put down the Styrofoam cup. "How did you find him? And where?"

"He still lives in his childhood home. I didn't search him out or interrogate him. I met him socially. Nothing to do with you."

"So why was he, of all people, vouching for my character?"

"He heard about your husband's death."

"Alex betrayed me." Fulvia closed her eyes.

"A lifetime ago." Marisa paused.

"What's the point of this?"

John shot Marisa a glance, as if he too wondered. Marisa's heartbeat was elevated. She was kicking into high gear. She said in Italian: "Alex never forgot you. He never got over you."

"He said that? To you?"

"I swear he did. And I saw it for myself. He still carries a picture of the two of you in his wallet."

"Tell me. Is he married? Children."

"He's alone. He hasn't moved on."

"Alex betrayed me." Fulvia's voice was low. She barely moved her lips.

"You were children. Alex said you were a beautiful flower when he met you. Pure and true."

"Why are you telling me this?"

"Because Alex's words helped convince me that you aren't like the other Arcuri. You have a moral centre. You want to do the right thing. Your uncle had your husband, the father of your daughters, killed. You must know that or suspect it."

"No."

"You know what your uncle is. A hint, anything I could use against him?"

John nudged Marisa's foot. He'd written *it won't work* on his notepad.

Fulvia's face was parchment white, her neck a purple-red alarm. Marisa calmed herself, taking a mouthful of warm tea. John was right: she could interrogate the woman for hours and get no further.

Silence. Marisa waited for Fulvia to say "enough," to stand up and walk out. Instead, she handed Marisa not what she wanted, but a gift nevertheless. "Turn off the recorder." Fulvia's voice was no longer flat. Life, animation, had flooded back into her eyes. "Drugs are not the only cargo worth smuggling."

"Tax-free cigarettes," Marisa said, impatient.

"*Clandestini.*"

"Human trafficking? That's in the *Guardia*'s jurisdiction. Besides, the *clandestini* may be dumped on our shores, but they quickly go north where there's employment. So not our problem."

"There could be a sweatshop, very much in your territory, a few kilometres southwest of the edge of Alcamo. Illegals, working day and night turning out knockoffs, fake handbags."

Marisa and John exchanged glances. "Don Antonio does have a variety of interests," Marisa said.

With a grimace, Fulvia pushed herself to standing. "No, not my uncle. It's Davide Arcuri who has moved into what he calls fashion."

John was the one who jumped up to open the door. He insisted on walking Fulvia Mazzolin back to her car.

"She was a little unsteady," he said when he returned. "You threw her, bringing up the old boyfriend."

"You obviously understand more Italian than you say you do."

"It was easy enough to follow. You said the guy she thought betrayed her was still madly in love with her."

Marisa was making notes. "Madly."

"But I didn't get why he would tell you."

"You and I have something in common. I'm drawn to the wrong type."

"You dated him." John was stacking the foam cups.

"A mistake. But, it turned out, a useful one." Marisa stood and picked up recorder, paper, and pen. "I'm glad to have met her. I understand now why she elicits such strong reactions, good and bad."

27 Banff National Park

For the first few hundred metres of the incline, John and Marisa walked in silence. As usual in the summer, the trail from Château Lake Louise to Lake Agnes, particularly in the opening gentle ascent, was well populated. They quickly passed a strolling family and a group of Japanese tourists. John could feel himself start to sweat. His leg had healed, but there was still a pull, a twinge.

At the first switchback, he paused to tie the laces of his runners tighter and snuck in a quick massage to the back of his leg. A few metres further along, Marisa stopped and waited, framed in spruce and alpine fir. "How's the leg?"

"A-okay," he said. To prove it, he lengthened his stride. "And yours?"

"Sore, but it won't interfere."

John couldn't help smiling at her. She was so prepared, so eager, in her new shorts, runners, and baseball cap, *never had one of these before*, her leather backpack, equipped with mineral water, suntan lotion, a bar of chocolate, bug spray. "If we need it, I have it." Across her white T-shirt, a Latin quote she translated for him. *I sing of arms and of a man: his fate had made him fugitive.* "It's Virgil," she said. "I found it at the giant mall."

John had suggested the excursion to the mountains as a diversion. He had four days off, and Marisa was frustrated and itching to go back to Italy and follow up on Fulvia Mazzolin's tip on the illegals and the sweatshop. "But my *Questore* warns me against returning. He is telling me to wait." She made a face. "I'm in limbo."

The mountains did distract Marisa. She was appreciative, enthusiastic throughout their time in Banff, which had included a stroll to Bow falls, a gondola ride, and a swim at the Upper Hot Springs, before the two drove north to Lake Louise. Over an after-dinner Scotch on the second evening, she steered the conversation to their respective careers. And she dwelled on how her boss had withdrawn his support. "He seems to be punishing me," she said.

"He had your back and now he doesn't," John said.

"My back? I like that expression. Indeed, Lanza no longer protects my back."

"I've got it here—your back."

"You're saying I should relax and enjoy the scenery?" Marisa nodded at the view on the other side of the floor-to-ceiling window.

"Always," he said.

Four switchbacks up the Lake Louise hike, John re-opened their ongoing discussion of the Fulvia Arcuri interview. "She's an angry woman," knowing he didn't need to attach a name.

"I suppose, but controlled, contained. I liked her. I didn't expect to."

"So you said. You don't think she could be responsible."

"You didn't either. Not a predator, you said."

"I changed my mind during the interview. Because of her anger," John said.

"I can't believe she would cause the death of the father of her children."

"You've never been married," John said. They both paused at a parting in the trees. The turquoise lake was a banner of brightness below them. "Sometimes, if you feel betrayed, you surprise yourself."

"Betrayal is a common experience. Murder is not. I think Mazzolin challenged the authority of the Arcuri."

"Agreed. But when you first arrived you kept insisting it must be more personal. For the Don to go after you."

"If it was his men who came after me."

They picked up their pace. His leg was throbbing, his pulse elevated, but he was determined to keep up. "Did you try to find the car? The one that forced Inzerillo's car off the hill? It must have had some damage. Paint? Scratches?"

"I think I told you. We checked the garages in Alcamo and two nearby. That's all we had the time for. We have no computers and too many cadavers." Was she reminding him of how much more important, more fraught her job was? "Do you need a rest?"

"No," he said. But he slowed. "Some water." John pulled out his bottle of water and took a long swig.

She gestured toward the lake. "*Favoloso!*" She didn't linger. She began to power walk.

John was forced to address the back of her head. "As the glacier retreats, it grinds rocks into a fine-grained powder, which ends up in the lake, scatters the light."

She turned and walked backwards as she answered. "So no magic, just dirt."

John trailed Marisa as they sped past the pale green waters of Mirror Lake, up a steep, shaded climb. He gained on her during a scramble over a cascade of fallen rocks, and caught up on a crest of rock suspended in thin, blue air. Far below, Lake Louise was a bright spot in an expanse of green. Marisa's face was flushed, her breath short.

"We should slow down," John said.

"I was thinking," Marisa said.

"Let's put the case away. We don't have enough evidence. Our intuitions clash."

"*Allora?* One of us is right. Either Fulvia Arcuri is guilty or she's not."

"You think I'll give in," John said. Now he was the one in front, leading the way. They climbed up and up through the rumble of a waterfall, up a long ladder of stairs. One last surge, and he stood in the hanging valley.

A few feet back, Marisa's face was pale under her tan. She took a woozy sidestep. "Marisa." He leapt and caught her as she collapsed. She went limp, a weight on his arms. He eased her onto a rock ledge and pushed her head forward.

After several long seconds, her eyelids flickered. "*Ma cosa... dove...*"

"Keep your head down between your knees. That's right. We came up too fast."

"I don't understand," Marisa said ten minutes later. "I don't faint." They were sitting at a table on the porch of the Lake Agnes teahouse.

"You insisted on walking fast." Trying to make a point? "You didn't take into account the altitude change."

Marisa looked disgruntled. "I wasn't going too fast."

"The perfect policewoman: can't give in or give up."

Marisa busied herself with the just-delivered teapot, swirling the tea bag, fishing it out, pouring. "You want to give up on Mazzolin and Inzerillo? On Fulvia?"

"Life isn't a whodunit where everything is resolved and justice done."

She smiled, "Or where the person we least suspect is the guilty one and the one we most suspect is innocent." Marisa was leaning over the table, her hand an inch away from his.

"And the murderer always exposes his or herself with a wrong phrase or move."

"In Sicily, bad guys don't make those mistakes. Or if they do, we can't use them in court because of some technicality."

Suddenly, he wanted to kiss her, to touch her face, as he had the other day, but this time for real. Even then, when he was putting on a show, he had liked it.

Marisa leaned back, moved her hand, broke off a piece of the apricot loaf he'd insisted they order. "Witnesses, judges, and juries are threatened," she said, her face suddenly grave. "Sometimes eliminated."

To temper her view that the Canadian justice system was the polar opposite of the Italian, a shining example, always blind, swift and true, John described several cases of innocents who were convicted. "Don't think the law is applied impartially, if you're poor, mentally ill, or Aboriginal. Natives are what they call overrepresented in the criminal justice system."

She wanted him to kiss her—he felt it. Or was he projecting? It could make things awkward. She must be several years older than him; she was a chief of police. Though not his chief. But what if she was offended? Felt he was harassing her like that captain who waved his cock around. Better to relax and soak in the elements: hot tea, sunshine, crystalline air, and the backdrop of mountain peaks. John brushed Marisa's hand. "You okay?"

"Why? Because of that moment of *girotondo*? I'm fantastic. Well, a little light-headed, but it might be the strain of thinking in English."

"On the way down, no racing. We'll take it slow."

As they walked into the Post Hotel, bags in hand, Marisa said to John, "We don't need two rooms, true?"

John stood still.

"I will not be offended if you say no," she said. "It could be a good story, ours, short and sweet."

"A story?"

"You don't want me." Her face was expressionless. She was walking away, headed toward the check-in desk.

He had to sprint to arrive before Marisa. "We have a reservation for two rooms under the name Buonaiuto." He spelled it out. "But we only need one." He glanced at Marisa. After some back and forth with the clerk, they were given a small stand-alone cabin, which cost more than the two rooms combined.

"*Un ragazzo e una ragazza,*" Marisa said, as soon as she stepped through the door. "And a little house in the deep, dark woods."

John felt awkward. They were moving too fast, crossing first the border between colleague and friend and now between friend and lover. He wanted to hang back, slow down. What did she want—expect—him to do next? Order champagne? Manoeuvre her into his arms?

She had pulled off her runners and socks and stepped onto the bed. Face beaming, she bounced up and down, as if it were a trampoline. He got it. She was playing at being young and uncomplicated, but it felt forced to him. Forget making this oh-so-casual, he thought. Let's get down to business. Instead, they discussed dinner, drank a beer, took separate showers.

He was sitting in the armchair, dressed in clean clothes and reading the paper, when she walked out of the bathroom, naked, dewy. Now or never, he told himself, crossing over.

Past midnight, John lay in the steaming oversized tub,

Marisa's back against his chest.

"The hot water should be good for your hamstring," she said.

"And your leg." He ran his hand over her hip and thigh. "I was thinking about your boss—Lanza."

"He doesn't exist here."

"But when you go back."

"Stop."

"Be ready. Find a way to force him to get rid of that pig of a captain."

She drifted to the other end of the tub, so she was facing him. "If only."

"You'll figure it out. I saw you with Fulvia Mazzolin."

"Are you exhausted?" Her stare was direct, obvious.

"Refreshed, relaxed," he said, smiling almost in spite of himself.

IV
Fire

S'I'fosse foco, arderei 'l mondo
S'I'fosse vento, lo tempesterei

If I were fire, I would burn the world
If I were wind, I would storm it
                    —Cecco Angiolieri

The prince finally recognized Maruzza when she spat into his face. "Yes," she said, "I'm your Maruzza, and I wanted you to feel the sorrow and grief you caused me. Now we're even."
                    —"The Green Bird"

28

Edmonton
WINTER 1989

Five days after Fulvia's mastectomy, Sam announced he had booked a flight. He had an opportunity he would lose if he hesitated or delayed. He was leaving; in a week he'd be gone for good. He paused, giving her a chance to reply, but she couldn't. Her tongue was a weight, a stone.

The home care nurse had just left, and Fulvia was lying exhausted under the duvet on their bed. On her left side, under the bandages, three drains and a raw sutured wound that stretched from her breastbone up to her armpit. "You're going to be fine." Sam said. "Stop with the tragic face. I told you I was going." But he hadn't, not straight out.

After his company went under in November, he made no effort to find a job or come up with another idea. She suggested that Persephone could use renovation; the decor was a hold-over from the last tenant. Sam built and tiled and painted. He took over some of the care of Anna and

Barbara: rides, lunches, supervision of homework. How was she going to manage? How? In the last few weeks, he had begun to spend even more time with the girls, teaching them gondolier songs, though he never could hold a tune, rhapsodizing about the magic of Venice and the lagoon, challenging them to Super Mario Brothers or Space Invaders on the Nintendo, so their shrieks and laughs echoed through the house. Playing at being the loving father while he planned to abandon them.

Anna and Barbara would suffer from his going. Did she have the power to keep Sam here and to prevent their pain?

Fulvia pushed herself up into a sitting position, half-turning to settle the pillows behind her. She forgot to protect her left arm, and flinched under the wave of pain, but she made no sound. Sam stayed a metre away from the bed, watching her. Since she had returned home, he had kept his distance, hovering beyond her reach, as if she were contagious or disgusting close up. His words dropped from his mouth, green frogs and garter snakes, and infested the room.

He—they—had a chance to enter the other Venice, the one he used to resent, where the privileged lived, the hidden gardens, the private beaches, the water taxis and yachts. She and the girls could come in the summer, when the school term and her treatments were finished. By then, he'd have an apartment for them. It wouldn't be like the last time. They would be a happy family. "You'll have to sell Persephone. But you'll restart your design line there, where they appreciate style and quality."

Liar: he didn't want them there, not in the foreseeable future. He wanted to get as far away as possible from her. She saw it in his eyes. He didn't care if his daughters grew up without a father. He was planning a different life, the charmed, semi-bohemian life he imagined he could have had if he had never emigrated. With Daniela, his slut of an old girlfriend. Deluded. He was already trying out the Italian artsy look: he hadn't shaved in three days, and his hair was shaggy, lapping the back of his collar. Coward. He was afraid she would beg or scream. He should know she wouldn't humiliate herself in that way. He continued to talk, reassure, promise. "You have the Belmondos, Frannie, your aunt, if you need help."

Fulvia had friends. She was a grown-up. She had made a life. But she was as powerless, as helpless, as she had been at nineteen. Confined to a room. Freezing yet burning.

Fulvia broke her silence with a line from a poem she memorized in high school.

If I were fire, I would burn up the world.

Sam flew away, and Fulvia held her daughters close. Of necessity, she made her bed a centre, a refuge, a lifeboat on the waves of uncertainty. They watched television, Anna on one side of her, Barbara on the other. They played Uno or Hearts. She read to them, *Matilda*, *Ramona*, *Harriet the Spy*. Anna complained the books were too young for her, though she liked hearing them again, liked listening to her mother's voice. Fulvia also read from the volume of Sicilian folk tales, skipping certain sentences: *As for the false bride, the king had her cut into pieces, salted, and stuck into a barrel, her head placed on top.* Fulvia disposed of all the evil characters by sending them to live far away in the woods: "And they lived happily ever after."

Barbara complained of stomach pains. "I don't wanna go to school," she said. In the middle of a game or a story, for no apparent reason, she would burst into tears. Anna had new compulsions. She counted aloud each step she took. She touched everything first with her left hand, then her right, then again with her left. She grew agitated if the pillows were not lined up exactly, if the covers were not tight and straight, or if the books on the side table were not piled neatly, with the biggest on the bottom and the smallest on top. Anna reorganized Fulvia's closet, then the bottles, jars and framed photos on top of the dressing table. "Are you going to get a wig?" she asked Fulvia.

"Heavens, no." Fulvia glanced into the mirror opposite. Her hair had lost its shine, but it still hung thick and dark to her shoulders. "Why would you ask that?"

"You're starting the treatments tomorrow, aren't you?" Anna said

"Yes, but—" Fulvia resumed tugging a comb through Barbara's long and curly hair.

Barbara half turned and stopped Fulvia's hand. "Are you going to wear scarves and funny hats like Jessica's mom?"

"I don't need to."

"Your head will get cold," Anna said. "And everyone

will know you're sick."

"Don't worry, sweeties. I'm having radiation, not che-motherapy. My hair won't fall out."

Barbara cuddled up beside Fulvia. "Mamma," she said, "Papa asked how you were when he phoned."

"You told me that." Fulvia reached out to caress Bar-bara's face with her left arm and regretted it.

"Why didn't you talk to him?" Anna said.

Fulvia rested her head against the pillow and immedi-ately felt as if she were sinking. "It's expensive talking on the phone to Italy. They charge by the minute." At her centre, nothing, three breaths of air, while the left side of her chest, her arm, ankles, and the skin between her eyes were heavy, aching. Anna's left hand was in her hair, yet another bad habit, twirling a curl, then tugging hard.

How to reassure them? Before she could decide what to say, she dropped off to sleep.

And saw her mother. And smelled her, gardenias and smoke. Fulvia was little again. She held up her arms to Mamma, and Mamma said "not now." She was party-pretty, dressed in blue, her hair puffed and sprayed, her lips and nails red. Fulvia pulled at Mamma's skirt. She needed to be held, right now, in Mamma's lap, to suck her thumb and stroke the silky blouse, to be rocked, to be safe.

Fulvia surfaced. Since the cancer, she had been prey to these dreams that took her back to the time before Fulvia began to run away, when her mother could still comfort her.

If I were wind, I would storm it.

Anna stood holding the wicker tray with the Japanese

teapot, a china cup and saucer, and a plate of ginger snaps, waiting for Fulvia to adjust herself. Fulvia eased herself up. "I was dreaming about your grandmother."

Anna placed the tray over Fulvia's thighs. "Does she drink tea? I can't remember."

"She does. She thinks it's chic. No one else in the family ever did." Fulvia took a sip of tea, gardenias and smoke.

"Did your Mamma brush your hair like you do ours?" Barbara said.

"She did. She liked to tie the top back with a big white satin ribbon. I'd untie it. She put me in starched, frilly dresses, and I'd squirm and grumble."

The girls both smiled. Anna's hand was back in her hair.

The broad corridors of the cancer clinic were dazzlingly bright; the walls painted in candy-floss mauves and yellows, and the floors waxed and buffed to a high gloss. The staff, from the parking attendants to the radiation technicians, were uniformly cheerful, coaxing conversation and smiles from the patients. The ill were near invisible at first glance. They seemed to eat up the light. Too many shuffled in their faded hospital gowns and housecoats, their shoulders slumped, hair limp or gone, eyes wary. Fulvia nodded to the two she had seen every weekday morning for three weeks: an elderly man in a wheelchair with a hovering wife, and a middle-aged woman with a red scarf wrapped around her head and a daughter by her side.

Sam shouldn't have left her when he had.

The nurse had a pink, smiling face. "What a storm, eh? I nearly ended up in the ditch. Highway 16 was treacherous. Did you have any trouble getting here? Can you stand another month of this? 'Cause that's what we're going to get."

Fulvia shook her head, accepted a hospital gown. Behind the canvas curtain, she peeled off her scarf, coat, boots, and wool pants. She sank onto the bench. Her head lolled against the wall and her eyes closed. A tremor in her left thigh.

If I were water, I would drown it.

On her eyelids, the black-clad crone, her Nonna, silent, observant. Conjured up by the hospital smell of wax, sickness, and disinfectant.

"Blame your Nonna," Fulvia's mother had said after the mastectomy. "She had a tumour the year you were born. And both Nonna's parents were stricken. Their deaths were long and painful."

"Enough," Fulvia said.

"The point is, you didn't inherit it from my side."

"I'm going to hang up."

"Wait." Lela offered to help. She would pay for household help or a nanny for the girls. She would arrange for Fulvia to go to a top-notch hospital and be examined by a world-famous oncologist. "France, Switzerland, or the United States. Wherever you want." For a few seconds, Fulvia was tempted to give in, stop battling alone and make sure she was getting the best treatment. She had to get healthy, not so much for herself but for her girls.

Lela's offer was typical, extravagant, and with a subtext. Fulvia couldn't possibly be getting the correct treatment in Edmonton. After all, wasn't it free? Available to all?

"No," Fulvia said. "Thank you, but it's not necessary."

Fulvia would have liked to have kept both Sam's leaving and the cancer private, but word spread, and a range of acquaintances knew. A few avoided her; others avoided mention of Sam or the illness. Friends recounted stories of survival or brought her books and pamphlets on so-called natural ways of healing: apricot seeds, mistletoe, Chinese herbs, extracts of bark or root. Frannie was the most insistent. "You have to purge yourself of toxins: coffee enemas, a macrobiotic diet, and no sugar; sugar feeds cancer. Pay attention, Fulvia. Positive thinking." Frannie read aloud from the latest book. "Rid yourself of unproductive feelings." As if it were easy. As if you could toss rage and pain out with the trash. How sensible, how tidy. "For those negative feelings are the root cause of the disease." Possible, probable, Fulvia's body was a minefield of blocked energy too dangerous to release.

If I were fire, if I were water. If I unleash my anger, I will blast the world.

Fulvia looked down at her swollen arm and the gauze where her left breast used to be. Underneath, a livid scar and a bull's eye drawn on by a marker pen. The skin from mid-chest to left armpit was tight, itchy, and hot, partially cooked. *Baste me, I'll soon be done.* She pulled on the hospital gown, fumbled with the ties.

Her turn, through the swinging doors, down the hall,

into the cavernous room, empty except for the monstrous machine. She lay down on her back, the gown over on the good side. Hands pushed and pulled her into place. She was sexless, characterless, a drawing board, a sack of flesh. A young man, his face intent, pulled the tape off the bandage and touched up the blue lines with his thick pen. Hold still. He rushed off to his place behind the shield. Don't move. The machine buzzed and hissed, then a metallic whine. She sensed, then felt the penetrating rays.

"Don't put this on me," Sam had said when she shared the diagnosis.

"I didn't get cancer to keep you here. Not everything is about you. Still, since you're the one with the memory, in sickness or in health, remember that."

"That husband of yours should be made to live up to his vows," Zio Antonio had said.

How? By a magic spell? A brain transplant? "No," Fulvia said.

During the next phone call, after Sam had arrived to visit the Arcuri, Zio offered to give Sam a job or a loan. "He would have to learn discipline. The family would be investing in both him and you, together."

Fulvia was resolute.

"You could open a proper design house. In Milan, for example. Even Venice."

Again, a moment of temptation: she envisioned a catwalk, an atelier, herself as the new, female Armani. "No," she said. There was a few seconds delay on the line, and she heard herself, *no*.

"He should not have left you, especially not now," Zio said, offering his form of justice. Her answer was equally indirect. "Anna and Barbara respect and love their father."

But then this morning, after the girls left for school and while Fulvia was getting dressed, Zio called again. "Sam hasn't returned to Venice. My sources in Tunisia tell me he and his friend intend to go into business for themselves." Zio spoke in a casual tone, but Fulvia heard his rage. "Under my nose. In my territory."

It must have been Sam's plan all along. And as Fulvia understood where Sam was determined to go, she panicked. Anna and Barbara must never feel the taint, the shame, she had.

"I have been indulgent out of respect for you."

"I know, Zio."

"Your husband's sins multiply by the day."

"He has crossed the line." And now, she was about to, as well.

"No more patience?"

"Do what you think is best, Zio."

Another one massacred, Nonna said when she heard that Zio Vincenzo was dead. A cousin beheaded, Enzo strangled, a *picciotto* dissolved in acid. Papà disfigured by thirteen shots, his head blasted, his coffin closed.

It was his time, her time, their time, your time, my time, the clank of the metallic machine, the keening of women in the night.

She could call Zio back, call before he gave the order.

29 Sicily

APRIL 1989

Easy.

Sam could have journeyed with maps, without instruments, without even the dependable diesel engine beneath the floorboards. He could have made the crossing, both ways, relying on his sense and his skills; he could have sailed to Tunisia, harnessing the winds. He is no hobbyist; he is a true sailor, able to read the chart of the stars, the language of the swells and currents. He can sense the land beyond the horizon.

Easy. He is a man of the sea, salt water in his blood, in his DNA. He is, after all, a Venetian, he reassures himself as he stands at the helm. And he has been landlocked too long. He has wasted years. From now on, he will always have his own boat, make that boats: a sloop to sail the lagoon and a crewed yacht to explore the Adriatic, Mediterranean, and Tyrrhenian seas. Why not? Thirty feet? Fifty? Moored at the Venice Yacht Club, tough to get in, but surely with a well-placed bribe? And if he continues in the importing business, a cigarette boat that can evade radar and cut through the waves faster than this too-large motorboat.

The last two nights, he revelled in following the ancient route from Europe to Africa and back, in being alone on the dark sea with the throb of the engine, with the promise of riches, alone, alert, in control. He is in his element, invisible, untouchable. A disappearing streak of light on the water.

His job is to avoid other boats, to leave no record, to get in and get out quickly and unobtrusively, and he has. He guided the boat from Sicily to Tunisia in seven speedy hours, docking by the early morning light at a private marina Silvio knew near the resort of Sidi Bou Said. Dry clothes and breakfast under a palm tree, a cab ride, a hole-in-the-wall café, two cups of mint tea, and then a fleshy man with olive-green eyes.

A well-planned trip. Fuck that asshole Arcuri, so smug. He could pull this off once a month if needed. He made sure he blended in with the tourist hordes, linen shirt, sunglasses, and a big camera. If the fleshy man was under surveillance, if Sam was observed or photographed, there are no mug shots, no paper trail, to identify him. And no harbourmaster or customs agent in Tunisia and no *guardia fiscale* here in Italian waters. Sam wishes he could flaunt his success in Don Antonio's sneering face. Look at what this loser, this freelancer, pulled off under your crooked nose.

Sam rechecks the instruments. He adjusts the angle

of the approach slightly. Almost there, and as the boat again slams down onto a wave, the fatigue pushes up to his brain. Fulvia hovers in the core of the darkness before him. She hovers, eyes reproachful: *you shouldn't have left me when you did.*

"Go away," he says. "I was dying there." She is pulling on his jacket. "I had to get away from the cold and dark and that sickness growing inside you." He is ashamed of how he couldn't stop himself from flinching at her maimed body, part of her softness, her womanliness cut away. *Coward*: her cool breath is part of the wind on his face. He is ashamed of his revulsion at the bandages and the blood, at the livid scar, the plastic tubes and the draining fluids. His reaction was physical, unstoppable—flee. So he lied, the competition for the job wasn't till the summer; he lied and he left. *I knew it*: her words a breath in his ear. *Loser*: she is leaning so heavily on his right arm, he will topple overboard.

"Let me go." He pushes back. Shakes his head. She's gone. Pours himself more coffee from his thermos and drinks. Grasping the helm, he makes another adjustment; he must be rounding the peninsula of San Vito. He can smell land through the salt tang of the sea, a whisper of lemon and myrtle, broom and rosemary. He slows the engine, counts to ten, and flicks the bow light off and on. He scans the darkness, waits, then signals again, off-on, off-on. Where is Silvio? Dickhead, Mamma's boy. Off-on, off-on. At this rate, every busybody and his dog will know he's arrived. Where the hell? Is this the wrong bay?

No, he recognizes the dim outline of the crescent beach and cliff. Silvio probably overslept; he's cozy and comfortable in bed while Sam waits, wet, tired, and hungry. Sam can do some of it on his own, jettison the crate and the box. He'd already attached the floats. He can cruise the few kilometres to the small marina where Silvio's family moors the boat. But then what? There's no phone at the beach house. Don't fuck things up, not when we've gotten this far. Sam has wagered too much. And job or no job, he needs the payoff.

At last, an answering light: three faint but regular flashes.

An hour later, through the grey light just before dawn, Silvio and Sam speed away from the beach house. They use a secondary road that will take them up and over Monte Bonifato. Silvio is driving; Sam is draped over the passenger seat, his legs stretched as far as the small car will allow. His body feels as if he were still riding the waves. "You sack of garbage," Sam says. "You were supposed to be waiting for me. I nearly panicked."

"You were early."

"Not that early." Sam arches his back and groans theatrically. "Despite all evidence to the contrary, I'm human. I need my sleep. Forty-eight hours, *per bacco*. And you left me out there, floating."

"Yeah, you did good. Speedy." Silvio's eyes remain focused on the mountainous road. "No one saw you?"

"No, the sea was mine. Well, I saw the ferry from Trapani on my way there, but no one paid any attention to me." Sam opens his eyes wide. "When I was approaching the south coast of the island, I saw what looked like a standard fishing boat. They must have heard me, maybe seen me, but they turned their lights off and stood still."

"Ah, colleagues, I bet," Silvio says. Taking a cigarette out of his jacket pocket.

"No sounds. When I passed, I strained my eyes. It was packed with people, huddled together on the deck. I swear I could smell their stink." Sweat, piss, and dirt, Sam thought: fear.

Silvio lit his cigarette with the car lighter. "Illegals, Africans, Albanians. Lots from Sri Lanka. Very lucrative, I hear."

"But ugly."

"Why? I would have said the opposite." Silvio glances into the rear-view mirror. "Give the poor bastards a chance." Inhaling a mouthful of smoke, he checks the side mirror.

"What is it?"

"There's a car, hanging back."

Sam looks over his shoulder out the back window. "Look, they're turning off."

He closes his eyes and falls into a dream. He is almost home. He is on a boat speeding across the lagoon to the floating city, the beloved city, to the palaces of shining stone, to the cupolas and towers. Almost home, the boat plunges up and down, up and down. Bang.

High beams in the rear-view mirror, one sharp turn, another, his body is shoved against the door, then bounces off Silvio's shoulder. "*Porco cane*." Sam shouts, "Silvio, we can't outrace this fucker."

The Innocenti is a bobsled, slaloming down the mountainous road. Silvio's eyes don't veer from the road. He is breathing hard, panting. "The brakes," he says between gasps. "The car. On the side road."

A bang from the back, a big grey bastard of a car pulling up, a hit from the side, an ear-splitting shriek of metal on metal. Another hit.

Then air, earth, fire.

30 Sicily

The third week of September, and the streets of Alcamo were still suffocatingly hot and dusty. Only in the early morning, when Marisa walked to the station, did she feel the touch of a cool wind and the promise of fall. "I'm not done."

Her time in Canada, with and without John, had refreshed and rearmed Marisa. But her route back to her *commissariato* was circuitous. As ordered, she flew to Rome and reported to central headquarters, where she was informed she'd been accepted, though she had never applied, to an intensive program on the theft of art and antiquities. She said, "I'm not done in Sicily. I have an important tip." And, "This is ridiculous." And, "Am I forbidden?" The answer lay with her boss, take it up with him, *Questore* Lanza, who was unreachable, sailing down the coast of Dalmatia. Unreachable—even if he had been sitting before her. She was on her own.

She took a train to Milan and on to her hometown of Cremona and squeezed in a duty visit to her aunt and a second cousin who'd had twins a few months before. Then by plane to Palermo, where she checked into a three-star hotel with air conditioning, near the green space of the *Giardino Inglese*.

She went first to see Roselli, who was about to be discharged from the hospital and sent back to his Calabrian hill town. He was in worse shape than she expected, gaunt and in a wheelchair.

"They're giving me six months paid leave," Roselli said. "At that point, I'll be examined to see if I'm fit to return to duty." He grimaced. "I'm still in pieces." He enumerated his injuries: a shattered leg, cracked pelvis, two blasted fingers, a broken collarbone and cheekbone. A scarred face and a patched eye. His voice was different, deeper and rougher, and he spoke as if he were describing someone else's body. "I probably won't regain my sight in this eye."

Marisa was wheeling Roselli down a corridor to the outside and spoke to the back of his head. "It should have been me. It's my fault."

"You didn't set the bomb."

"I should have been more careful, more circumspect." Marisa said. She was near nauseated with guilt. "But you will get better. I'm sure of it." She stressed hope, faith, and the healing power of home. She pushed him out to the courtyard, but even in the shade of the open arcade, the heat was unbearable. So a turn and back inside to the small and cramped room that served as the hospital café. And all the while, she spouted inspirational clichés and smiled. "We'll work together again, the dynamic duo." Roselli shrugged, his face skeptical. "If you want to," Marisa said.

"You're going back to Alcamo? Is that wise?"

"I'm not done yet."

Marisa stayed in Palermo. While she waited for Lanza, she worked out her strategy. She was going to use Lanza's complicity and Antonio's Arcuri's revelation about the government's deliberate sacrifice of Aldo Moro as ammunition. She would threaten her *Questore* with exposure. And to ensure she could carry out the threat, if she needed to, Marisa met with the media couple from the dinner party in the spring. Her plan was to arouse their interest and even extract a semi-commitment without delivering any specifics. To Marisa's surprise, Giada, who worked for RAI TRE, and Danilo, the correspondent for *L'Unità*, caught her hints and ran with them. They claimed everyone knew—or at least, everyone in a select group of lefties knew—that Moro's execution was not what it seemed. Everyone suspected that certain forces within the government, together with or ordered by the CIA, had encouraged, even initiated, acts of terrorism in order to create a false state of emergency. It was a conspiracy, they said, a conspiracy. Of course, they were interested in being the ones who exposed the truth, wrote the articles, filmed the documentaries.

"Give us your story," Danilo said.

"You could remain anonymous," Giada said. "We can alter your voice."

I'll wear a mask, Marisa thought. I'm used to that.

She stopped in at Palazzo Sclafani, police headquarters, every weekday until she was told Lanza had landed and would see her. Lanza greeted her at the door of his office with a rare smile. "You look so much better."

"It did me good, my respite in a distant garden."

"I told you so. Nothing like a vacation." Lanza himself looked refurbished: imitation Gianni Agnelli, extrawhite teeth, a tobacco-brown tan, a suit that spoke not of Zegna but of bespoke Neapolitan tailoring, chunky gold cufflinks and signet ring.

"Of course, the relief is temporary," Marisa said. Like a cool drink or a fresh breeze on a summer day.

"You should have gone when I told you to. I hope you have finally learned to follow orders."

Did he expect her to re-pledge her fealty? Obey the way she used to before Sicily?

"Be patient and discreet, and you can return to your station."

"I can resume my command? I'm not being exiled to the art fraud program?"

"Not this term. It wouldn't look good—your being transferred out so fast."

"On my CV?" Could he still be invested in her career? Unlikely.

"It is safer now that your obsession, that double homicide on Monte Bonifato, has been solved."

"Excuse me. Solved? When?"

"The report with all the details must be on your desk in Alcamo. But if I may summarize: in early February, Silvio Inzerillo flew to Venice to visit Samuele Mazzolin, and together they hatched a plan to import hashish from Tunisia and distribute it to cities in the north and the south. Inzerillo travelled to Tangiers and Tunis in March, stayed a couple of weeks, found a source for the drug. As you discovered, in early April, Mazzolin drove the Inzerillo's family powerboat all the way to Tunisia and loaded up. Logic tells us that he had the backing and help of his uncle-in-law, Antonio Arcuri."

"I disagree. He's the only one with the power to order the hit. Why would he, if he were involved?"

Lanza lifted his hand, palm out to silence her. "Let me finish. In the end, Inzerillo and Mazzolin were amateurs. They got the go-ahead from Arcuri but ignored Enzo Montinelli, who runs the hashish trade in Tunisia. They were punished."

"Why bother with the car crash? Why not kill Mazzolin over there in Montinelli territory? Where did you get this story come from?"

"One of Montinelli's men. A Tunisian, arrested here for a rape and a serious assault."

"No, I don't believe it." Marisa was hot with anger. Her boss was protecting Arcuri. And she was no longer considered a threat or even an irritant. That was why she was being allowed back.

Lanza was starting to look bored "Accept it, *Dottoressa*. Believe it, tick-tack, file closed. Move on."

She spoke almost inaudibly. "Handy, no real evidence. And Montanelli is beyond our reach."

"We know the truth. You can relax." His smile glittered.

"The truth?" Her mouth felt prickly, as if she'd bitten into a lemon.

"Your Captain Brusca notified the Inzerillo family, so they can set their hearts at rest. We thought it would be best if you informed Mazzolin's wife and his mother."

"What about the bombing? In your version of events, the Arcuri had no reason to threaten me. So who was it? Some of my men?"

"You did blunder into Arcuri's house, scattering insinuations."

How do you know what I did, she thought.

"If the Arcuri wanted you dead, you'd be dead." So she should accept the bomb as a Mafia equivalent of a slap on the wrist? Accept Roselli maimed? How would Lanza know anyway? Was he covering for Brusca and his group? Had he encouraged the rebellion and been shocked the cabal had gone to such extremes?

"You sent me to Alcamo to fail," Marisa said.

"Don't be ridiculous. Why would I do that?" A perplexed expression on his face.

Because you're bored and arbitrary. Because you're dishonest and compromised. Because at some time I must have questioned you. Or your guilty conscience made you fear that I would question you, would find you out, Marisa thought but did not say. The silence stretched between them. Lanza flicked the end ball in the Newton's-cradle desk ornament. Click, click, click. They both watched and waited. For every action, there is an equal and opposite reaction. Click, click, click.

"Brusca must be removed before I go back," Marisa said. "Transferred to somewhere he would hate to go. How about the Tyrol?"

"*Dottoressa*, we settled this the last time."

A deep breath and she spooled it out: Lanza and his colleagues knew or could have found out where Moro was but chose not to rescue him. They allowed, maybe encouraged, certain acts of terrorism, so they could justify an attack on the left wing. "*Facevi piazza pulita.*" In order to clean up, eliminate certain troublesome elements.

Her words cracked his reserve. He stood, he sat. He blustered, denied, swore on his honour that her accusations were groundless. There was no conspiracy. And if there were, he'd known nothing about it.

Marisa was not convinced by Giada and Danilo's claims that the American puppet masters had directed the Moro kidnapping and murder. But Lanza himself could have been a puppet, a dupe, of others higher up. Marisa almost brought up Roberto Valente. You made me trick him. You made me a whore, a dupe, a dupe of a dupe.

But no, keep it cool, impersonal. Magazine articles, news shows, she threatened. Implicating you, but casting aspersions farther up. "You'd endanger your career to avoid transferring Brusca? I didn't know you cared so much for the man."

"That's all you want?"

"Yes, for now."

"You didn't need to hit so hard for such a trivial thing."

"Now you know I know."

"Nothing, you know nothing." Lanza had looked unnerved, even frazzled, but now *l'uomo di mondo*, the man in charge, was back.

Three days later, Marisa was again in command of the Alcamo *commissariato*. The men did not welcome her back, but they listened to her address without interrupting or complaining. The continual underlying tension, the resistance, seemed gone. Brusca's transfer made a difference, and not just because he'd been the ringleader. Those who remained knew that the *Commissario* had brought about the Captain's sudden removal. She had pull.

Marisa was eager to follow up on Fulvia Mazzolin's tip about the illegal workers and the sweatshop. The widow had been vague about the location—west of town. But Lo Verde and a new arrival, Battista, quickly pinpointed an area of lightly inhabited land with a number of deserted farmhouses. With further observation and a few stray rumours, they found their target. Marisa ordered twenty-four hour monitoring of what and who went in and out of the fortified farmhouse and outbuildings. The goal was not to capture and deport the poor wretches but to arrest the guy in charge and, even more important, to implicate

Davide Arcuri.

The second night she joined Lo Verde and Battista; they hiked in about a kilometre from where they left the unmarked car. They crept over parched land, through an abandoned olive grove, and took up separate covered positions. Like the others, Marisa had a gun in a holster under her arm and a camera with a telephoto lens hanging down from her neck. It was what she had dreamt of when she was posted to Sicily: a clear target, a shared purpose, though the feeling of comradeship was still missing.

The surreptitious pictures, along with the results of the surveillance and the information from the unnamed but reputable source, led to a warrant for wiretaps on the phones of Davide Arcuri and two of his *picciotti*. And soon after, the loss of the operation. The *Guardia di Finanza* was brought in to provide support; instead they commandeered the investigation. They had jurisdiction, as she well knew, over borders, immigration, organized crime, and international fraud. She'd been derelict in her duty. She should have involved the *Guardia* from the start.

Marisa had waited until she was back in the station house in Alcamo to call Sam Mazzolin's mother and inform her of the closing of the case. Predictably, the woman insisted her son would never have smuggled drugs. Fulvia must have given him the idea. "The witch set him up," the older Mrs. Mazzolin wailed, "and her people did him in."

Marisa phoned John from her apartment. "Hey there," he said. His voice made her spirits rise. "I wondered when or if I'd hear from you."

"I'm finally back at work. Listen, the Inzerillo/Mazzolin file's been closed. You're going to have to let the widow know."

John was as sceptical of the offended Tunisian gangster theory as Marisa. "You're kidding me."

"I wish. There are so many holes to the story. Weak plotting. The point is for me to accept the findings. Stop poking around."

"You weren't getting anywhere anyway."

"Unfortunately. I did have a partial success." She told him about locating the sweatshop, continuing on with an edited version of the last two weeks.

"Congratulations, you managed to get rid of the bastard of a captain," John said.

"Lanza saw the light," she said

"I hear you," he said. And later, before she hung up, "I miss you."

Marisa sat at her desk, tackling six weeks of paperwork. She was distracted by the sunlight pouring through the window, by the fan perched on the filing cabinet. If she put it on maximum, it roared and ruffled the piles of papers; on low, she could not breathe. What was she doing here? What use was she? Not much.

On the edge of her desk, the day's paper and a front-page headline:

"32 Chinese Nationals Living And Working In Makeshift Factory: Boss's heir faces five penal charges."

None of the reports in either the local or national papers mentioned the work of the Alcamo station house. On the TV news, an inspector of the *Guardia* took full credit. Besides, Davide Arcuri was already out on bail, and who knew when the case would go to court. And would the judge be paid off or terrorized? Or would the Arcuri lawyers twist and turn the laws until most, if not all, the charges were dropped?

Marisa's white blouse was damp and wrinkled with sweat. She tried to summon the glowing green lake, the glacier-clad mountains, the sound of the tumultuous river a few metres from the cabin. John's smile, John's eyes, John. And for the first time she understood the Sicilian phrase *fuocu all' arma*, fire to the soul: the fresh breeze that brings relief and hope was not just temporary but dangerous. Once it passed, you felt the heat even more intensely. Everything was worse.

The ring of the phone cut into her reverie. On the line, the receptionist and then Samuele Mazzolin's sister, Luisa Taviani. "It's her, *la Siciliana*," Luisa said. "You have to stop her. We tried the police here, and they said nothing could be done."

"Is your sister-in-law there in Venice?"

"She has no shame. This will kill my mother."

Marisa could hear the sound of a second voice without being able to make out the words. "*Signora* Tavani, tell me, please, what did she do?"

"She took him. She said it was her right. What about Samuele's right?"

A half-muffled shriek, a "let go" from the other voice, and Mrs. Mazzolin senior had gained possession of the telephone. "That witch has stolen my boy," she yelled. Marisa lifted the receiver from her ear. "She didn't even warn us. The cemetery called." She let out a low, deep moan. "Samuele always said he didn't want to die in Canada. He wanted to come home."

A rustling and Luisa Taviani was back on. "When I got to San Michele, he was already disinterred."

"What?"

"Fulvia was standing over the coffin, her hands full of official papers. She wouldn't listen to anything we said. She kept saying, 'He's my husband.' She had made arrangements to have him cremated that afternoon."

The women's anguish travelled over the telephone lines and, like a cold wind, chilled the back of Marisa's neck. "I do understand your agitation. But I don't see what I can do to help."

"Talk to Fulvia. She's down there now. With my brother's ashes."

"Perhaps it was your brother's expressed wish." Besides he had been reduced to bones and cinders the night he died.

"Never, *Dottoressa*. My mother's right. Samuele would have wanted to rest here in the city he loved. It cost us a lot to buy him a place on San Michele. Unfortunately, we couldn't afford a view of the lagoon; that's over fifty million lire. But he's in—he was in—*Gesù Cristo*, a lovely spot in a prominent row."

"What's done is done. And as the wife, she does have the legal right."

"My mother's afraid the witch will throw him into the garbage. Or have him entombed in Alcamo. She's capable of anything, that one," said Luisa.

When Marisa interviewed Fulvia in Edmonton, she had judged her strong, talented, and independent. Now Marisa questioned that impression. Was Fulvia Arcuri so vengeful that not even Sam's death was enough?

Fulvia answered the phone at her mother's house. She didn't seem surprised to hear from Marisa. Fulvia suggested they meet in the cemetery of the nearby village of Balestrate. "Tomorrow at three o'clock, by the family vault," she said in a half-whisper.

A canny choice: at that time of the afternoon, possible visitors were in the midst of their post-lunch nap or, at least, avoiding the sun. There was little room for trees here; the graves, individual family crypts, and a long wall of a mausoleum were all jumbled together. The narrow paths were straight, but the place was labyrinthine with no clear sightlines. To blend in, Marisa was dressed in off-duty white linen pants and tunic and carried a bouquet of yellow chrysanthemums. The pungent autumn smell carried her past a multitude of headstones, new and old, straight and crooked, past a host of elaborate family monuments: mock Gothic, mock Norman, pseudo Greek; columns, crosses, pediments of marble, limestone, and cement; stained glass, iron grills, and bronze doors.

Fulvia stood before a structure different from its neighbours only in degree: bigger, more bullying, a leaden gothic-Baroque. On the roof, a squat angel loomed. Over the gate, the name ARCURI carved in large letters.

Fulvia was wrapped in a gauzy, silver cloud of a dress. A matching scarf was draped around her neck, so Marisa couldn't see if Fulvia was still plagued by radiation burns. Her face, even in the bright sunlight, was less strained and lined than when Marisa had questioned her in Edmonton. She extended her hand to Marisa. "I appreciate your coming here."

They stepped into the meagre shade of the front portico. Marisa laid the bouquet of flowers against the wall. "You didn't want to be seen with me?"

Fulvia pulled off her sunglasses. "I didn't want anyone to suspect that we'd met in Edmonton."

"Because of your brother? That's not why I asked to see you."

"I was present when he was arrested." A small, tight smile. "You did a good job with what I gave you. You even covered your tracks, kept yourself out of it."

"Not deliberately." A wave of heat washed away Marisa's concentration. She didn't follow what Fulvia said next, not until she heard "Davide was humiliated." And Marisa thought: so that was the point of your tip.

"Mrs. Mazzolin," Marisa said, "I'm here to inform you that your husband's case has been solved. Unfortunately, we cannot bring the man who ordered his death to justice. At least not at this time. But you may be happy to know, the case is officially closed."

"I know," Fulvia grimaced. "My Uncle Antonio was informed by a friend."

"I should have guessed he would be. I presume you have heard the official details, yes? I won't waste your time and mine reviewing them." Then, despite herself, Marisa said, "The report was worked up while I was away. I have no choice but to accept it, though I don't believe a Tunisian drug lord decided to take your husband and his friend out."

"So you've closed the investigation unofficially as well as officially? You're not going to follow me back to Canada? Question me again and again?"

Marisa knew what she must say. "You have my word."

"My uncle said you were as sharp as a newly honed knife."

"A sinister simile. Don't tell me the powerful Don Antonio is threatened by someone like me?"

"He respects you. Mentioned how much he enjoyed debating with you." Fulvia was using her scarf to pat dry her sweaty neck.

"I'm flattered. He's a well-read man."

"My father was too. Doesn't fit the stereotype, does it?"

"Don Antonio knows what goes on in his territory."

"Enough, you gave your word."

"This is just between you and me. For Samuele's sake."

"Once my husband came up with his hare-brained scheme, once he entered the criminal world, the rest was inevitable."

Marisa was wet under her breasts and down her back. "The criminal world. In Canada, you insisted you had escaped, yet here you are. That tells me something."

Fulvia shook her head. "Do you know the Lampedusa quote about everything needing to change in order for everything to stay the same?"

"Is that what you're doing?"

"In a way. Sometimes you have to compromise on one thing, to keep another, more important one pure."

Marisa had a sudden urge to kick Fulvia. "Come on. It's too hot for these vague pronouncements."

Fulvia was staring at an elderly couple inching their way down a parallel walkway. "So why are you still here, Chief De Luca? You said what you had to say. And the heat is dreadful."

"I told Sam's mother and sister that I would talk to you."

Fulvia hesitated then pointed to the vault. "It'll be cooler inside." She pulled a large key from a hidden pocket and unlocked the decorative iron gate. She gestured at Marisa to enter. "And more private."

31   Alcamo
SEPTEMBER 1989

Fulvia guided Marisa through the doorway, down three stairs, then between two sarcophagi to the small patch of open space. The light in the sepulchre was dim, the ceiling low, the air cool and damp. Marisa was turning her head, taking in the stacked tombs, the altar with a plain crucifix and tall vases filled with purple chrysanthemums. The scent so sharp, so overwhelming. Was she frightened? Fulvia's own heart was quickening.

"Take a good look," Fulvia pointed at the row of urns. "My husband isn't here."

Marisa looked, peering at the names. "I didn't think he would be."

"But my in-laws did."

"They did."

"Even if I asked, he wouldn't be allowed in."

"Your husband's family are deeply disturbed by your having Sam disinterred. They view it as sacrilege. And now they are terrified you will dump his ashes."

"What idiocy. I'm taking him home to his daughters. That's the whole point."

Marisa blinked and took a deep, audible breath. "Maybe if you emphasized you were carrying out Sam's wishes. You could send his family a token portion of his ashes."

That would have been Sam's wish: to be at least partly there. Though not in a drawer in a wall. Scattered over the waters of the lagoon. Too bad. "I'm taking him home. You can reassure his mother the hysteric. His daughters will never know their father died a criminal, running drugs. He was in a car accident just when he was about to come back to them, to me. He loved us more than anything in the world."

Fulvia felt no urge to confess; she didn't need absolution. But she longed to tell the story of her long and perilous journey. *I was born a princess, my father a king, both loving and cruel, and my mother a queen, both foolish and cold. And like the other princesses in the desolate and wild kingdom, I was kept locked in a tower. But I was determined to escape. And I tried, but I never ran far enough or fast enough.*

Marisa would listen and understand.

A prince strove to release me, but fear defeated him.

For she too must have needed courage and cunning to set off into the wide world.

Finally. I found the magic rhyme to free myself.

Stop it. Fulvia told herself. Keep quiet. Swallow the words. Silence, with courage and cunning.

The words and the power had been there all along—in my own heart.

And she gasped. Marisa was staring at her. She couldn't catch her breath. The dust of the dead stinging her lungs, passing through the air sacs into her blood. But weren't the Arcuri—Zio Vincenzo, Nonna, Papà—already in her blood, in her DNA? Fulvia coughed and wheezed until she was doubled over.

"You have asthma," Marisa said, as she grabbed Fulvia by the shoulders and propelled her up and back into the sun and heat.

Still coughing, Fulvia shook her head, squeezed out, "I don't— I've never… had an attack."

Marisa took hold of her elbow. "We'll walk slowly." Her tone was light. "You must be allergic to the dead."

Last night, the Sirocco, with its load of sand from the Sahara, blew hard, hot, and gritty. *If I were wind.* In the small hours of the night, Fulvia lay awake on her narrow childhood bed. *I would storm the world.* Did anyone in the path of the witches' wind sleep? Or was everyone tossing and turning, their nerves raw and lungs irritated. The ancient poem played in a loop: *If I were water / I would drown it.* She missed Anna and Barbara, though in their fragile state, better for them to be there with the Belmondos, loving and familiar, than here or, worse, Venice. A few more days, that was all, a few more of this duty visit, and she would be home with Anna and Barbara. If she didn't expire in this hot box of a room smothered from the lack of oxygen. She opened the window a few inches, and a small gust of wind brought the smell of smoke. Inland, kilometres away, vineyards and orchards were burning up. *If I were fire.*

And she was eight again, and Davide had conjured fire from air, and the pasture and garden were collapsing into ash.

Fulvia yearned for the girl she used to be, a flame of hope and possibility.

It was Sam's fault.

If I were God / I would throw it into the abyss.

For five minutes, as she paced up and down, Fulvia entertained taking maybe a third of his ashes to the mountainside where he had both fallen to earth and vaporized into the sky. Ashes to ashes. But the thought of driving to that place was nauseating.

It was Sam's fault, Zio's fault. Papà's fault. Her fault. *My fault.*

She would take the ashes home to Edmonton and put them in a stone urn. She would make a small shrine in her bedroom, a photograph, a crystal vase the girls would take turns filling with fresh flowers. Barbara and Anna would grieve for their father, but their love would remain untouched, uncomplicated. They would make him into the man they'd need him to be.

Could she make herself into the mother her daughters needed her to be?

She tasted the granules of doubt on her tongue. Her heart hesitated, stuttered.

She would; she would protect them. She would keep the family there and here at bay.

She would do for them what she hadn't succeeded in doing for herself.

Their hearts unscarred, free.

ACKNOWLEDGEMENTS

The story of Ninetta the Brave is excerpted from the Sicilian tale "Gràttula-Beddàttula," collected in the second volume of Italo Calvino's *Fiabe Italiane* (1956). The translation from the Italian is mine. The other tales quoted or referenced, "Betta Pilusa," "The Daughter of the Sun," "The Green Bird," and "Sorfarina," are all taken from *Beautiful Angiola: The Great Treasure of Sicilian Folk and Fairy Tales*, collected by Laura Gonzenbach in the nineteenth century and translated from the German by Jack Zipes (2004). The resourceful, indominable heroines of these tales helped inform the portrayal of Fulvia. The Sicilian proverbs were found on the web, as was the Angiolieri poem. The Sicilian sayings and riddles came from Leonardo Sciascia's *Occhio di Capra* (1984), translated by Marco Lo Verso.

I am grateful to the Sicilian cousins for their hospitality and patient responses to my endless questions: Marilia and Enzo Cirincione, Maricetta and Rory Cigna, and Vito Tuzzo. I am also indebted to Rosabianca Lo Verso, who left Sicily a lifetime ago but remains thoroughly *sicula*. A particular thank you to a lady from the Veneto, Ausilia Contessa, who gave me inspiration.

Detective PJ Duggan graciously explained the procedures of the Edmonton police force, as did Detective Fabio Bonetto, who also shared some of his experiences as an Italian-Canadian policeman. In Italy, Questore Vicario Luigi d'Aquino took a day out of his busy schedule to illuminate in detail the inner workings of the Italian state police.

Many thanks to Liz Grieve, Ann Cameron, and Kay Stewart, who commented on two versions of the novel, and to my writing group, Mar'ce Merrill, June Smith-Jeffries, Debby Waldman, and Lorie White, who shared their insights on yet another draft. I owe Mary Irey for her sharp-eyed editing. And I feel privileged to have Linda Leith as a publisher.

Marco, Tatiana, and Antonia Lo Verso accompanied me on two of my research trips to Sicily. On the last one, they withstood a month in an apartment with no air conditioning in central Palermo. The temperatures hovered in the high thirties to low forties and the windows opened either to the roar of traffic and stink of diesel fuel, or to a courtyard with banana trees and 52 feral cats. As always, their love and encouragement made the writing possible.

Over the years, I have been lucky to receive some financial support for the writing of this novel from the Edmonton Arts Council, the Alberta Foundation for the Arts and the Canada Council for the Arts.